Edge of the Past

by
Jennifer Comeaux

To Jennifer Herd for helping me find the light when I was lost in the dark. Thank you for giving me your honest thoughts, being my "Emotion Police," and listening to all my rambling ideas. I wouldn't have been able to finish this book without your help!

CHAPTER ONE

February, 2003

LAST PRACTICE BEFORE GRAND PRIX FINAL. *No mistakes!*

I repeated that over and over in my mind as Chris pulled me into our pairs spin, our blades tracing tight circles on the ice. We whirled around, and I caught a glimpse of Sergei, our coach and my fiancé, keenly observing us. In two days I'd be visiting his home country of Russia and meeting his parents for the first time. All while trying to win one of the biggest competitions of the season. *No sweat!*

"Em! Emily!"

Chris's voice jolted me back to our program and the gentle orchestral strains of "Clair de Lune." We'd come out of the spin, and I was doing the steps but not looking at my partner. I focused on Chris's steady brown eyes, keeping the connection through the final seconds of our run-through. After we cooled down by stroking lightly around the ice, we met Sergei near the boards.

"You were a little shallow on the footwork," Sergei said, rubbing the slight stubble on his chin. "But everything else was solid."

I nodded and blew an errant strand of hair off my nose while Chris grabbed his water bottle from the boards. "Time to start the weekend, then!" he said and hopped off the ice.

I smiled up at Sergei. He smiled back but with a hint of concern in his deep blue eyes.

"You've seemed a bit distracted the last few days," he said.

I twisted the end of my long ponytail around my finger and looked toward my training mates motoring around the rink. "I guess I've been thinking a lot about the trip."

"Just remember…" He squeezed my shoulder, and my skin warmed from his touch. "Competition first, everything else second. We'll have plenty of time after the event for family and sightseeing."

I let out a long breath. As usual, Sergei held the key to calming my nerves. It was the reason he'd been the perfect coach for me the past four years. And one of the reasons I loved him beyond words.

Since we liked to maintain a professional appearance at the rink, I couldn't give Sergei the kiss I wanted to give him at the moment. But I'd have more than enough opportunity later during our dinner date.

"I need to get home and do some more packing." I reached for my bottle of orange sports drink. "See you at seven?"

"I've been looking forward to it all day," he said, dropping his voice low.

I shot him a grin and stepped through the ice door, ready to unwind and not stress about the Final for a few hours.

SURROUNDED BY TWO LARGE suitcases and over half the contents of my closet, I stood with my hands on my hips, mentally scrolling through the wardrobe I'd need on the trip. My bedroom, which I normally kept as neat as the rest of the townhouse, looked like it had been hit by a tornado of clothing and accessories. My mother would give me a look of disapproval if she saw the room's current state. The house on Cape Cod had been a summer retreat for my parents and me until I moved into it full-time to train on the island.

I snapped my fingers as I thought of the leather boots I needed to pack. My roommate Aubrey had borrowed them, so I jogged down the two flights of stairs to her room and found the boots strewn across the beige carpet. The distant chime of my cell phone quickened my return trip upstairs. I grabbed the phone from where I'd tossed it on the bed and saw my mom's name on the tiny screen.

"Hey, sweetie," she greeted me. "Guess what I have in my hand? Your wedding invitations."

I gasped. "They weren't supposed to be ready for another two weeks."

"Just picked them up. They look beautiful."

I smiled at Mom's enthusiasm, remembering a time not long ago when she thought I was too young at twenty-two to get married. But during the past few months, she dove into the wedding plans and helped me organize the chaos amid my busy competition schedule.

"Can you bring one on the trip to show Sergei's parents?" I asked.

"Already planned on it." Shuffling ensued in the background. "I've been going over my Russian words and phrases every night. But you said Sergei's parents' English is getting better, right?"

I cradled the phone between my shoulder and ear so I could fold a pair of stretchy warm-up pants. "His mom's is. Last time she called Sergei, I talked to her and we could understand each other pretty well. His dad hasn't been quite as dedicated to learning." *Because I don't think he's interested in talking to me*. Mom didn't need to know that detail, though.

"Well, I guess as long as we can talk to one of them, we can get by."

And oh, how Mom could talk. I had visions of her rambling to Sergei's poor mother, who'd be totally confused. Hopefully, Dad would rein Mom in like he usually did.

"Can I call you back tomorrow?" I asked. "I want to finish packing before I have to get ready for dinner."

"Sure, go ahead. We'll catch up tomorrow."

I surveyed the mess around me and set to the task of putting together outfits and transferring them to the luggage. By the time I ducked into my bathroom to shower and change, I had two tidily packed suitcases.

Sergei arrived a minute before seven, and my stomach fluttered at the sight of him through the narrow foyer window. His short golden brown hair and his blue eyes shone under the porch light as he stood casually with his hands in his pockets. Tall and lean with the perfect amount of muscle, he was in the same superb physical shape as the elite athletes he trained. I wondered if I'd still feel the butterflies long after we were married. Taking another glance at Sergei's handsome face, I decided the answer was yes.

I opened the door and didn't let Sergei speak as I locked my lips on his. He circled his arms around my waist, hugging me against his soft leather jacket.

"That's a nice hello," he said with a smile.

I gave him another quick kiss. "Let me get my coat."

Sergei helped me slip my lightweight trench over my sweater, and soon we were in his SUV, traveling toward Hyannis's Main Street. An earlier rain shower had slicked the roads and added dampness to the chilly evening. As we pulled up to the Roadhouse Café and walked across the parking lot, I could feel the long waves of my hair frizzing.

Inside the restaurant, the hostess seated us at a cozy table beside the brick fireplace. We ordered matching glasses of red wine and laughed when we correctly guessed each other's entrée choices. The comfortable predictability never bored me. With so much drama in the skating world, I relished stability in my personal life.

Sergei took my hand, and our clasped fingers rested on the white tablecloth. "Did you get more packing done?"

"Almost finished. I just need to pack the gifts I bought for your parents."

"My mother's going to love you. Every time I talk to her, she tells me how excited she is about our visit."

"She's so sweet. I'm really looking forward to meeting her, too. It's your dad I'm nervous about…"

Sergei's face clouded over, and he gripped my hand tighter. "Once he meets you, he'll see this is a completely different situation from what happened years ago."

I took a sip of wine and cleared my throat. What happened years ago was something Sergei didn't usually talk about much—his relationship with his skating partner Elena and her resulting pregnancy, which had ended their partnership. Sergei hadn't seen or spoken to her since her wealthy and powerful father had sent her away and made her give up the baby.

"I understand he's skeptical because you're mixing your career with a personal relationship again." I looked up into Sergei's eyes. "But he needs to forget about the past. That was ten years ago. You're not eighteen anymore."

Sergei brushed his thumb over the solitaire diamond on my ring finger. "I know. I'm hoping he'll be reasonable."

"If my mom could get on board with us, then anyone should be able to." I gave him a crooked smile. "No one's more stubborn than her."

"I'm very glad I'm on her good side now." Sergei chuckled and took a long drink of wine. "It's much nicer than the days when she thought I was going to break your heart and ruin your career."

"I'd suggest she talk to your dad, but with her flimsy Russian and his limited English, that could be a disaster."

"Well, like I said today, I don't want you worrying about it during the competition."

I nodded and toyed with the tea candle on the table. "It's kinda crazy that our first competition in Russia will be in the same arena where you skated for the last time."

Sergei turned his attention to the crackling fire. "That night feels like a thousand years ago."

Knowing that time wasn't a favorite topic of discussion with Sergei, I was debating whether to continue when our waiter appeared with our dinner, placing a steaming plate of shrimp and asparagus ravioli in front of me and a platter of baked scallops in front of Sergei. We set aside the serious talk while we ate and chatted instead about the various landmarks in St. Petersburg and Moscow that Sergei planned to show me.

The lingering smell of rain met me as we left the restaurant, and I huddled close to Sergei's side to block the strengthening wind. He wrapped his arm around me, nestling me to him.

After the short drive to my house, we snuggled together on the living room couch and found an 80's comedy to watch on TV. Not long into the movie, the double run-throughs Chris and I'd done at practice that morning caught up to me, and my eyelids began to droop. Sergei kissed my forehead.

"I'll let you get some sleep."

I lifted my head from his shoulder and yawned. "I'm sorry. Somebody worked me too hard today." I poked his firm chest.

He caressed my cheek as his adoring eyes gazed upon mine. "Four months and two weeks until I don't have to say goodnight anymore."

"Why do I have the feeling you'll want to leave our wedding reception as early as possible?" I giggled.

"I might slip the DJ some money to hurry up the last

dance."

"We don't have to stay until the last dance," I said, fingering the collar of his shirt.

"That is excellent news."

Sergei kissed me, and I ran my fingers along the nape of his neck and through his hair. His lips traveled from my mouth to the delicate spot below my ear, sending a shiver through me. I wrapped my arms around his strong shoulders and sighed as he decorated my neck with more kisses.

We eventually made the slow walk from the sofa to the foyer, where we shared another long embrace. Every night it got harder to let Sergei leave, but waiting until marriage to be together in every way was important to me.

My family took our Catholic faith seriously, and I had always known I wanted my first time to be with my husband. Sergei respected my beliefs and had been so patient, waiting over two years and counting. We'd set boundaries for our physical relationship, but there'd been times we'd come very close to crossing them. Sergei had probably taken enough cold showers for a lifetime.

I waved at Sergei as he drove out of the parking lot and rubbed my hands when I returned to the warmth of the house. On my way upstairs, I peeked at my watch. Aubrey wouldn't be home from her late movie date for a while.

After I got comfortable in my pajamas, I climbed into bed with my laptop to check email but never made it to my inbox. Thinking back to the conversation at dinner, I pulled up a search engine and typed *Sergei Petrov and Elena Gorshkova*. With a click on the Images tab, I landed on a page of photos from Sergei and Elena's competitive days.

I'd looked at the pictures before—Sergei and Elena with their World Junior Championship gold medals, action shots from their winning free skate, and their celebration in the kiss and cry when they received their scores. But now I studied them longer, knowing I'd soon be in the city where all the history had taken place.

Elena and I had the same petite build, perfect for pairs skating, but our other physical features differed greatly. Her raven hair, cut in a bob, contrasted with my long, dark blond locks. And her eyes were brown, almost black—the total opposite of my blue ones.

Even though Sergei and I had a lifetime together ahead of us, a twinge of something—perhaps jealousy, perhaps curiosity—hit me as I stared at the photos. Elena had given birth to Sergei's child. His first child. They'd always have that bond, no matter the time and distance between them. Going back to Russia would surely trigger old memories for Sergei, especially since his father was obsessed with past mistakes.

I shut my laptop and burrowed deeper under the blankets. *The ghosts must finally be put to rest.*

CHAPTER TWO

"How should I greet your dad? A hand shake? A kiss on both cheeks?" I asked, fidgeting beside Sergei on the couch.

He rested his hand on my knee, his fingertips brushing my jeans. "Anything you do will be fine."

My parents sat across from us in the lobby of our St. Petersburg hotel, the lodging headquarters for the Grand Prix Final. Having them at my competitions always gave me a feeling of comfort, so I was glad spring break came early at Boston University. Mom and Dad only had to miss a few days of work for the event and our side trip to Moscow afterward.

Dad flipped a page in his Russia guidebook and adjusted his glasses, while Mom patted her short brown hair and smiled at me.

"I'm sure Sergei's parents are just as anxious about meeting us as we are about meeting them," she said.

A tiny laugh escaped my lips. I doubted Sergei's father was anxious. Except maybe to bring up Elena and chastise Sergei for mixing business with pleasure again.

"Do the trains from Moscow generally run on time?" Dad asked with a glance at his watch.

Sergei looked toward the entrance. "Usually. The taxi from the train station might run into traffic, though."

I followed his gaze. "I hope they won't be too delayed. I have to get ready soon."

The impending start of the competition was also shaking my nerves. I had a routine I followed before every event, and being off schedule would make me even more jittery.

As if on cue, a woman carrying a suitcase, the old-fashioned kind without wheels, stepped through the revolving glass door. I immediately recognized her bright blue eyes and sweet smile from photos Sergei had shown me.

Sergei jumped up, and my parents and I followed. Anna set down her bag and walked toward Sergei with outstretched arms. Her eyes glistened as she held fast to her son.

Since Sergei had only been able to return home once in the past eight years, Anna's emotion was understandable. When Chris and I had toured the U.S. with the Ice Champions show the prior summer, my heart ached every day Sergei and I were separated, and we were only apart a few months.

Sergei and Anna spoke quiet words in Russian to each other before Sergei stepped out of the embrace. "Where's Papa?"

Anna's smile tightened, and she paused a moment. "Could not leave work. Will try to take train tomorrow, but plant very busy."

"Oh." Sergei slowly bobbed his head. "Well, if he can't make it, we'll see him in a few days."

Some of the tension drained from my shoulders. Not sure I bought the work excuse, but I'd take any reprieve I could get.

"Emily." Anna beamed at me and took me into her slender arms. "So wonderful to finally meet you."

I returned her warm hug. "I know. I've been looking forward to this for so long."

She cupped her hands around my face as she looked on the verge of tears again. "You are beautiful angel. So happy you will be family."

My own throat swelled, and I could barely squeak out, "Thank you."

Sergei motioned to my parents. "Laura and Jim, this is my mother Anna."

The three of them exchanged double-cheek kisses and a jumble of pleasantries. Mom spoke in a voice even louder than her usual powerful tone, as if that would help Anna understand her better. Sergei and I sent each other amused glances behind her back.

While Sergei accompanied Anna to the registration desk, Mom said, "It would be a shame if his father can't come."

"Yeah, it's a real shame," I said, hoping I didn't sound as insincere as I felt. "I, umm, I should go upstairs to do my hair and makeup."

Dad put his arm around me and kissed the top of my head. "Have a great skate. We'll see you at the arena."

Mom gave me a hug, and I hurried to the elevator. The absence of Sergei's father eliminated a bit of stress, but the pressure of being the favorites to win remained. Chris and I hadn't lost a competition since the Canadians, Madeline Hyatt and Damien Wakefield, had beaten us at the last World Championships. I'd fallen on the triple Lutz, my best jump, and the fatal error had gnawed at me for the past eleven months.

The Canadian champions were in St. Petersburg, as were all the top pairs in the sport. Chris and I had learned at Worlds that having "2002 Olympic silver medalists" under our names wouldn't earn us bonus points from the judges. If anything, the expectations were higher. There was no room for mistakes.

IN THE COLD, GRAY underbelly of the Ice Palace, I flexed my knees and bounced up and down on my skate guards to stay warm. Waiting for our turn to skate was the hardest part. It gave me too much time inside my head.

Sergei stood a few feet from me, staring down the hall. He had a faraway look in his eyes, the one he got on the rare occasions we talked about his days as a skater. The last time he'd stood in this corridor, he was part of Russia's brightest young pair. He and Elena were already being talked about as future Olympic champions. But then one careless moment had ended it all.

Chris's hands massaged my neck, and I jumped. Craning my head up, I expected to see my partner's usual confident smile. Instead, his jaw was set, his dimples hidden.

"I'm not liking our chances here," he said.

"What?" I spun around to face him. "What are you talking about?"

He held the serious expression a moment longer before a huge grin appeared. "Just kidding."

I smacked his arm. "Don't ever do that again."

"I had to see your reaction if you thought I was freaking out."

"You're not allowed to freak out." I straightened the rolled-up cuffs of his burgundy shirt and then brushed my fingertips over his short dark hair, making sure it was neatly in place. "There's only room for one worrier in this partnership."

"And you handle that role very well."

"It's an unfortunate gift from my mother."

"You have nothing to worry about." He returned his hands to my neck and lightly squeezed. "We're gonna skate this program lights-out."

"How did I end up with the coolest partner in the universe?"

"That's a pretty big title to live up to... but I think I can handle it." He grinned.

Sergei snapped out of his daze and wandered over to us

just as our team leader beckoned us toward the ice. He gave us a reminder about the overhead lift and a few other elements, but he still looked a bit distracted. *Is he thinking about what might have been?*

Chris and I hopped onto the ice as the top Russian team exited. I fiddled with the skinny straps of my glitzy black dress and tugged on the short skirt. My hands never stayed still in the moments before a performance. Neither did my brain, and despite Chris's reassurances, I couldn't turn off my anxiety or the image of Sergei and Elena skating on this very ice.

Chris took my hand, and we stopped at one end of the rink for our introduction. I closed my eyes, and the announcer's rich Russian accent presented our names.

"Emily Butler and Christopher Grayden—United States."

Polite applause received us as we skated to center ice and locked into our opening pose, our eyes fixed on each other. The music began, and I let myself get lost in Sergei's passionate choreography. The strong piano notes provided the perfect backdrop for the emotions he wanted us to portray. Sergei and I had found the music, "Victoria's Secret" while watching one of my favorite TV shows, *Due South*. The story of our program was a couple fighting to be together. Chris and I had become pros at faking a romantic connection.

The elements flew by in a blur of clean jumps and centered spins. Approaching our final move, the star lift, Chris grasped my hip and I pushed against his shoulder to raise myself into the air. I started to exhale, but a loud grunt from Chris halted my breath. The noise had a painful groan to it.

We kept moving across the ice but not with our customary speed. Even though I had complete trust in Chris to keep me safe, a panicky shot of adrenaline shook me. I changed positions above his head and gripped his hand like a vise. When he set me down, I looked to him for a positive sign, but he winced through his nod.

The music stopped a few seconds before we struck our

final pose, a result of our cautious pace during the final moments of the program. Disregarding the applause, I grabbed Chris's waist and darted my eyes over his face.

"What's hurting?"

His mouth twitched with discomfort. "My shoulder."

A thousand possible arm injuries flew through my mind as we took quick bows and skated over to a very concerned Sergei. He hugged Chris and held his elbow as he snapped his skate guards over his blades.

"Did you hear anything pop?" Sergei asked.

Chris shook his head. "I don't think so. Just a really bad pain."

While Chris walked to the kiss and cry with his right arm hanging by his side, Sergei hugged me and kissed my forehead.

"You did a great job, Em."

I rested my head against his shoulder. Having my fiancé as my coach was sometimes a tough balance, but at times like these, it was wonderful to meet Sergei's comforting embrace at the boards.

I sat beside Chris on the small bench and put my arm around him, while Sergei reached behind me to pat him on the back. The red light on the camera in front of us blinked, and I thought of Chris's parents watching in Baltimore. They were probably already calling his cell phone and leaving messages. I knew he must really be hurting because he ignored the camera and didn't give his girlfriend Marley a wave or a shout-out.

The scores were good but not our best—5.8's for both technical and artistic merit. We'd racked up a number of perfect 6.0's over the course of the season. The other teams must've made mistakes, however, because our names flashed into first place on the scoreboard. Sergei applauded, and Chris and I stood to acknowledge the crowd's cheers. I showed everyone a bright smile, but inside I churned with worry.

Our team doctor led Chris toward the medical room as

soon as we stepped backstage. There was no time to waste because the first of our two required long programs was scheduled later that night. If Chris needed treatment, the medical staff only had a few hours to tend to him. I didn't want to think about a more serious injury—one that could cause us to withdraw from the competition.

I slipped my jacket over my dress and went to meet the media alone. Since I couldn't provide any information on Chris's condition, the interviews didn't take long. After I changed out of my costume, I found Sergei and the doctor huddled in the corridor.

"How is he?" I asked as I rushed up to them.

Sergei hesitated before answering, and my stomach plunged. "It might be just a strain, but it could be a torn rotator cuff. He'll need an MRI when he gets home."

A torn rotator cuff? Being a Red Sox fan, I knew that injury was very bad news for a baseball pitcher. I couldn't imagine it was any better for a pairs skater who had to lift a hundred pounds over his head every day. My stomach dropped further.

"He can't skate with that, can he?" I asked.

Dr. Parker scratched his beard. "Well, he could with treatment if the pain was tolerable, but without knowing the extent of the injury, I'm advising against it."

"And we don't want to chance anything with Worlds in less than a month," Sergei added.

Chris came out of the men's locker room, pulling his rolling bag with his good arm. He wore a rare glum look. As I hugged him, he said, "I've never had to pull out of a competition. Ever."

"We can't risk hurting you more," I said, keeping my arms around him. He always took such good care of me on the ice. I needed to make sure he took care of himself now.

Sergei accompanied us as we officially reported our withdrawal to the event referee. On our way upstairs to meet my parents on the concourse, Chris called his mom and was still on the phone when we reached the main level of the arena. My parents were with Anna in front of a popcorn stand, and Mom was jabbering and gesturing to Anna, communicating in some kind of sign language. Anna was just nodding in reply.

Dad broke away from them and hugged me. "You skated great."

"Thanks, Dad."

"Did Chris hurt his arm?" Mom asked, shooting a worried glance toward him.

"Dr. Parker thinks it's his rotator cuff. We won't know more until he has some tests at home. But we had to withdraw."

"You not skate tonight?" Anna asked.

"I'm sorry. I know how much you've been looking forward to seeing us compete."

She clutched my arm and shook her head. "No, no, Chris need to get well. I see you skate short program. So beautiful. So much better than watching on TV."

I smiled. "Thank you."

When Chris wrapped up his phone conversation, we all headed to the hotel. Without an event to prepare for later, we could have a leisurely dinner. In the lobby, everyone streamed into the restaurant except Chris, who paused and jerked his thumb toward the elevator. "I think I'm just gonna get room service."

"Are you sure?"

"Yeah, I need to call Marley. Besides, listening to your mom try to talk in some half English-half Russian language might be more painful than a bum shoulder." A hint of a smile surfaced—a most welcome sight.

"Sadly, that's probably true," I said.

His face turned solemn again. "Even if this turns out worst case scenario, we're not missing Worlds. I'll deal with it after. There has to be a shot or something they can give me to get me through it."

"I'll be saying lots of healing prayers tonight before I go to sleep. And you know my mom will say like ten rosaries for you." I jabbed his stomach.

Chris's phone jangled in his pocket, and he retrieved it. "That's Mar. I'll catch up with you later."

The back of his navy Team USA jacket disappeared into the elevator bank, and I rubbed my temples. Chris might think he was Superman, but what if he messed up his shoulder even more trying to skate at Worlds with the injury? Usually he had no problem backing up his confidence, but he'd never had to deal with this big of a physical handicap.

"You are Emily," a thick Russian voice said behind me.

I whirled around and found a middle-aged man peering at me. My blank stare prompted him to continue, "I am Sergei's father."

Of course! I saw it then in his strong cheekbones and slightly crooked nose. Since Max didn't like to be photographed, Sergei hadn't been able to show me any pictures of him.

"I... I didn't think you were coming so soon. Anna said you couldn't leave work, that you were very busy at the plant," I babbled, so caught off guard I didn't think to speak in Russian. *He probably doesn't understand a word I'm saying.*

Indeed, his eyes narrowed and he appeared to be concentrating hard. I realized I hadn't offered a handshake or a kiss or any greeting, but the time for that seemed to have passed.

"Sergei and his mother here?" He scanned the lobby with his piercing green eyes.

"Restaurant," I said in Russian and pointed to the large arched doorway. *Now I'm using sign language, too.*

Max picked up his suitcase, which matched Anna's, and walked toward the dining room. My legs took a moment to move, but I soon trailed after Max's tall figure. He had the same posture and long stride as Sergei.

Max found the table where my parents, Anna, and Sergei were seated, and Sergei shot to his feet. "Papa."

My parents and Anna rose also with matching looks of surprise. Anna asked Max a question in Russian that I vaguely understood as, "You were able to leave work?"

I couldn't decipher Max's mumbled reply, but he still wasn't smiling. His stern face didn't look like one that easily smiled. Anna swept her fingers through her long graying hair and cleared her throat. Sergei had a habit of clearing his throat whenever he was anxious.

"This is Emily's parents," she spoke slowly. "This is Sergei's father."

After handshakes were done across the table, Max looked at his watch. "Competition start in few hours?" He glanced at Anna then Sergei and me.

Anna's mouth creased into a frown. "Emily's partner is hurt, so they not skate."

Max gave her the same confused stare he'd given me in the lobby. Anna switched to Russian and patted her right shoulder. In turn, Max grunted and spewed out a frenzy of agitated Russian I couldn't follow.

"What's he saying?" I whispered to Sergei.

He didn't answer me. His cheeks had reddened, and the color was spreading down to the collar of his dress shirt.

Anna and Max continued to converse while the rest of us watched in uncomfortable silence. Finally, Max shifted his suitcase to his opposite hand and nodded to us.

"Good to meet you. Long on train, so I rest. Have good night."

And with that farewell he left. Anna gave us an apologetic smile, and I sensed that was something she was used to doing.

"He work many hours. Very tired," she said.

Too tired to even give his son a hug? He'd barely acknowledged Sergei's presence in the room. The bad car accident Max had been in a year ago obviously hadn't made him appreciate his family more.

"We understand," Dad said. "Traveling is always tiring, especially after a long day at work."

Mom's eyebrows were still raised as she returned to her seat. I stayed standing and tapped Sergei's arm. "Can we talk for a sec?"

I led him away from the table to a quiet spot near the entrance. A couple of Canadian ice dance coaches passed us, and we swapped brief hellos. I retreated further into the corner and looked up at Sergei.

"What was your dad angry about?"

Sergei rubbed the back of his neck and let out a frustrated sigh. "He wasn't happy that he left work and now you're not skating."

I laughed dryly. "So, now he has something else to hold against me."

"No, it's not you." Sergei touched my cheek. "He doesn't even know you. It's just him… and the way he is."

"When you said he's not a ray of sunshine, you weren't joking. He didn't even shake your hand."

"He's never been good at expressing emotion."

"I'm sure glad you got your mom's personality." I tugged on the end of Sergei's purple tie.

He smiled and wrapped his arms around me, but I could feel the tension in his body. What else could go wrong on this trip? With two days left in St. Petersburg and three more in Moscow, I was almost afraid to ask that question.

CHAPTER THREE

"Morning, sweetie." Mom pecked my cheek. "How's Chris doing?"

"He's feeling okay. He said he's going to skip sight-seeing with us, though."

"Do you think Max will join us? He didn't seem very social last night," Mom said while fiddling with her leather gloves.

We hadn't discussed Sergei's father's behavior at dinner, but it had been like an invisible unwanted guest at the table all night. Across the lobby, the decorative golden elevator doors slid open, and Sergei and his parents exited.

"I guess that answers your question," I said.

Sergei kissed me, and I eyed Max warily as he shook Dad's hand. He looked more at ease than he had upon his arrival, but his smile still seemed forced.

Anna came over to me, buttoning her long coat. "We go to museum first?"

"If that's okay with all of you," I said.

"Yes, yes. We enjoy to be tourist. We are not here in many years."

Since money was tight for Sergei's parents and they rarely took a vacation, I wasn't surprised Anna was soaking up every minute of the trip. I couldn't wait until her visit to the States for the wedding. She was going to love the colorful seascapes of the Cape and the historic charm of Boston. From what I knew of Max, he wouldn't be as impressed. Or if he was, he wouldn't show it.

We set off for Palace Square, the famous landmark seen in most pictures of St. Petersburg and the site of the State Hermitage Museum. Sergei and I strolled behind our parents, and I noticed Max kept his hands shoved in his pockets, not offering Anna any warmth. Dad had linked his arm through Mom's as soon as we stepped outside.

As we walked through the expansive Square, I gaped at the long stretch of ornate structures. The layers of snow on the ground surrounding the palaces added to the area's majestic feel. We stopped in front of the Winter Palace, and my eyes swept over the three-story green and white building.

"It kinda looks like a big wedding cake," I said to Sergei.

He laughed. "I've never thought about it, but it does a little."

We made our way into the museum and started our tour of the numerous collections. Max seemed interested in a sculpture of Adonis, so I formulated a comment in Russian in my head and approached him.

"It must take so much patience to complete a detailed work like this."

"Yes, it must," Max replied and shuffled over to another sculpture.

Nice talking to you, too. Deciding to make another attempt, I followed Max and did my best to engage him in conversation, but he gave me only short responses. Sergei watched us from a close distance, and the glare he aimed at his father could turn mortals to stone.

I wandered away from the group and stared at a row of

Italian religious paintings, admiring the deep colors and precise brushwork. Mom joined me with a backward glance over her shoulder.

"Am I imagining it or is there some tension between Sergei and his father?" she asked.

I focused on the da Vinci painting before me so I wouldn't have to face Mom with a lie. "They've never been very close, so it's probably just awkward spending time together." That might not be the main reason, but there was some truth to it.

"Anna is such a lovely person. She's really embraced you. But Max seems so distant to Sergei and to you, too."

Sergei walked up to my side, so I took that opportunity to leave Mom and the discussion of Max. I wasn't going to share the reason for his coldness. My parents knew Sergei had been involved with Elena, but they thought his career had ended because Elena's father didn't approve of the relationship. They didn't know about the pregnancy, and I wanted to keep it that way. If Mom found out Sergei had fathered a child as a teenager, she'd switch into judgmental mode in a hot second.

After we viewed all the collections we wanted to see, we left the museum and settled on a nearby eatery for a late lunch. I sat between Sergei and Max, squirming from the tension radiating between them.

The young waiter took our orders, which turned into a complicated process when Mom tried to stray from the menu and ask for a different type of sauce on her pasta. I'd thought selecting an Italian restaurant for the meal would make things easier. Not so much. Max shook his head and made some sort of noise as Mom battled the waiter in broken Russian. Sergei quickly intervened and relayed Mom's request.

Anna smiled at me across the table. "Do you finish all plans for wedding?"

"Almost. The seamstress who makes my costumes is making my dress, and she has some alterations left to do.

Other than that, there are just a few little things to take care of."

"You finish honeymoon plans also?"

I nodded. "All set. I'll have to show you pictures of the house we're renting. It has an amazing view of the water."

"It is nice you not have to travel far."

Sergei took my hand, and I squeezed it as I replied, "That's why we chose Martha's Vineyard. We travel so much with skating that we wanted to go somewhere without a lot of hassle. We can take the ferry and be there in an hour."

"Where do you live after wedding?" Max asked.

My head jerked toward him at his sudden willingness to speak to me. Sergei answered before I could recover from my surprise.

"We're going to stay at Emily's parents' summer house until we find a place."

"It's where I live now," I added.

"House cost much money in Cape Cod?" Max asked.

Is he making small talk or is he going somewhere with this question? I looked at Sergei then back at Max. "Some are very expensive, but we'll be looking for something small... since it'll just be the two of us for a few years."

Anna smiled and touched Mom's arm. "Yes, no grandchildren for us until after Olympics."

"Hrrmph," Max grumbled and mumbled in Russian, "Unless he messes up like he did with Elena. We may have a grandchild next year."

I sucked in a breath and threw a quick glance at my parents, praying they hadn't understood what Max had said. Sergei's grip on my hand tightened. I waited for a reaction, but neither Mom nor Dad looked shocked, so I finally exhaled.

Anna scowled at her husband but didn't say anything. Mom leaned toward her. "I'm sorry, I didn't quite follow that."

"It is not important," Anna replied with a wave of her

hand.

But Mom knew something was off. She set her brown eyes like lasers on Max throughout the remainder of lunch even though he uttered only a handful of words. When we left the restaurant, she steered me ahead of the others and dropped her voice.

"What was that comment Max made that upset everyone? I know you understood him. I could see it on your face."

I groaned inwardly. I knew she was going to ask me that, so I'd prepared an answer while I ate my pasta. I hated lying, but I wasn't going to let Max blow open a big mess four months before my wedding. It had taken Mom such a long time to accept my relationship with Sergei since he was my coach. Now was not the time to undo the goodwill between them.

"He said something like, 'They might not win.' I guess he was implying I'd keep skating if we don't win gold at the Olympics, and that would delay having kids."

"Would you keep skating?"

"I don't think so. I mean, I can't say how I'll feel then, but right now, I can't imagine competing past two thousand six."

With Mom's concerns addressed, I hung back for Sergei and cozied into the crook of his arm. "We're okay," I said quietly. "She didn't understand him at all."

"I can't believe he said that," Sergei muttered. "It took everything in me not to go off on him."

"Do we have to worry about him bringing it up again in front of my parents? What if he tries to say it in English next time?"

"I'll talk to him. I would've said something earlier, but I didn't think he'd mention it in casual conversation."

"Does he really think I'd be stupid enough to get pregnant before the Olympics?"

Sergei stiffened, and I touched my fingers to my mouth. "I'm sorry, I didn't mean..."

"It's okay. Elena and I *were* stupid." Sergei glared at the back of Max's head. "And my father thinks he has to constantly remind me. As if I could ever forget."

I slowed up to put more space between our parents and us. Sergei sounded like he wanted to talk about his past, so I wanted to give him the chance.

"Do you think about it a lot?" I asked. "How things would be different if you hadn't made that mistake?"

"I don't think about what might've been because I know I'm right where I'm meant to be—with you." He hugged me closer to his side and kissed the top of my head. Looking up, he paused and stared at a young family crossing the street. "But I do think about the baby."

His wistful tone made me want to hold him tighter. I cinched my arm around his waist and stayed quiet, allowing Sergei to continue talking at his own pace.

"I've never told anyone this, but when I travel different places and I see a kid with some of my features, I wonder if they could be mine." He rubbed his hand through his hair. "It's ridiculous, I know."

"No, it's not," I said softly.

"I just wish I could see if he's happy. Or *she's* happy." He shook his head and let out a slow breath that smoked through the frigid air. "I don't even know if the baby was a boy or a girl."

"I would hope that Elena's father arranged for a good home for it... the baby."

"I hope so." Both Sergei's voice and his gaze shifted downward.

I never knew Sergei thought about his child so much, and I wondered how much more emotion he held inside. I stopped walking and slid in front of him. Placing my hands on his face, I looked into his eyes but didn't speak. I just wanted to connect with him.

Sergei drew me nearer and rested his forehead against

mine. His lips were closing in for a kiss when Mom called my name behind me. I turned, and she pointed at the small shop ahead.

"We're stopping in this bakery."

I faced Sergei again. "Do you want something sweet?"

He kissed the tip of my nose. "I have my sweetness right here."

I smiled and hugged him, warming my face against his wool scarf. Hearing Sergei talk about the baby made me sad but also a little uneasy. That part of his past still weighed on his mind, and he might never come to terms with it. I could only hope that if he opened up more and more, he would find some peace.

SERGEI HAD A CHAT with Max that kept him from making any more inappropriate comments, but it didn't ease the strain between them, and it didn't make Max any friendlier toward me. When Monday morning came, I happily packed for the train ride to Moscow. Max would be returning to work, and Sergei and Anna could show us their hometown without any negative vibes around us.

Outside the train window, the icy landscape blurred into a haze of white as we sped away from St. Petersburg. With our parents seated in a different car, Sergei and I were enjoying some rare alone time. I turned to him and brought my knees up onto his lap.

"This is going to be so much fun. I finally get to see where you grew up, where you skated…"

"My air of mystery will be gone," he said with a sigh.

"Especially after I see those baby pictures your mom promised to show me." I giggled.

He groaned. "She'll probably have them waiting next to the dinner table tonight."

"I'm excited for my first home-cooked Russian meal. I told your mom I'd return the favor with an Italian feast when she comes for the wedding. All the best of my grandma's recipes."

"Maybe you can win over my father with your cooking. He does love a good meal."

"I got *your* attention with my spinach lasagna." I winked, thinking back to the first time I'd cooked for Sergei.

He smiled and angled his head down, his mouth inches from mine. "It was more than the lasagna."

He gave me a slow, soft kiss and treated me to several more during the four-hour trip. Upon arrival in Moscow, the train took us into the center of the city, where we parted ways with Anna and Max. They boarded a bus to their apartment, while Sergei, my parents, and I snagged a taxi to our hotel.

Mom and Dad said they wanted to take it easy for the afternoon, so I suggested Sergei and I visit the sports club where he'd trained for twelve years. He hesitated a bit, and I considered proposing another activity, but then he nodded. "Yeah, we can do that today."

Thick traffic made our taxi ride long. The time passed fast with Sergei playing tour guide through the cab's windows, but as we neared our destination, he grew quiet.

I laid my hand on his thigh. "We can turn around if you're not up for this."

He squinted out his smudged window and cleared his throat. "No, I want to see if it's changed any."

The cab pulled up to the large multi-rink complex, and we plodded through the snow to the entrance. Sergei swung open the door, and I tugged the zipper on my coat higher. The building didn't offer any relief from the cold.

"It still smells the same." Sergei looked around the lobby.

Cases packed with medals and trophies adorned the walls. Above them hung hockey jerseys and red banners celebrating the club's many successes. Two tiny blonde girls in pink skating dresses emerged through the double doors to our right, and I caught a glimpse of an ice surface.

"Is that the main rink?" I asked.

Sergei nodded and showed me inside. Music from the ballet *Spartacus* reverberated off the tall ceiling. On the ice, a number of girls and boys were working on elements and consulting with coaches. There were no bleachers like we had at our rink on the Cape. The few spectators stood on a balcony overlooking the ice.

We drifted toward the edge of the rink. Sergei spread his hands on the boards and stared at a spot on the ice. "My coach used to stand right there for the entire session. He wouldn't move. But we could hear him yelling at the other end of the rink."

"Sounds like a fun guy."

"He hated when we asked questions. If we didn't understand something the first time, we had to figure it out on our own because he refused to repeat himself."

"Wow. That makes your accomplishments even more impressive then. You were practically coaching yourself."

"The little kids used to come to me for help, and he would yell at me for teaching them." Sergei shook his head. "When I decided to quit skating after Elena and I split, that was one of the hardest things—leaving all the kids."

I rubbed the back of his leather jacket. "One good thing came out of his awful teaching methods. You learned how to be an amazing coach."

His gaze traveled to the students on the ice, and we watched the action in silence for a few minutes. Sergei's eyes had that faraway look again.

"What are you thinking about?' I asked.

"The last day I skated here." He swallowed, and his jaw tensed. "The day Elena told me she was pregnant."

An uncomfortable heat flushed my cheeks, and I loosened the scarf knotted around my neck. "Did she tell you here?"

He nodded. "After practice. There was a spot behind the building where we used to meet so our coach wouldn't see us. He would've gone straight to Elena's father if he'd known we were together, and I've told you how Ivan felt about me."

"He didn't want you anywhere near Elena off the ice. He didn't think you were good enough."

"When she said she was pregnant, I thought, 'Ivan is going to kill me.'"

"From what you've said about his power and his reputation, that was probably a valid fear."

Sergei looked down at the boards. "I can't believe how careless we were. With everything that was at stake… I disappointed so many people."

I wanted to say something comforting, but my stomach was turning at the images of Elena and him flashing through my head. The fact that it had all happened years ago didn't make it any less unpleasant for me to think about.

Sergei's phone rang, and he fumbled through his pocket to check the caller. "It's my mother."

I glanced around. I needed a couple of minutes to myself. "I'm gonna look for the restroom."

"They're at the end of the hall." He pointed behind us and peered at me. "Are you okay?"

Was my face red? Probably green. "Yeah. I'll be right back."

As I walked along the dank corridor, *Spartacus* faded, overtaken by tinkly piano music. Behind a large window to my left, a class of little girls and boys stretched through ballet positions. Gathered next to the window were a couple of ladies cloaked in fur coats. Their pungent perfume followed me down the hallway like a floral fog.

An exterior door next to the washrooms was propped open, revealing the rear of the complex. Was that where Sergei and Elena used to hide? What did they do back there? Make out? *Well, you know they went way beyond that.* I gulped as more images flooded my brain.

I slipped inside the restroom, where another fur-clad woman stood facing the stone wall, her phone to her ear. She lowered her tone and continued her conversation as I washed my hands and splashed water on my cheeks.

I reached for a paper towel from the rusty dispenser, while the woman snapped the phone shut and spun around. We came face to face, and her eyes widened. I froze in place and gasped.

It couldn't be.

But there she was right in front of me.

Elena.

CHAPTER FOUR

SHE WAS GORGEOUS. HER SILKY BLACK hair still had the bob cut, softly framing her face. Not one blemish could be found on her porcelain skin. She resembled the teenager I'd seen in photos but with a sophisticated maturity. Everything about her, from her delicate makeup to her manicured nails, gave off a feeling of perfection.

I can't believe it's really her.

Elena blinked and returned my examining stare. She looked as alarmed as I felt shocked. I said in Russian, "You know who I am."

She paused, pressing her red-stained lips together. "Yes."

"Do you speak English?"

"Yes," she repeated.

A drop of water slid down my cheek, and I remembered the paper towel in my hand. I patted my face, which had grown hot again. *Nothing like being a mess when meeting your fiancé's ex-girlfriend, especially when she looks flawless.*

"Sergei's not going to believe you're here," I said.

Elena shook her head and walked around me. "I should not see Sergei."

I wasn't keen on them having a reunion either, but Elena's reluctance baffled me. "Why not?"

"Too many bad feelings. It is best to leave past."

"I can't not tell him I saw you."

"I do not want to see him," she stated forcefully.

Ten years had passed since they'd split, and she still hadn't gotten over it? Whatever her reason, I wasn't going to push her. I had no desire to watch Sergei reconnect with her.

"Okay. If that's what you want."

I marched out the door but stopped in the hall. Maybe I shouldn't tell Sergei about Elena. He was already feeling down enough, thinking about all the disappointment he'd caused. Telling him Elena refused to talk to him wouldn't make him feel better. But how could I face him and pretend nothing out of the ordinary had happened?

I walked slowly toward the ice where Sergei had resumed his position at the boards, watching the skaters. I joined him, and he turned his body to face me.

"I'm sorry I brought up that stuff about Elena," he said. "Being here is just kind of… intense."

"You don't have to apologize. You can talk to me about anything."

He enveloped me in his arms, and I pressed my face to his neck, breathing in his spicy cologne. *You don't have to tell him about Elena.* He held me tighter, and I took a deeper breath. *No, I can't do it. I can't keep this from him.*

"I have to tell you something unbelievable," I said, pulling away. "Elena is here."

"What? Where?" Sergei's eyes dashed around the rink.

"I ran into her in the restroom. I told her you were here, but she said seeing you would bring up bad feelings."

"She won't even say hello? After all this time?"

"I don't understand it either."

Sergei stood with his mouth agape. "Why would she even be here?"

"I don't know. Maybe she's coaching? You heard from a friend that she doesn't have any kids, right?"

"Yeah, that was a few years ago." He scratched his head. "What did she say to you besides not wanting to see me?"

I started to reply, but the appearance of Elena stole my words. She quickly clicked across the concrete floor in her stiletto boots and stopped in front of us. She'd looked poised on her walk over, but now that she was next to Sergei, she shifted from heel to heel, and her fingers fiddled with her silver bracelets. Sergei gave her a subtle once-over, and the uncomfortable feeling returned to the pit of my gut.

"Sergei," she said softly in Russian. "You look well."

He studied her, delaying his response. "So do you." A deep V formed between his brows, and he switched to English, "I thought you didn't want to see me."

"I do not want to bother you. You have very successful life now. No need to bring up past." Elena fidgeted and looked over her shoulder.

"I hope all is well with you? You are married?" Sergei asked.

"No, I divorce two years ago." She glanced again at the corridor as she continued to jangle her bracelets.

"I'm sorry," Sergei said.

"Are you coaching now?" I asked.

"I am here with my cousins' daughter. She wait for me, so I must go." She started to back away. "It is good to see you, Sergei. I am happy you have good life."

She hurried toward the ballet studio, leaving Sergei and I to share bewildered looks. I'd only known Elena for a total of two minutes, but she'd left a lasting impression.

"That was very strange," I said.

"She practically ran out of here."

"I can't get over the fact that she's here when we were just talking about her."

Sergei stared down the hall. "There are so many things I

wanted to ask her… about when she went away and…"

A group of kids and parents streamed into the area from the studio, among them Elena with a young girl beside her. Elena rushed the girl to the exit as she helped her put on her pink jacket. We watched them pass through the gray double doors with the rest of the crowd.

Sergei rubbed his hand over his mouth and made a move for the door. "I'll be back."

"Where…" I asked to his retreating figure. I hesitated but then jogged after Sergei. When I caught up to him, he said, "I have to talk to her."

Outside in the parking lot, Elena shut the rear driver's side door of her dark SUV and was about to climb behind the wheel. Sergei called her name and she paused behind the open door, stricken with a startled look.

"What do you want?" she asked shakily.

"I haven't seen you in ten years and you can't spare a few minutes?" Sergei asked.

I peered at the back window, but the tinted glass prevented me from seeing inside. Elena took a step closer to the vehicle. "There is nothing more to say."

The rear door opened, and the girl in the pink jacket jumped out. A white knit cap covered the top of her long black hair, and a matching scarf circled her neck. She gawked at me and said quietly, "You're Emily Butler."

That's when I saw them. Her blue eyes. Eyes the color of crystal azure seas. The same eyes that mesmerized me on a daily basis.

Sergei's eyes.

"Liza, please sit in car. We need to go," Elena ordered.

But Liza didn't move. She continued to stare at me, just as Sergei and I did back at her. Luckily, she was too enamored with me to notice Sergei. An unconscious movement shot my arm forward toward the girl.

"Yes, I'm Emily. You're Liza?"

Her face lit up as she shyly took my hand. "I watch you on TV all the time."

She didn't have any hint of a Russian accent. I cocked my head to the side. "Are you American?"

"She is," Elena answered for her. "She live in New York until last year."

A jumble of thoughts confused me as I tried to make sense of what I was seeing and hearing. Sergei couldn't tear his eyes away from Liza, and he'd lost the ability to speak.

"We're going to America for the World Championships," Liza said. "It's my birthday present."

"You're going to Washington D.C.?" Sergei asked, finally finding his voice.

"Yes," Elena said. "Liza's parents buy tickets last year… before they pass away."

My hand went to my heart, while Sergei said, "I'm so sorry."

"Liza live with me now, and we need to get home, if you excuse us."

The petite girl looked up at Elena with pleading eyes. "Can I get Emily's autograph first?"

Elena pursed her lips and waited a few moments before turning to me. "This is okay?"

"Sure, of course," I stammered.

Liza hopped into the back seat and reemerged with a purple backpack. She pulled out a small notebook and pen and handed them to me.

"Is it L-E-E-Z-A?" I asked, holding the pen above the paper.

"L-I-Z-A," she said.

As I wrote her name, I asked, "How long have you been skating?"

"Since I was four."

"And how old are you now?"

"I'll be nine in two weeks." She bobbed up and down.

The quick math in my head brought me to a date circa summer nineteen ninety-three. The summer Elena had gotten pregnant. My hand started to shake and not from the bone-chilling cold. I steadied the pen and finished the autograph.

"There you go." I returned the book to Liza with a quivering smile.

She gazed wide-eyed at the paper. "Thank you."

"Time to leave." Elena herded the girl into the SUV. "Again, it is good to see you, Sergei."

"Elena, we need to—" Sergei said, but Elena shut her door. She reversed out of the parking space and zoomed away before I could blink.

My heart beat as fast as the speed of Elena's SUV. I slowly pivoted toward Sergei. He stood with his hand atop his head, staring down the road.

"Do you think… could Liza possibly be…" My voice trickled into a whisper.

Sergei's eyes showed both pain and confusion. "My daughter?" he croaked.

I shivered and wrapped my arms across my chest. His *daughter*. Hearing Sergei say it out loud made my suspicion all too real.

"Could Elena have given the baby to her cousins?" His forehead wrinkled.

I looked down at my boots and closed my eyes for a moment. *What is happening here? We just came to visit the rink and now we might have discovered Sergei's child?*

"Could that be what her father made her do?" Sergei rambled on.

"She didn't want us to see Liza," I said, raising my head.

"I can't…" Sergei ran his hand through his hair. "I have to find out if she's…"

"Do you think Elena will tell you the truth?"

He stood taller with determination. "She has to. I'm not leaving without answers. If Liza trains here, then she'll be back tomorrow. And I'll be here waiting."

I chewed on the inside of my lip. "I'd like to come with you, if that's okay."

"Of course." He grasped my hand and intertwined our fingers. "I just assumed you'd be with me."

"We have to keep this to ourselves tonight at dinner."

Sergei nodded. "Until we know anything for certain."

I knew one thing for certain—Elena had secrets. Secrets that could turn everything in our lives upside down.

"WELCOME! WELCOME!" ANNA EXCLAIMED. "Dinner ready very soon."

Sergei and I stepped inside ahead of my parents, and I was struck by the size of the apartment. Sergei had described it to me, but words hadn't adequately conveyed the small dimensions.

I shed my jacket, and Sergei hung it on one of the dining table chairs. The table sat almost in the doorway. There was no separation between the eating area and the living room. The entire space could fit inside my parents' den in Brookline.

"Papa's working?" Sergei asked.

"Yes, he work late shift," Anna said and motioned to the short couch and two mismatched parlor chairs. "Please sit. We have drink."

Sergei accompanied Anna to the kitchen, and Mom and Dad sat in the chairs. I sank into the old brown sofa and noticed the bed in the tiny alcove across the room. The space had to be Sergei's old bedroom from what he'd described. I'd seen closets bigger.

Sergei and Anna returned, carrying glasses of liquid that resembled cider or beer. Dad accepted one from Anna and examined the drink. "Is this Kvass?"

"Yes, like you try in St. Petersburg," Anna said.

I hadn't sampled the malt-like drink at any of the restaurants in St. Petersburg, so I took a tentative taste from my glass. An initial hint of lemon hit my tongue followed by the lasting flavor of beer. I hid my dislike behind a smile.

"Where in Moscow do you want to visit tomorrow?" Anna asked. "Red Square? Cathedrals? I can show you good market for shopping."

"Em and I need to go back to the rink in the morning," Sergei said, sitting beside me. "We saw Elena there, but she didn't have time to talk today."

Anna gasped. "You see Elena?"

Mom leaned forward in her seat. "This was the first time since you quit skating, isn't it?"

"Yes. So, obviously, I wanted to talk to her, but she couldn't stay."

"Does she work at the rink?" Mom asked.

"She was there with her cousins' daughter." Sergei's voice dropped on the last word and he stared at his glass.

Mom watched me with a worried frown. If she only knew the situation could be much more complicated than just running into an ex-girlfriend.

A bell dinged in the kitchen, and Anna rose with her drink. I took a tiny sip of mine, concentrating on the frayed rug under my feet. Sergei hadn't said much after we'd left the rink. He was understandably stunned from meeting Liza, but I wondered what he was thinking about Elena. Was he having flashes of their years together? He'd said he didn't have any thoughts of "what might've been," but did seeing the beautiful Elena and their possible daughter make him feel different?

Both my parents had their eyes on me now, so I gave them a little smile as I took another sip of my Kvass.

"We can check out the area around the hotel in the morning," Dad said to Mom. "Looked like there were some interesting shops and cafés."

God bless my father. Nothing ever fazed him. I was going

to need his calmness if Liza turned out to be Sergei's daughter. I cringed on the inside just thinking about telling Mom the news.

Anna called us to dinner, and we helped ourselves to the first course, a cabbage soup Sergei introduced to me as shchi. The table, sized for four, was set with plain ivory-colored china and a small bouquet of white lilies in the center. It would've been a tight fit if Max had been there.

Each course gave my palette a new experience, and I enjoyed the meal more than I'd anticipated. The entrée, beef and pork-filled dumplings called pelmeni, had me humming with appreciation. The thin and translucent dough melted in my mouth, and the filling was well-seasoned and juicy. Anna detailed each step of the recipe and promised to give me a copy. Talking food with her pushed thoughts of Elena and Liza to the back of my mind.

After dessert of Russian fruit cake, my parents helped Anna clear the table while Sergei and I went over to his room, if one could call it that. We stood between the bed and a tall wooden cabinet, and there was barely enough space for us to move. I thought of my bedroom in my parents' house—the four-poster bed, my own bathroom, the window seat where I loved to read. Sergei hadn't enjoyed any such comforts growing up.

"This bed looks even smaller than a twin," I said. "How did you fit in this?"

He laughed. "When I had my growth spurt at fifteen and hit six feet, it got tough."

"I can't imagine not having a door for privacy. There were many times I needed to shut out my mom's nagging."

"I guess since I never had a door, I didn't know what I was missing."

"Where'd you keep all your stuff?" I asked.

"My clothes were in here." Sergei tapped the cabinet. "Everything else got crammed under the bed."

"It's nice you had a window," I said, running my hand along the sill. My fingers stopped when I reached a carving—one Russian word etched into the wood.

Elena.

"Did you do this?" I asked.

Sergei's chest bumped my back as he looked over my shoulder. "No. Elena did."

My neck tensed, and I pulled my hand away from the window. "So, she was here. In your room."

Sergei turned my waist so I faced him. "A very, very long time ago."

"It didn't seem so long ago today."

I moved past him into the living room just as Anna came forward with a picture album.

"Here are photos I promise to show you," she said.

I wiped the irritation from my face and sat with Anna on the sofa. Sergei perched on the arm as I opened the album to a black and white picture of him as an infant.

"Sergei such good baby. Cry very little," Anna said.

"That's how Emily was, too," Mom said.

"We used to keep checking on her in the nursery to make sure she was okay because we couldn't believe a baby would be so quiet." Dad chuckled.

I sharply flipped the page. All the talk about babies was just reminding me of Elena in Sergei's bedroom. The alcove had probably been another one of their hiding places.

I concentrated on the photos of toddler Sergei—ones of him playing in a snowy playground, showing off a toy truck, and smiling next to his traditional Russian birthday pie. As I looked at the pictures I'd wanted to see for so long, my nerves relaxed and my heart softened at Sergei's adorableness. His hair was blond then, and his blue eyes practically popped off the page.

"You were so cute," I said, grinning up at Sergei.

He glanced down with an embarrassed smile. I resumed

paging through the album and gushing over the images until I arrived on one of Sergei and Elena as pre-teens in matching glittery blue costumes. They were posing in what appeared to be the lobby of the rink, and Sergei's arm was locked around Elena's tiny shoulders. He looked protective of her, which made sense considering how much Elena feared her father.

I lingered on the page, my chest tightening more the longer I stared at the photo. Seeing the two of them together as kids—Elena with her fair skin and dark hair next to Sergei with his striking blue eyes—I became convinced Liza was their child. I peeked up at Sergei, and his dazed look said he was thinking the same thing.

CHAPTER FIVE

THE DOOR TO THE SPORTS CLUB swung shut behind us, and I stomped my boots on the rug to shed the wet snow. Sergei did the same while keeping his eyes fixed on the lobby. A few women congregated near the far wall, but Elena wasn't among them.

We made our way further inside, where a group of about ten kids occupied the ice. I looked for Liza and finally spotted her on the opposite end of the rink executing a layback spin. Her back was beautifully arched, her right leg expertly turned out. The long dark hair that had hung over her shoulders the day before was pinned into a tight bun.

Sergei gazed up at the spectators on the balcony. "I don't see Elena."

"She has to be here somewhere," I said, tapping my fingers on the boards. I wanted to be there so I didn't feel left out, but I'd like the conversation with Elena to be over as soon as possible.

Liza repeated her spin three more times for her coach, a diminutive older man with his arms crossed and a stern eye trained on his student. When Liza skated closer to him, he said a few words and her head drooped. Sergei stepped toward the boards, watching the lesson with a concerned stare.

A rapid click-clack of heels behind us became louder, and the hairs on my neck rose, anticipating the confrontation. Sergei and I both turned at the same time.

"Why are you here?" Elena asked in Russian.

Bundled in a different fur, she wore the same agitated look she'd had when we last saw her in the parking lot.

"You must know I'd have questions," Sergei replied in English.

Elena glanced at me and snapped, "There is nothing to question."

"I think we should talk outside," Sergei said. "This isn't the place to discuss this."

"What is to discuss? Nothing."

Sergei inhaled deeply. "We can either talk outside or I'll wait here until Liza's finished and say it in front of her."

Elena narrowed her dark eyes and pivoted on her five-inch heels, stalking toward the exit. Sergei placed his hand on the small of my back, and we followed Elena outside to the sidewalk. Her anxious breaths showed as white puffs in the frosty morning.

I stayed close to Sergei's side. I might be mostly an observer during the conversation, but I wanted Sergei to feel my presence.

He stood in front of Elena and shoved his hands in his jacket pockets. "I don't even know how to ask this except to just ask it." He swallowed slowly. "Is Liza our daughter?"

Elena burst out a laugh. "It is ridiculous. She is my cousin. I raise her only past year."

Her too-quick response raised my suspicions even more. It sounded rehearsed, and Elena was staring over Sergei's shoulder rather than at his face.

"Lena, I took one look at that girl and could see how much she resembles us," Sergei said.

Lena? Maybe he thought using childhood nicknames would open her up. I shuffled my feet on the pavement, watching helplessly as Sergei's frustration grew. There was nothing I could do to make this easier for him.

"Liza's father had blue eyes," Elena said sharply.

"*My* blue eyes?"

"You make mistake." She started to walk away, but Sergei blocked her path.

"I don't think so," he said. "I think the reason you didn't want to talk to me yesterday and the reason you tried to run out of here with Liza was because you didn't want me to see her."

"Liza is not your concern. You have life in America. I have life here. You marry soon." Elena waved her hand at me. "Stop with questions!"

A pair of skaters and their mothers came through the glass doors and gave us curious stares. I returned them with my own icy glare, hoping it would drive the onlookers away. It worked.

"I have a right to know if she's my child," Sergei said, sounding more desperate with every word. "Why would you deny me that?"

Elena's chin began to tremble and she turned away from us, staring across the snow-covered parking lot. The sick feeling I'd had since the previous afternoon spread from my stomach to my heart. I couldn't blame Elena for wanting to be left alone. But Sergei deserved to know the truth.

"What do you do if she is yours?" Elena asked in a shaky voice.

Sergei took a slow step forward. "You're saying it's true."

"What do you do?" Elena faced Sergei, her eyes burning with her question.

"I'd want to be part of her life."

There was no hesitation in Sergei's response. He'd apparently moved from shock to certainty in a short period of time. I wished I could do the same, but I was stuck in amazement at the turn of events.

"She do not know I am her mother," Elena choked. "My father think it best—"

"Your father!" Sergei exclaimed. "You're still letting him control your life?"

"No, he is gone now!"

Sergei's face froze. "He's...?"

Elena settled her chin and spoke quieter, "He suffer illness long time. He pass away six months ago."

Sergei slowly rubbed his hand through his hair. "I'm sorry."

I opened my mouth to add my condolences but decided Elena probably wouldn't hear me. She was singularly focused on Sergei, and Sergei looked only at her. I felt like an even more distant observer.

"I do not tell Liza she is mine," Elena said. "It is not right for her now."

"I know it will be hard for her, but she should know the truth," Sergei said.

"It give her so much confusion." Elena shook her head. "How can I tell her everything is lies?"

"Don't you want her to know who you really are?"

"I take care of her as mother. That is enough."

"I don't think you really believe that. You were robbed of all those years just like I was. We can make this right."

Elena covered her face with her hands. "I cannot think what is right."

My head spun from the emotional exchange. Things were happening too fast. Someone needed to slow down the runaway train of confessions and demands.

I touched Sergei's forearm. "Can we talk for a minute?"

Sergei kept his eyes on Elena for a moment before he moved down the sidewalk with me, leaving Elena sniffling to herself. I placed my hands on both sides of Sergei's face, caressing his prickly stubble with my thumbs.

"We don't have to make any big decisions right now," I said.

"We're only here for two more days," he said. "There's no time to take it slow. I can't go home without resolving this."

"I don't know that Elena will agree to resolve anything."

"I need Liza to know who I am. I can't just leave without..." He shot an anxious look toward the rink.

My hands slid down the front of his jacket. "If you go to her now, then you have to leave her in two days. This is going to be such a shock for her. Maybe it would better to wait."

"I've lost nine years already. I don't want to lose another day."

I sighed in exasperation. Sergei sounded so certain he was ready to be a father, but he hadn't even asked how I felt about it. He was caught up in emotion and not thinking. Somehow, I had to make him understand the consequences of what he was suggesting.

"It sounds like Liza has been through a ton of changes in the past year with her parents dying, then moving to a different country... Adding another huge change might not be a good idea."

"But this would be a good change. She'd have parents again."

Excited optimism filled his voice, and the hope in his eyes was so pure. I couldn't imagine what he must be feeling. But I knew what I was feeling—fear. Fear that our future was about to change in a massive way.

"Sergei," Elena called.

He looked up over the top of my head, and I turned to see Elena approach. She dabbed at her eyes and asked, "Why you ask me to do this? Why this is so important to you?"

Sergei paused and wet his lips. "I've never stopped thinking about what happened to our child. I've always wanted to know if they had a good family—"

"Liza have everything," Elena interrupted. "I give her everything she needs. Best tutor, best coach… When my cousins pass away, my father help me bring Liza here and make sure she have good life."

"How did they die?" I asked, curiosity getting the better of me.

Elena's eyes misted over again. "Terrible car accident. When we receive phone call, I do not believe it. They take Liza as baby and give her good home. They let me see her."

"So, she's always known you as her cousin," I said.

"It is good she know me so when I bring her to Russia, she is not with stranger."

"You've been in contact with her all these years and you couldn't let me know?" Sergei asked. "You couldn't call me and tell me she was okay?"

"If I tell you, you want to see her and my father not allow it. You know I do not cross him."

"Of course. He always had to keep me away," Sergei said, his words as biting as the cold stinging my face.

I reached for his arm and gave it a squeeze. He looked down at the frozen ground, closing his eyes. We stood motionless until Sergei slowly lifted his head.

"I don't want to fight. I just don't know what else to do except to beg of you to please talk to Liza." He took a deep breath. "Lena, please. All I want is to get to know her, to show her she has someone else she can call family."

Elena set her glistening eyes on Sergei. "Do you try to take her from me?"

"No. I would never do that. She needs both of us."

"You promise?" she spoke louder. "You swear that?"

"Yes. You could always trust me. I know it's been a long time, but that hasn't changed."

They stared at each other, and my throat tightened as I witnessed a flicker of the connection between them. The connection of all those years, partnering on the ice and loving each other off it. Their time apart hadn't completely erased it.

"Okay," Elena whispered. "I try. I try tonight to tell her."

"Thank you," Sergei said hoarsely. "We're here only a couple more days, so I'd like to see her as soon as I can."

"I tell you good time to come. I do not know how she take this." Elena pulled a tissue from her purse and patted the corners of her eyes. "I go inside. Liza may look for me."

"Let me give you my phone number so you can reach me," Sergei said.

Elena took out her cell phone and tapped in the digits. Sergei asked for hers, and she hesitated before relaying them.

"Are you living in your father's house?" Sergei asked.

"Yes. It is good place for Liza and me. It is home." She emphasized the last word, seemingly as a reminder to Sergei in case he thought of breaking his promise.

Elena hurried inside, and I expelled a long breath. Sergei turned to me, and we stood in silence for a minute.

"What are you thinking?" he asked.

I'm thinking we should've discussed this before you set it all in motion. I'm thinking the more I'm around Elena, the more uncomfortable I am.

"Em?"

I looked up into Sergei's thoughtful gaze and remembered how emotional he'd been when we talked about his past. He wouldn't be making such rash decisions if they didn't come from his heart. I had to try to understand how he felt. He needed my support more than ever.

"I think you should prepare yourself for Liza's reaction," I said. "When Elena gives her the news, she might not be open to seeing you right now. I just want you to be ready for that."

"I hope Elena tells her it wasn't our choice to give her away."

"I doubt she's going to tell her that her grandfather was the one who orchestrated it all. But hopefully she'll explain it was out of your control."

Sergei brought me into his arms and buried his face in my hair. "Thank you for being so understanding. You are amazing."

I held onto him, willing myself to ignore my swirling emotions and to look at the situation objectively. Sergei had been given such a wonderful gift. We'd always conquered challenges together, and we'd do the same here. I had to stand strong by Sergei's side because who knew what was going to happen once Liza found out the truth.

CHAPTER SIX

"ARE YOU READY FOR THIS?" I asked Sergei as we walked hand in hand up to his parents' door.

"Are *you* ready?" He squeezed my palm. "Your mom's not going to be happy you weren't honest with her."

"I don't think that's going to be her biggest issue with all this."

Sergei knocked on the door, and Anna opened it with a smile and kisses for both of us. My parents sat in the tiny living room, drinking more Kvass. Dad had his big camera bag in his lap, ready to play tourist.

"You have good visit with Elena?" Anna asked.

"Yes," Sergei said. "It was very… surprising."

"How's that?" Mom asked.

Sergei started to answer but was distracted by Max emerging from the kitchen. "You don't have work today, Papa?" he asked in Russian.

"I worked all night. I'm about to sleep."

Oh, man. I hadn't planned on Max being there. His attitude wasn't what we needed in this conversation.

"Can you sit with us a few minutes?" Sergei asked in

Russian and then switched to English. "There's something I need to tell everyone. About our visit with Elena."

Mom set her drink on a coaster on the small side table and braced her hands on the arms of her chair. Sergei and I took deliberate steps toward the sofa while Anna brought two chairs from the dining table into the living room.

Sergei leaned forward and pressed his hands together, taking a moment before he looked up at my parents. "There was more to my split with Elena than we've told you. Elena's father didn't break up our partnership just because he didn't want us involved. He sent her away because she was pregnant."

Mom's mouth opened, and there was a pause before she emitted, "Huh!" I glanced at Max, and he'd folded his arms tightly across his chest.

Sergei continued, "I apologize for not telling you the truth, but it's something I thought should stay in the past."

I rubbed Sergei's shoulder, and Mom raised her chin as she peered at me. "So, you've known all along."

It amazed me how even though I was an adult, one disapproving look from Mom could still make me squirm. "I didn't know when you first asked me about it. I told you everything Sergei had told me at that point."

"He lied to you?"

"At first, yes, and we went through a really rough time because of it, but that's long behind us."

"The reason I'm telling you now is because of what we learned when we saw Elena." Sergei stopped and glanced at me. "Her cousin that lived in the States adopted the baby, but she and her husband died last year in a car accident, and Elena is raising our daughter now."

"Daughter?" Anna squeaked. "It is girl?"

Sergei nodded weakly. "Her name is Liza."

I thought of the little girl looking at me in wonder as I gave her my autograph. She didn't know she was about to receive a much bigger surprise.

"We met her," I blurted out.

"You see her?" Anna gasped.

"Does she know Elena is her mother?" Dad asked.

"No, but Elena's going to tell her tonight," Sergei said. "I really want to talk to Liza before we go home."

"Elena has husband?" Max asked in his gravelly voice.

"She's divorced," Sergei replied.

Max grunted. "Her father likely cause."

"He passed away recently," Sergei said. "I don't know if he did more damage to Elena's life before he died."

"He damage many life," Max said.

Mom held up her hand. "What else did he do? Besides send Elena away?"

"He threaten to take away Max's job when he learn Sergei is with Elena," Anna said. "He has many connections, and he use his money all for no good."

"What was he, some kind of Russian mafia?" Mom asked with wide eyes.

"Something like that," Sergei muttered.

"And you knew that and got mixed up with his daughter anyway? What were you thinking?" Mom demanded.

"Mom." I gave her a hard stare.

"I ask this ten year ago," Max said.

Mom nodded at him with respect. I should've known they'd bond over their disappointment in Sergei.

"None of that is important now," Sergei said. "What's important is Elena letting me into Liza's life."

"What do you want with this child?" Max asked in Russian. "How can you be a father when you are not here?"

"I can't go home and pretend she doesn't exist. I'm not going to ignore the fact that I have a daughter. I'll find a way to spend time with her."

Mom rose and started for the door. "I'd like to speak with you in private, Emily. Please excuse us."

Dad stood, too, and I reluctantly followed my parents into the dimly lit hallway. The smell of onions cooking wafted out from another apartment and further turned my flip-flopping stomach.

"Are you just blindly supporting Sergei in this?" Mom asked. "Do you want this child in your life?"

I didn't know what I wanted. I couldn't deny Sergei a relationship with his daughter, but the thought of Elena in our lives forever twisted my insides.

"It means so much to him," I said. "He never thought he'd have this chance."

"Why didn't you tell us the truth when you found out?"

"Because I know how quick you are to judge. Sergei made a mistake, and he paid dearly for it. He doesn't need to be punished any more."

"As long as you're certain you're comfortable with everything," Dad said. "You don't want to start your marriage with anything unresolved between you."

"I know. This is what Sergei wants and this is what I want." I nodded, trying to convince myself.

"You're incredibly calm about all this," Mom said. "Or maybe you're putting up a good front."

"Freaking out isn't going to help the situation."

Mom pursed her lips. "I knew from the beginning that getting involved with Sergei would bring you nothing but trouble. Having to hide it from everyone for so long because he's your coach, that whole fiasco with the skating federation and Ethics Committee, and now this..."

"Why are you bringing all that up?" The last thing I wanted to think about was how Sergei's career had almost been ruined when our relationship was exposed.

"To remind you how much turmoil you've had to deal with because of Sergei. Maybe you should think about whether he's worth—"

"Don't even go there." I opened the door to the

apartment, ending the conversation.

Sergei and his father were now standing, and I caught the end of what sounded like harsh words coming from Max. Sergei walked away from him and stood at my side.

"Mama, are you still coming with us to Red Square?" he asked.

She snuck a peek at Max before answering, "Yes, yes."

"We should go then." Sergei scowled at his father.

Max vanished into the kitchen, and we gathered up our coats and headed out into the light snow. Mom had on her I-want-to-say-something-but-don't-want-to-start-an-argument face, while Sergei also walked in silence, his eyes filled with thought. *This is going to be a fun day of sightseeing.*

Through the slushy snow, we trekked briskly to the nearest subway station. Since everyone in our group was playing the quiet game, I spent the time on the train watching the passengers and dreaming up stories about their lives—anything to avoid thinking about the problems in my own life.

As usual, Dad took charge of easing the tension, directing Sergei and me to pose for funny pictures in Red Square. Sergei raised me up into the air, and I demonstrated some of my overhead lift positions as Dad photographed us with the multi-colored turrets of St. Basil's Cathedral in the background. Holding me aloft with one arm, Sergei spun in a circle as if he was rotating on the ice. The other tourists around us applauded, and Sergei brought me down into his arms. A smile crept across his face. I cupped my hands around his neck and gave him a tender kiss, melting the tiny snowflakes on his lips.

"I love you," he said, his breath warm against my mouth.

I echoed his sentiment but in Russian, and his smile widened. We joined our gloved hands and walked toward the cathedral, taking our time and pointing out various sights for Dad to photograph. Sergei and Anna showed us through St. Basil's, and Mom's fascination with churches got her talking as we wandered through the maze-like corridors. She chatted with Anna about the large murals and dark floral-patterned walls. I hoped she'd keep her deeper thoughts to herself and not ruin our precious moment of relaxation.

We moved on to the Kremlin, which contained two more churches to explore. As we toured the historic buildings, my mind drifted to the future and how I might be visiting Russia more often if Liza became part of our family. Would Elena let Liza come to the Cape to stay with Sergei and me? I might be a stepmother very soon. What did I know about being a mother? I didn't even know how to be a wife yet.

My moment of relaxation was gone, clouded by the unsettling questions.

THE DEEPER THE SUN set, the antsier Sergei became waiting to hear from Elena. He and I sat in a small bar downtown, and Sergei picked up his phone from the table more than once, scrolling to Elena's number. On the latest instance, I covered his hand with mine.

"She'll probably just get irritated if you call her first," I said.

"I need to know what's going on," he said, keeping his left hand on the phone and lifting his drink with his right.

I caressed the soft skin of his wrist. "She'll call soon. She will."

He nodded but didn't let go of his cell. I looked up as the door to the bar opened, and a dark-haired woman in a sleek leather coat sauntered into the room with a burly older man. The woman's cool beauty reminded me of Elena.

I sipped from my wine glass and watched the couple sit at a nearby table. The woman gave the man a flirtatious smile, and I shifted my eyes from them. I didn't want to think about Elena ever giving Sergei a look like that.

Sergei flipped his phone around and around in his hand. "It's crazy that Liza was living in New York, so close to me all that time. I never thought Ivan would give her to someone in their family. I thought he'd make sure Elena never saw her again."

"Did you know Elena had relatives in the States?"

"Yeah, her mother was actually American."

"Really? She seems thoroughly Russian."

"Well, she didn't know her mother since she died when Elena was so young, but she does have U.S. citizenship. I remember her father making sure she kept her American passport so it would be easier to travel to the States for competitions. She doesn't consider herself American, though. When a lot of Russians started defecting to the U.S., Elena said she'd never move there."

Hmm... so it doesn't sound like Elena will be interested in leaving Russia anytime soon. That's a bit of good news.

A melodic ring trilled, and Sergei looked at his phone even though he knew it was my ringtone. I pulled my cell from my purse.

"Hey, Chris. Did you see the doctor?"

"I just left his office." He paused, and I heard his car radio in the background. "It's a partial tear of the rotator cuff."

"What does that mean exactly?"

"I have to do some major physical therapy between now and Worlds. He said I could compete if my shoulder feels stable enough, but I'll need surgery right after."

I shivered with unease at the thought of Chris going under the knife. Neither of us had suffered any serious injuries during our four-year partnership.

Sergei leaned over the table, his forehead creased. "How did it go?"

I frowned. "Partial tear."

Sergei continued to look worried as I resumed talking to Chris. "Are you in a lot of pain?"

"It hasn't been bad unless I move my arm a certain way. Don't worry, Em. I told you I'll be good to go for Worlds."

He kept saying that, but a partial tear could turn into a full tear once he started lifting me over his head and throwing me into the air.

Sergei tapped the table. "Tell him I'm going to call the doctor tomorrow."

I relayed the message, and Chris asked, "How's it going with Sergei's parents? Has his dad loosened up?"

"Uh, no. We've had some bigger issues on our plate, though. It's too much to get into now, but I'll tell you when I get home."

"Sounds like it's not much of a vacation."

"That would be correct."

Sergei's phone vibrated, and we both froze and stared at it. "Chris, I have to go. I'll talk to you soon."

Sergei pressed the answer button while I hung up my phone and took a long drink of my red wine.

"Elena?" he said.

As Elena spoke, Sergei closed his eyes and rested his forehead on his fist. In Russian, he said, "I'm sorry" and later, "Did you tell her I want to see her?"

He raised his head and made eye contact with me, clearly distressed. "I want to come over," he said into the phone. "Maybe I can help."

I massaged his sleeve and gave him a questioning look. Sergei moved the phone from his mouth and whispered, "Liza locked herself in her room."

That poor girl. Everything she knew to be true had just been blown apart. I questioned again whether Sergei should've taken more time to think this through.

"I'm coming over so we can talk in person," Sergei said.

Elena's rising voice filtered through the phone before sudden silence took over. Sergei winced and disconnected the call.

"She doesn't want you there?" I guessed.

"She's so upset she can barely speak. She wasn't making much sense. I need to talk to her face to face."

I wrapped my knit scarf around my neck. "I can get a taxi back to the hotel."

"Can you come with me? If we see Liza, you might make her more comfortable. She seemed to be a big fan of yours."

Confronting an angry Elena and an emotional child didn't sound like a particularly pleasant experience. But Sergei needed me, and I didn't like the idea of Elena and him potentially being alone.

"Sure," I said, wishing I hadn't tried the herring appetizer earlier. It was now swimming upstream in my stomach.

We jumped in a taxi and were at Elena's building as soon as the evening traffic allowed. The plain gray tower rose high above the busy street. We took the elevator up to the eighth floor, and when we stepped into the hall, Sergei halted. He turned his head both ways before aiming for a door to our left.

Sergei rang the bell, and frantic footsteps sounded from inside. The door popped open, and a tear-stained Elena huffed, "I tell you to stay away."

"We have to deal with this," Sergei said.

"She do not come out of her room," Elena cried. "She say she never come out."

"Can you let us in so we don't have to discuss this out here?" Sergei pleaded.

Elena looked too defeated to put up a fight. Her shoulders sagged and her dark bob shielded her face as she shuffled aside for us to enter.

The inside of the apartment was much more impressive than the exterior. Marble floors stretched from the foyer into the living room ahead of us. The air smelled rich, like polished wood and fragrant roses. I couldn't tell from the immaculate furniture that anyone lived there. The room resembled a museum more than a home.

"I should not do this stupid thing," Elena wailed. "Why I listen to you?"

"She had to know the truth," Sergei said. "It wouldn't have been any easier later on."

"I need time to prepare. Maybe I find better way to explain to her."

"Did you tell her we didn't want to give her up? That we had no choice?"

Every time Sergei said he didn't want to give up the baby, my heart pulsed with jealousy I was ashamed to feel. If Elena's father hadn't intervened back then, Sergei would've married Elena. He'd admitted that to me when I discovered his secret. Knowing there was another woman who could've been his wife…

Elena sat on the cream-colored couch and wiped her eyes with the crumpled tissue in her hand. "I tell her we are too young and we cannot care for her. Then she ask why my cousins lie to her. Now she think bad of them. And she is so angry with me because I not tell her sooner."

She balled up her tattered tissue and resorted to using her fingers to blot her eyes. Her efforts only resulted in smearing more mascara across her ivory cheeks. I rummaged through my purse and fished out a packet of Kleenex, offering it to Elena.

"Thank you." She sniffled and plucked a tissue.

"She's not going to be angry with you forever," Sergei said. "She'll—"

He gaped over my shoulder, so I turned to see what had startled him. Liza stood at the edge of the hall, just as sniffly as Elena. Her beautiful blue eyes looked like large swimming pools of tears. I felt the urge to go over and give her a big hug.

"You're my father?" she asked, barely above a whisper.

Sergei's Adam's apple slid down slowly. "Yes," he croaked.

Liza stepped further into the room and faced Sergei, her

chin trembling and her fingers fidgeting together. "Will you take me back to America with you?"

CHAPTER SEVEN

OF ALL THE REACTIONS I EXPECTED from Liza, asking Sergei to take her with him wasn't one of them.

"Liza, this is your home…" Elena rose and moved toward her.

"I hate it here." Liza's voice broke. "I never wanted to come here."

Sergei's eyes shot to Elena. "What is this? Why is she so unhappy?"

"She is upset. She never say before she is not happy."

"I miss my friends. I miss my school." Liza craned her neck up to Sergei. "Please, I promise I won't be any trouble."

The pools in her eyes overflowed, and a stream of water trickled down her pale cheeks. I bit down on my lip, holding in my own tears. Sergei's face was white with pained shock.

"Liza, I know you are mad with me, but I make it better. I give you anything you want," Elena said.

"I want to leave," she replied.

Sergei sniffed and cleared his throat. Then he crouched on one knee in front of Liza.

"I am so happy to finally meet you," he choked out. "And

I want to spend as much time with you as possible, but the law says I can't take you with me."

"But you're my father," she said with teary confusion.

Sergei's jaw shook as he tried to keep from crying, and my heart couldn't handle the sight. I bent my head and blinked as stinging tears flooded my contact lenses.

"I am." Sergei's reply dripped with pride. "But since I just found out the truth, it's a little complicated. There's some stuff Elena and I need to discuss."

"Liza, you wait in your room while Sergei and I talk?" Elena asked tentatively.

Sergei straightened up, looking so tall next to the tiny girl. She gazed up at him with wet eyes. "You're not going to leave, are you?"

"No, I'm not going anywhere. I promise."

Liza slowly turned and retreated to the hallway. Sergei covered his face with his hands, and I went over to him and clutched the front of his jacket.

"Are you okay?" I asked, though I knew he wasn't. But I had no idea what else to say.

He dropped his hands and put his arms around me. I touched my fingers to the nape of his neck, gently rubbing and lending him warmth. After a few steadying breaths, Sergei slid close to my side and gave Elena a questioning stare.

"Why didn't you tell me how miserable she is?"

"She still adjust. She need time."

"Does she have friends? Does she enjoy skating?"

"It is... difficult, with different language. Girls at rink, they do not speak much English. But Liza loves to skate, and she have much talent."

"What about her coach? Does she like him?"

"He is good coach. Tough, but all good coach are."

"You didn't answer my question."

"We do not like our coach and we succeed."

"So, she doesn't like him." Sergei left my side to pace

along the shiny floor. "Which means she's probably not enjoying skating as much as she should, and she probably feels alone because she can't talk to the other kids."

"You make it sound so horrible when it is not," Elena snapped.

Sergei stopped pacing and stared at an abstract painting of red and black streaks hanging on the wall. "You're still going to Worlds?"

"Yes, I promise Liza."

Sergei put his gaze back on Elena. "Would it be possible for her to come stay with me until then?"

Say what? I studied Sergei's eyes, trying to get a read on them. What was he thinking?

Elena gawked at him. "You are crazy."

"It's only a couple of weeks. It would give us a chance to get to know each other."

"You promise not to take her from me and now you ask to take her!"

"I'm not trying to take her away from you. This would be a visit, that's all. A few weeks until you meet us in D.C."

"How do you care for her? You work all day at rink."

"She can come to the rink and skate." Sergei sounded more determined and excited with each breath. "There are so many kids there her age. She'll love it."

I lifted my hand to my mouth. *Oh, my goodness. He's really serious.*

"No. Never," Elena said. "She not go to America without me."

"Then come with us," Sergei said.

Every part of me went numb. Sergei had truly lost it. He was on his runaway train again, making plans while leaving me at the station.

I walked over to Sergei and said quietly, "Maybe we should talk."

He took my hands and squeezed them. "This makes the

most sense since they're already coming for Worlds. It's the perfect opportunity."

"How do we go so soon?" Elena sputtered. "And where do we stay? In hotel for weeks?"

Sergei rubbed his chin, his wheels turning. No way he'd offer to let them stay in his one-bedroom apartment, would he? He wasn't exactly thinking clearly at the moment. Even if Elena and Liza were at a hotel, Sergei would be spending time with them without me. I had to do something…

"You can stay with me," I blurted out.

Sergei looked at me with one eyebrow lifted. "Em, you don't have to…"

Elena shook her head. "We do not bother you."

"I have plenty of space. I live with a roommate, but we have an extra bedroom and bathroom. And Sergei's apartment is only a few blocks from my house."

Elena folded her arms and followed the path Sergei had paced. "All is so sudden… Liza is so upset now. And she have schoolwork and skating—"

"Her tutor can give her work to take with her, and like I said, she can skate at our rink." Sergei took a few steps toward Elena. "This trip might be just what Liza needs. To have both of us with her as she deals with everything."

I fiddled with the small silver cross hanging around my neck. My emotions were fighting each other again. I certainly didn't want Elena in my house for three weeks, but if she refused to bring Liza, Sergei would be crushed. There were no easy answers to the growing mess of complications in our lives.

"I want Liza to know I do anything for her," Elena said.

"You can show her by doing this," Sergei replied.

Elena closed her eyes and stood very still. Neither Sergei nor I moved, waiting for a response. When Elena looked at us again, she said, "We go if we find flight."

Sergei exhaled and grasped her shoulders. "Thank you."

A gleam of light shone in Elena's dark eyes. It was the first time Sergei had touched her since we'd run into her at the rink. I clamped my hand around my cross, the sharp edges digging into my palm. The pain was nothing compared to the stabbing in my heart.

"Can we tell Liza the news?" Sergei asked.

The sound of a rattling cough and the heavy front door shutting pulled my attention from Sergei and Elena. An older woman carrying a paper sack entered the room and stared wide-eyed at Sergei.

"Olga," Elena said in Russian. "You remember Sergei?"

The woman walked over to him and lifted her bony hand to his cheek. I shuffled closer to translate her scratchy reply. "It is good to see you after so many years."

Sergei echoed the sentiment and continued in Russian, "This is my fiancée Emily." Turning to me, he switched to English. "Olga's worked for Elena's family for a long time."

She gave me a nod and a long appraisal, and I mumbled a greeting. I felt like I was being sized up by one of the hard-nosed Russian skating judges.

"I bring Liza out," Elena said.

She left us, and Olga angled her head as she questioned Sergei. "You met Liza?"

"Elena told me everything. She told Liza, also. I assume you know the truth?"

"I do."

I raised my eyebrows. Olga had to be more family than employee if she knew all the dirty little secrets.

Elena returned with Liza, and Olga ambled toward the hallway. "I finish dinner."

Elena touched Liza's long braid while she spoke to her. "Sergei and I have talk, and he invite us to visit with him few weeks before Worlds, if you like to do that."

Liza's teary eyes brightened, and she almost smiled. "We're going to America now?"

"Yes. We leave very soon."

The smile fully appeared on Liza's face, and she turned to Sergei. "Thank you *so* much."

He beamed and tipped his head. I couldn't imagine what was showing on *my* face. Probably some combination of fascination and disbelief.

"Sergei, it is late. I think it best if you and Emily leave," Elena said. "You call me with detail of trip?"

"Definitely. I'll get you our flight information. Hopefully, there are some open seats." Sergei approached Liza and took a moment before speaking. "It's been so great to meet you, Liza. I can't tell you how much I'm looking forward to your visit."

She smiled shyly. Elena walked Sergei and me to the door, and as he opened it Sergei said, "Thank you again for doing this. I really think it will be good for Liza."

Elena had more strength in her posture than when we'd arrived, but worry still darkened her face. "We see."

Sergei and I were both quiet as we waited for the elevator. The doors opened and shut us inside, and Sergei leaned against the back wall with a look of wonder.

"I can't believe I just talked to my daughter."

The magnitude of what had just occurred started to sink in, forming a lump in my throat. "She's a beautiful little girl," I said, my voice cracking.

We walked outside, and I tilted my head up to watch the snowflakes swirling around the streetlight. My nerves were dancing a similar pattern. Sergei stopped on the edge of the sidewalk and faced me.

"Do you think I'm crazy, doing all this?" he asked. "I don't know how to explain it, but the first time I saw Liza, I felt this instinct to protect her. I couldn't walk away."

That fatherly instinct he'd suddenly acquired added to my confusion about the situation. It was somewhat unnerving but at the same time incredibly appealing. Watching Sergei with Liza had made my heart flip-flop in a whole new way.

"You're not crazy," I said, putting my hands on his waist.

He tucked a few strands of hair behind my ear and caressed my cheek. "I told you this before, and I have to say it again. You are truly amazing."

He kissed me softly, and I pressed my lips harder against his, trying to block out my thoughts.

Was I amazing or a total fool?

CHAPTER EIGHT

WITH A DEEP SIGH, I THREW back the comforter on the bed and sank into the stack of pillows. I was more worn out than I'd be if I'd skated back-to-back long programs. Since Sergei and I had just rehashed the scene at Elena's to my parents, I didn't feel like reliving the day's events again, but I had to call Aubrey to tell her about our impending guests.

I slid my phone off the nightstand and scrolled to Aubrey's cell number. Glancing at the clock, I calculated the time difference and hoped I'd catch her leaving the rink. She should be on her way to ballroom class, an extra off-ice requirement for ice dancers.

"Hey, Em," she answered.

"Hey, do you have a few minutes?"

"Yep, class was cancelled so Marley and I are going out to Mashpee to shop in a bit."

I pushed my damp hair away from my face and laid my head back against the starchy pillowcase. Oh, to be at home with my friends, doing trivial things.

"Some crazy stuff has been going on here," I said. "You're never going to believe it."

"Uh-oh. Did Sergei's dad do something?"

"No, he's the least of my problems. It's a pretty convoluted story, but I'll try to make it short."

I gave her a rundown of the situation, and nothing but silence came over the line. Finally, Aubrey said, "Back it all the way up. You met Elena *and* the kid she had for Sergei?"

Aubrey, Chris, and Marley were the only people I'd told about Elena's pregnancy and her father's threats. My friends had been there for me when I found out Sergei had lied. Sensing more trouble on the horizon, I suspected I'd need them once again.

"It's been a whirlwind two days," I said.

"So, why are Elena and Liza staying with us? Did Sergei ask you to put them up?"

I picked at my flannel pajama pants, wincing in advance of the expected reaction. "I invited them."

"Are you nuts?"

"You know the old saying—'Keep your friends close and your enemies closer.' I mean, I don't really know Elena so I can't say she's my enemy, but you get my drift."

Aubrey was silent again. I could picture her green eyes crinkling with concern. "This is so totally insane," she said. "How are you processing all this? Or are you still in shock?"

"I honestly don't know. We've just been going, going, going since yesterday when we first saw Elena. I'm sorta numb right now." Turning my head, I looked out at the lights of Moscow, visible between the half-drawn curtains. "I'm sorry I didn't check with you before I invited Elena and Liza. It was one of those things where I had to make a move fast."

"I know you, and you wouldn't have suggested something so crazy if you didn't think it was necessary. Besides, it's your parents' house, so you can invite whoever you want." Aubrey stopped and gasped. "Oh, no, you had to tell your parents everything. Your mom must've had a conniption."

"She wasn't pleased, especially when I told her about my invitation."

"Please tell me these people speak some English so I won't need you to translate for me the entire time."

"Elena's English is good. Liza actually lived in the States before her parents died, and I get the impression she knows very little Russian. I'm not sure how much she'll be talking, though. I think she's pretty mad at Elena for keeping the truth from her."

"Great, so we'll have their uncomfortable drama to deal with."

"I'm sorry. I know it's not the best time to throw our routine out of whack with Worlds coming up. Believe me, if I thought there was a better answer…"

"Is Sergei not thinking about Worlds and how this will affect you? How are you supposed to be on your A-game with all this going on around you?"

Hearing Aubrey's concern lifted a layer of my numbness, revealing irritation. "Sergei doesn't seem to be thinking about anything except Liza right now."

A quick knock came from the door. "Somebody's knocking," I said. "I really hope it's not my mom. I ran away tonight before she could corner me."

"Good luck. Call me tomorrow."

I put the phone on the nightstand and crept on my bare toes to the door. If it was Mom, I wanted her to think I was asleep. Peeking through the peephole, I discovered my visitor was Sergei.

I opened the door and Sergei glanced at my T-shirt and pajama pants. "Did I wake you? Sorry, I'm still so wired I couldn't sleep."

"No, I was just talking to Aubrey." I motioned him inside and shut the door.

"Is she okay with Elena and Liza staying with you?" he asked, stopping at the foot of the bed.

"She's worried this is a bad time for them to visit with Worlds in three weeks. And now that I've had a minute to breathe and think about it, she has a good point."

"They can stay in a hotel. You don't have to—"

"It's not just the matter of where they're staying." I folded my arms "It's the fact that you invited them to come at all without talking to me first."

Sergei stepped closer to me. "I'm sorry, Em. When Liza asked to come with us, it got me thinking, and I had to do something quickly. Elena was so upset that I was afraid she might make us leave."

"I understand you did what you thought was good for Liza, but you still should've taken the time to discuss it with me. It scares me that you're making these huge decisions without me. I hope this isn't an indication of what our marriage will be like."

"It's not." Sergei gently cupped his hands under my chin. "This was a crazy situation that I never thought I'd be in, and I just started reacting and saying things before I could even think them through myself."

I dropped my eyes to the silver pendant hanging around his neck, the one I'd given him for his birthday, engraved with *Always* in Russian. It was turned backwards, so I reached up and flipped it forward.

"You should've talked to me," I said, removing Sergei's hands from my face. "No matter how crazy things get, you have to remember that we're in this together. We should make decisions like this *together*."

"You don't want Elena and Liza to come with us," Sergei stated.

"That's not what this is about," I huffed. "It's about you doing things that impact me, that impact *us*, without considering my feelings at all."

"Why didn't you say something at Elena's?"

"I tried, but you kept rolling right along. Maybe I

should've said more, but I was still in shock over what was happening."

"I was in shock, too. I was just hoping Liza would see me, and then when she asked me for help..." Sergei's voice caught. "All I knew was I couldn't say no."

The emotion on his face nipped at my irritation. What if I was in his position? Would I be able to think rationally if I was suddenly looking into my child's eyes?

"You really feel a connection to her already," I said.

"It's crazy, I know. I've only talked to her for a total of five minutes, but I feel it." He took a slow step back and sat on the small bench in front of the bed. "And the idea of leaving her when I just found her... I couldn't do it. Not after all those years of wondering where she was and if she was okay."

He bent forward, dropping his head, and I sank onto the bench beside him. I put my arm around him and rested my chin on his shoulder.

"You'll never have to wonder anymore," I said.

He turned his face to mine and brushed the lightest of kisses on my mouth. Taking me in his arms, his hands settled around my waist while I ran my fingers up and down his back.

Sergei's lips grazed my hair and trailed down to my ear. "I'm sorry I didn't talk to you first."

The warmth of his breath and his words softened me even more, but I had to make sure he'd gotten my message. I shifted my head back so I could see Sergei's face.

"Promise me you won't spring any more surprises on me."

"I promise," he said, holding my gaze. His eyes searched mine, and I felt like there was something he wanted to say.

"What is it?" I asked.

"You didn't answer me earlier when I said you don't want Elena and Liza to visit."

The problem was I had two answers—"No" for the first

person mentioned and "Yes" for the second. I chose to reply with my other concern.

"I wish it wasn't at such an already stressful time," I said. "Besides the usual pre-competition crunch, we have Chris's injury to worry about, wedding stuff going on..."

"I wish it was a better time, too, but I couldn't count on Elena agreeing to let me see Liza later. I had to make it now."

"I want you to be able to spend time with Liza, but having Elena around..."

"It's asking a lot, I know," he said, combing his fingers through the damp waves of my hair. "I don't think she'll make things difficult, though. She's going to do whatever makes Liza happy."

I didn't have the same confidence he had, and it gave me pause again, thinking of Elena in my house. A woman I barely knew but who knew Sergei very well. Too well. The unsettled feeling that had taken residence in my gut flared up, and I pulled Sergei into another embrace, seeking comfort... if only temporary.

"I WISH YOU NOT GO HOME so soon," Anna said, hugging me for the fifth time since I'd arrived for dinner.

I couldn't get home soon enough. No offense to Sergei's mother, of course. I just wanted to get out of Russia before any more life-changing events could occur.

"Thank you for another wonderful meal," I said.

"Everything was delicious," Dad chimed in next to me.

Anna released me and gave Sergei an even stronger hug, patting his back over and over. "You tell Liza she have grandmother and grandfather who want to meet her."

Max rose from the couch with a grunt, and Sergei glared at him. "What, Papa? I know you've wanted to say something all evening."

"I do not know why you push this, why you always make things more difficult in your life." Max turned to me. "Why you do not stop it?"

My voice got lost in my throat, and Sergei jumped in. "Emily supports this. She understands why it's important to me."

Mom gave me a pointed stare, and I quickly looked away. Sergei made my support sound a lot stronger than I felt about it.

Sergei's cell phone buzzed, and he answered the call, "Elena?"

He wandered a few feet from us in the cramped living room, and Dad set a worried arm across my shoulders. I kept my ears tuned to Sergei's conversation, concentrating hard to translate.

"What happened since you bought the plane tickets this morning?" he asked. "You're not changing your mind?"

An unbidden ray of hope streaked through me. *Maybe all the plans will fizzle out.* If Sergei knew what I was thinking, he wouldn't be boasting about my support.

"You saw how excited Liza was," Sergei continued. "Please don't take this opportunity away from her."

"He's going to keep pushing," Max said, throwing one hand up.

"Liza is our family," Anna said. "He's doing what is right."

My ears and my brain strained to block out their bickering and focus on Sergei. He put one hand on his hip and said, "I'm not going to make her choose sides. I want us all to do things together."

I stiffened, wrapping my arms around myself. Perhaps I was included in Sergei's definition of "us all," but the way he said it gave me a picture of their little family, me excluded. Add that to the pile of unpleasant pictures I'd imagined on the trip, and I had an entire album in my head.

Dad hugged me closer to his side as Sergei rattled on in Russian. I stopped trying to translate, growing tired of feeling on the outside. When Sergei ended the call, he ran his hand through his hair, expelling a slow breath.

"They're still coming. Elena was having some second thoughts."

I kept my face motionless, not wanting Sergei to see my disappointment. Anna moved toward him and placed her hands on his face. "Good, good. You should have this time with Liza."

"Wonderful," Mom muttered.

"Always making bad decisions," Max said and went into the kitchen.

Sergei jammed his phone into his pocket. "Mama, we have to get back to the hotel. Our flight is very early tomorrow."

Anna embraced him again. "I miss you and you not gone yet."

"The wedding will be here before you know it," he said.

Will it? It felt so far, far away to me.

Anna gave the rest of us more hugs, and I watched over her shoulder as Max quietly reentered the room. Dad approached him with his hand extended.

"Thank you for all your hospitality," he said in practiced Russian.

Max nodded. "You're welcome."

"We will return it when you come to Boston," Mom said, giving Max kisses on each side of his face.

I hung back, not sure if Max would welcome any affection from me. "Yes, thank you both."

He hesitated but slid over to me, bending to place kisses on my cheeks. When he faced Sergei, he simply said, "Good luck, Son."

The emotional distance between them tore at my heart. No wonder Sergei so badly wanted to show Liza she could count on him. And I had to show him he could count on me to help him through this, as trying as it might be.

CHAPTER NINE

THICK GRAY CLOUDS BLOCKED MY VIEW of the European countryside below as I peered out the narrow airplane window. I wished I could tap my heels together and be home. But my shoes were sneakers, not ruby slippers, and Dorothy just had Toto with her. I had my fiancé's ex-girlfriend and newfound child to tote with me.

Sergei yawned and unbuckled his seat belt. "I need to stretch my legs. Want to take a walk?"

"I think I'll read for a while," I said, pulling my paperback from the seat pocket.

"Oh, yeah, you need to finish that so we can talk about it. The end will blow your mind."

I smiled a little. Our afternoon coffee shop dates where we discussed our current reads might seem boring to some people, but I thought they were the perfect way to relax after training. It would be nice to get back to a normal routine. Although, with Elena and Liza coming to town, I doubted there'd be much normalcy at home.

Sergei started to get up but stopped and turned back to me, surprising me with a kiss.

"You plan on being gone a long time?" I asked.

"No, I just want you to know how much I love you."

When he said things like that, I forgot about the chaos he'd brought into our world. Then I remembered our traveling companions sitting ten rows behind us.

Sergei headed up the aisle, and I opened my book to its dog-eared page. I'd only read one paragraph when Mom dropped into Sergei's empty seat.

"You can't avoid me here," she said.

I sighed and shut the book. The entire previous day I'd dodged being alone with Mom. I couldn't listen to her question Sergei's decisions because I was trying to ignore my own doubts about them.

"You know, that is my house you're living in, so I have the ultimate say on who does or doesn't stay there," Mom said crisply. "I could override your offer to Elena and Liza."

"Please don't do that."

"Why do you want them there? They're only going to be a constant reminder of Sergei's past."

"It's better than if they were staying at a hotel. This way, I can have some control over the situation," I said, reaching up to adjust the air conditioning vent.

"Do you feel threatened? Is that why you need to control it?"

"No, I just... I'd rather Sergei come to my house to see Liza than have to go elsewhere."

"You'd rather he not see Elena elsewhere." Mom tapped her index finger on my leg. "Without you present."

Shifting in my seat, I stared at the clouds, remembering the look in Elena's eyes when Sergei had showed her a hint of affection. It was a look I didn't care to ever see again.

"I trust Sergei completely," I said. "But no, I don't want them spending time together. I don't think I'm irrational for feeling that way."

"It's perfectly normal. No woman enjoys seeing her

boyfriend with an ex. Especially when that ex is also the mother of his child."

Mom's frown spoke of disapproval. Before she could launch into a judgmental rant about Sergei's unplanned fatherhood, I steered the conversation to a new direction.

"I was watching them at the airport," I said. "Liza's still so upset that she's barely speaking to Elena."

"And you have to entertain them. That will be fun."

I laughed dryly. "When I called Aubrey to tell her we're having visitors, she said the same thing. Well, first she said, 'Are you nuts?'"

"I second that."

"It's not going to be easy, but I couldn't think of a better solution."

Mom pursed her lips. "Sweetie, I'm worried about you. I think you've let yourself get caught up in this and haven't thought how it could change things."

"They're only going to be with us for a few weeks, and then they'll go back to Russia and everything can return to normal." If I sounded convincing enough, Mom would have to believe me. And I'd have to believe myself.

"So, Sergei hasn't said anything about trying to get custody?" Mom asked.

"No, he wouldn't do that to Elena."

"Wait until he spends more time with Liza," she said with a voice full of warning. "He might have some other ideas then."

I couldn't think about that. I had to focus on getting through the next three weeks. I glanced down at my paperback and realized I'd bent the cover back and had smashed it into a creased mess.

Three weeks. One day at a time.

"WELL, THIS IS IT," I said, leading Elena and Liza into my foyer. "I hope you'll feel at home here."

Sergei helped us carry in our mounds of luggage, and I showed my guests their bedroom and bathroom just off the entryway.

"Let me give you a quick tour of the rest of the house," I said and turned to Sergei. "I'll see you at the rink in a bit?"

"I'll be there as soon as I shower and change."

"You go to rink?" Elena asked.

"Just for a little while," I said. "I'm going to skate and then Sergei and I have a lesson with our junior team."

"May we go with you? I like to see where Liza skate here."

"Umm…" I hesitated and looked at Sergei.

"That sounds like a good idea," he said. "Liza can meet some of the other kids."

My heart sank. I'd been looking forward to my first day back on the ice being a peaceful one, away from any personal drama. Everyone at the rink was going to have questions the minute Elena and Liza walked through the door.

I followed Sergei out to his SUV, knotting the belt tighter on my cardigan. Though not nearly as cold as Moscow, the air had a chilly bite to it with spring still a few weeks away.

"Are you going to take care of telling everybody at the rink what's going on?" I asked, setting my hands on my hips.

Sergei rubbed the back of his neck. "I talked to a couple of people late last night. Not sure if the word has spread yet, though."

"I'm sure it has. It was a miracle we kept our relationship a secret as long as we did."

Sergei kissed me goodbye, and I went inside to take Elena and Liza through the townhouse. I showed them the kitchen and small den on the bottom floor and then the second-floor living room. With its warm colors and comfy furniture, it was a striking contrast from the sterile living room in Elena's house.

We passed Aubrey's bedroom on the third floor and kept going up the stairs to my room. I deposited my carry-on bag inside, and Liza followed me into the doorway. Her eyes went straight to my Olympic silver medal, encased and hanging on the wall.

She went over and stared up at it. "That's so cool," she whispered.

"I have a whole box of stuff from the Olympics I can show you," I said. "I think I have a few extra keepsakes you might like."

Liza's eyes widened even more. "Really?"

"The T-shirts will be pretty big for you, but you can use them as nightgowns," I said with a smile.

Elena had also come inside, but her attention was on another item in the room—a photo on my dresser of Sergei and me at the Gay Head cliffs on Martha's Vineyard, the site of our first kiss. We'd taken the picture at sunrise, our favorite time to visit, and the orange sky glowed around us as we reenacted the kiss.

Elena stared at the picture so long that I was about to ask if she'd like to inspect it closer. Instead, I put on my formal host voice. "If you need me for anything, you can knock on my door anytime."

She finally turned away from the dresser. "Thank you."

"I'll show you my favorite part of the house next."

I led them back into the hall and to the sliding glass door across from my room. Pushing it open, I stepped onto the wood-planked terrace and shaded my eyes from the midday sun. The neighbor's wind chimes jingled a soft tune, while seagulls squawked to each other above us.

"The beach is right there." I pointed to the left, where a small strip of sand divided the large complex of townhomes from sparkling Lewis Bay.

"It is nice," Elena said, looking around at the wrought

iron table and chairs and the empty flower pots along the railing. "Very quiet."

"This is where Sergei proposed," I said. *What are you doing, trying to make her jealous?* I didn't like feeling so unnerved in my own home.

Elena had a wistful look on her face as she gazed out at the horizon. Liza moved next to the wooden rail, her head barely above it. She appeared to be watching a small sailboat cutting through the bay.

Before any more random things could slip out of my mouth, I showed Elena and Liza inside. They continued down the stairs to their room, while I went to mine to freshen up. Within an hour we were on our way down Route Six to the rink in South Dennis. Both Elena and Liza were quiet on the drive, and my brain was too tired from the trip to start a conversation. I just wanted the ice. *Get me to the ice.*

I parked my sedan next to Sergei's SUV, relieved he'd beaten us there. He needed to be in charge of our visitors. I didn't want to have to explain the messy details to anyone who might be in the dark.

Elena paused on the sidewalk and looked up at the building. "It is small, like where Liza skate in New York."

"It's not as big as your club in Moscow, but it has everything we need," I said with a slight edge.

We walked inside, and I smiled as the familiar cold blast of air hit my face.

Home.

I pointed out the snack bar and the skate shop in the lobby, and as we approached the ice, my fourteen-year-old student Courtney ran over and tackled me in a hug.

"I'm so glad you're back!" she cried.

"Me, too." I gave her a tight squeeze.

Courtney smiled at Liza and Elena, seemingly oblivious to the situation. I glanced around for Sergei. He was probably upstairs in the lounge getting coffee. Now, I'd have to do the introduction for him.

"Court, this is Elena and her daughter Liza. They're visiting from Russia." I decided to leave it at that for the moment. "This is Courtney. She's part of the junior pair Sergei and I coach."

"Hi!" Courtney waved and then turned to me. "I don't know any Russian except nyet and spasibo."

"Oh, they speak English. Liza actually grew up in New York. She's a skater, too."

"Cool!" Courtney said. "Are you related to Sergei?"

Liza looked to me for a cue, and I twisted my hands together. "Umm…" I cleared my throat. "Why don't you take a walk with me to the locker room? I need to stash my stuff." Turning to Elena, I said, "Sergei should be down in a minute."

I rolled my bag quickly toward the locker room with Courtney matching me stride for stride. Inside the musty room littered with skate bags and warm-up jackets strewn across the benches, I stopped in front of my locker and faced Courtney.

"Sergei is Liza's father," I said.

For once, my chatty student was speechless. Her mouth hung open, and her big green eyes were unblinking.

As I pulled open the locker door, I continued, "Liza's going to skate here while she's in town, so it would be great if you could introduce her to some of the other kids."

Courtney slowly raised her jaw. "Yeah… I can do that. Is Elena Sergei's old partner?"

"Yes," I said, shedding my jacket.

"How come Liza hasn't come to visit before?"

I shut the metal door and retied the laces on my sneakers. "We just met her in Russia."

"So, Sergei didn't know he had a daughter?"

"We knew. It's a long story, Court. Can you just make sure Liza feels welcome here? She's been through a lot, so she needs some fun."

"Definitely. I'm on it."

"Thank you." I gave her a hug, probably harder than she was expecting, but I felt the need to hold on tight to all things familiar in my life.

Courtney's long blonde ponytail bounced behind her as she left the room, and I followed soon after. I set off on my warm-up jog around the rink and saw Sergei taking Liza and Elena upstairs. They were in my house, they were in my room, they were at my rink. There was no escaping them.

Jogging with extra speed and intensity, I rammed into Chris as he exited the weight room.

"Sorry!" I exclaimed.

"You running away from something? Your house guests maybe?"

"You heard?"

"Aubrey filled me in. You've got Sergei's kid and his baby mama crashing at your place?"

I stared at him for a moment and then burst into laughter. Loud, body-shaking laughter. Chris looked at me like I'd lost it, and I covered my mouth with my hands. I felt as if I'd just been uncorked. As I continued to laugh, the release of emotion opened the door for more bottled-up feelings, and my laughter turned to sobs. Deep, rattling sobs. I spread my hands to hide my entire face.

"Em, what..." Chris said and quickly grabbed my waist. "Here, come with me."

I blindly let him guide me until I heard him open a door, and I peeked between my fingers. We'd gone through the side exit and were out in the sunshine. My tears continued to flow like a hard rain shower.

"I'm sorry, I shouldn't have said that," Chris moaned. "I'm an idiot."

I dropped my hands and shook my head. Through sputtering breaths, I said, "It's okay. It sounded really funny."

"But it's obviously *not* funny. This can't be easy for you."

"I was doing okay. I just..." My face crumpled again. "I

guess I've been holding a lot in."

Chris lightly took my arm. "Let's sit."

We sat on a low cement wall next to the building, and Chris rubbed my neck. "Vent all you need to."

I rested my forehead on my hands, slowing my breathing and sniffing back the tears. Picking up my head, I said hoarsely, "I just wanted to see what Sergei's life was like growing up in Russia. And I was hoping he could feel some closure on the stuff that went down all those years ago. Instead, we opened every closet and brought all the skeletons home with us."

"Everything must've happened really fast. You were only in Moscow three days."

"As soon as Sergei found out Liza was his, he went into Super Dad mode. He was on a mission to get her here, and there was no stopping him."

"What's she like? Liza?"

"She seems like a good kid, which makes this harder. If she was a total brat, I could hate her." I covered my face again. "Ugh, what's wrong with me? That was a horrible thing to say."

"No one would blame you for feeling that way. You've been thrown for a pretty big loop."

"If it was just Liza, it would be easier. But with Elena in the picture..." I dabbed at my eyes with my fingers. "Liza's going to be skating here, so that means Elena will be here every day, too. I'm never going to be able to get away from her. And I know I brought it on myself by inviting them to stay with me, but the other options just didn't work for me."

"You can ignore Elena while you're here at the rink. You'll be busy practicing without me and thinking how much you miss me and my awesomeness." He grinned.

I frowned. "It's going to suck practicing alone. I need your humor now more than ever."

"Except when I'm at therapy, I'll be around as much as

always. I started a killer new lower body workout program." He patted his thighs. "I'm gonna have incredible power down here."

I choked on a laugh. "I'm sure Marley will love that."

I cracked up and didn't start crying that time. Chris laughed and said, "I walked right into that one."

"It feels good to laugh. The last three days were one never-ending intense conversation."

Chris put his arm around me. "If you need a break from the craziness, you can hang out with me and Mar anytime."

"Thanks." I stood and wiped my face with the back of my hand. "I should go. The sooner I'm warmed up, the sooner I can get on the ice."

"I wish I could get out there with you. I don't know why I can't just skate without doing any of the high-risk stuff."

"Sergei said the doctor doesn't want you anywhere near the ice. If you fall, you could do more damage to your shoulder."

He sighed. "Yeah, I know. It's just annoying to be stuck on the sidelines."

I opened the heavy blue door. "But think about how *powerful* you're going to be from all your workouts."

He laughed and shoved me ahead of him. I resumed my jog, breezing past Sergei, Elena, and Liza as they returned from the lounge. A few parents on the bleachers were already whispering and staring at them and then me. It reminded me of when Sergei and I had gone public with our relationship a year ago. Mostly everyone at the rink had been supportive, but that didn't stop the usual gossipers from huddling and gawking at us. The novelty of our situation had worn off, but now we were at the center of a juicy new story. *Thanks, Sergei.*

After I'd run, stretched, and prepared all my muscles, I ditched my sneakers and donned my skates. My first few crossovers around the rink brought me a serenity I hadn't felt in forever. I unzipped my warm-up jacket and leaned over the boards, tossing it onto the bleachers. Building up speed again, I skated around my training mates and did a few easy waltz jumps. The icy breeze on my skin invigorated every part of me.

I practiced my jumps, spins, and footwork over and over until it was time to teach with Sergei. Courtney and her partner Mark glided over to me while Sergei finished putting on his skates. Elena and Liza had taken seats on the top row of the bleachers. There was a big space between them, which I guessed was Liza's doing.

"I showed Liza the locker room and we talked a little," Courtney said quietly. "She asked me about you and Sergei."

"What about us?"

"She said you guys seemed really nice. She asked if you're nice when you coach, too. Of course, I told her you're like the most super awesome coaches ever."

I smiled. "You remember that when we ask you to do triple run-throughs. Did she say anything else?"

"Hmm… not much. I told her about some of the fun stuff there is to do around here."

Sergei joined us, so Courtney and I cut our chat short and got to work. The hour of working on choreography for the kids' new programs flew by. When Sergei and I went to change out of our skates, he brought up dinner plans.

"I was just going to order a pizza or something," I said. "We have to unpack, and I'm sure Elena and Liza are tired from the trip. I'm waiting for the jet lag to hit me once I get home."

"Yeah, we should definitely keep it low-key tonight. I won't stay long at your place. I just want to spend a little time with Liza."

I nodded, but a twinge of jealousy struck again. *She's his daughter*, I reminded myself. She deserved all Sergei's attention the next few weeks.

But I was already missing him.

CHAPTER TEN

"Is dinner going to be super awkward? Maybe I'll take my pizza to my room," Aubrey said.

I pulled a bag of ready-made salad from the refrigerator and tore it open. "Please stay. I have no idea what to expect. Liza's been so quiet that I don't know if she'll even talk to us."

Aubrey brushed her long blonde hair to one shoulder. "It must be so weird for her, to all of a sudden find out your cousin is your mom, and this coach you've seen on TV is your dad. How does a kid process that?"

"She's still barely talking to Elena." I lowered my voice as I looked toward the stairs. "I haven't heard a peep out of them while they've been unpacking."

"I swear, this whole thing is like some really bad Lifetime movie."

I laughed and shook my head as I dumped the salad into a bowl and tossed it with oil and vinegar. Aubrey scooted past me in the narrow kitchen and reached into the oak cupboard, taking out five glasses. I'd never been so glad to have a roommate. I couldn't imagine dealing with Elena and Liza on my own. Aubrey had been my best friend since we met at summer skating camp on the Cape when we were thirteen. She'd told off some girls who were making fun of my dress, and she'd had my back ever since.

Elena appeared at the kitchen door, and I gave her a little smile. "All unpacked?"

"Yes." She came closer and glanced down at the salad before settling her eyes on me. "I need to speak about something with you."

I lifted one eyebrow. "Okay."

She threw a look at Aubrey, who returned it and then went back to gathering silverware.

"I know you and Sergei to be married, but I am not comfortable if he stay here with you at night. I do not want bad example for Liza."

Aubrey snorted. "Like the one you set getting knocked up at seventeen?"

My jaw dropped, and Elena's eyes crinkled, like she didn't quite understand what Aubrey had said but knew from the tone it wasn't good. I set down the silver tongs and coughed a little.

"Umm… Sergei doesn't stay here. We're—"

"Because Em stays at his place," Aubrey piped up. "It's more private."

I gave her a what-are-you-talking-about look, but she kept going, "I'm sure Em will be here every night while you're visiting, though. Right?" Her eyes appeared to be sending me a telepathic message.

"*Right*," I said slowly.

"See?" Aubrey said to Elena. "Nothing to worry about."

Elena continued to study her before backing toward the door. "I tell Liza to ready for dinner."

I waited a moment and then peeked up the stairs. With the coast clear, I turned to Aubrey. "Why'd you say that?" I asked in a hushed voice. "I'm not ashamed that Sergei and I aren't sleeping together."

"I know, but Elena doesn't need to know the intimate details of your relationship. She's got nerve, coming into your house and telling you how things are going to be around here. Don't give her any reason to feel like she has power over you."

I picked up the pepper grinder and paused with it over the lettuce. "I wonder if Liza's the only reason behind her request."

"You think she doesn't want to see you and Sergei together?"

"I don't know." I twisted the grinder. "She had a weird look on her face when she saw the picture of me and Sergei in my room."

The doorbell rang, and I wiped my hands on a dish towel before bounding up the stairs. Sergei stood on the doorstep with a large pizza box.

He gave me a kiss on his way inside, and we went down to the kitchen. Aubrey smiled as she passed us with an armful of plates. "Hey, Sergei. You know, most people just bring back souvenirs when they go on a trip. You went a little crazy there."

He slid the pizza onto the counter with a little smile. "Very funny."

Elena and Liza came down the stairs, and Liza wandered into the breakfast area where Aubrey was setting the table.

"Do you wanna help?" Aubrey asked.

Liza answered by picking up the forks and placing them precisely next to each plate. Sergei watched her over the bar, looking pensive, and I put my arm around his waist. He gazed down at me.

"Everything going okay here?" he asked.

I thought about Elena's concern over our sleeping arrangements but wasn't going to mention that conversation. "Yeah. They're just getting settled in."

After we all helped ourselves to salad and slices of the veggie pizza, we had the awkward moment of choosing seats at the table. I shuffled around Sergei so he could sit at the head, closer to Liza. Elena sat next to her, and I almost had to laugh at how surreal the whole scene was.

Sergei cleared his throat. "Liza, would you like to skate at the rink tomorrow?"

She lifted her eyes from staring at her pizza. "Yes, sir," she said quietly.

"Our rink's pretty cool, huh?" Aubrey said.

Liza nodded, a smile appearing on her lips. Beside her, Elena took the tiniest bites of pizza I'd ever seen. A bird could make a bigger dent.

"Maybe after skating we can show you more of the Cape," Sergei said. "Em, do you have anything going on tomorrow evening?"

"No, I'm free. Chris and I had a phone interview, but it got postponed until next week."

"You not take Liza without me," Elena said sharply.

Sergei set down his fork. "I wasn't planning to. I meant the invitation for both of you."

Oh, fun. I ripped off a piece of my pizza crust and shoved it into my mouth.

"We see how Liza feel after skating," she replied.

"I'd like to go," Liza said.

Elena pushed her silky hair behind one ear and took a miniscule sip of water. "Then I guess we go."

Liza could ask for a horse, six dogs, and a lifetime supply of chocolate, and Elena would probably give it to her. That was how desperate she seemed to get back in the child's good graces.

"We can drive out to Brewster," Sergei said. "It's a little town not far from the rink, and there are some good places to eat. Do you like seafood, Liza?"

"She is allergic," Elena quickly replied.

"Oh. Well, that's good to know."

"There is much you not know about her," Elena said.

"And I hope to change that," Sergei said.

Liza had dropped her head again and was picking at the black olives and artichokes on her pizza. I hated when my parents would talk about me as if I wasn't in the room.

"There's a really cool sweet shop in Brewster, too. I bet you're not allergic to candy," I said with a smile.

Liza's blue eyes met mine, and she chewed on her lip. "I'm not allowed to have too much candy."

I leaned my elbows on the table and angled toward her. "Yeah, neither am I, but we all need a treat every now and then."

She gave me the shy smile Aubrey had received earlier. I caught a glimpse of Elena as I sat back, and the sour look on her face had deepened.

During the meal, we gleaned more bits of information about Liza—she loved to swim, she'd once had a goldfish named Goldie, and much to Sergei's delight, his daughter was an avid reader. "She always have book with her," Elena said.

"What's your favorite story?" Sergei asked.

Liza chewed hurriedly, appearing very excited to answer once she finished. "*The Secret Garden.* It's *so* good."

Sergei smiled. "What's it about?"

"It's about this girl, Mary, who goes to live with her uncle in England, and she finds a secret garden at his house that's been locked for years. She and this boy, Dickon, fix up the garden, and then she finds out another secret when she meets her cousin..."

Liza couldn't talk fast enough as she spilled out more of the story. I hadn't heard her speak that many words since I'd met her. Sergei wore the biggest grin, and the more questions he asked about the book, the quicker Liza's answers came.

It didn't look like Elena was going to finish her dinner, so I started clearing the dishes. She and Aubrey carried some of the plates to the kitchen with me while Sergei chatted with Liza about skating.

I dumped the dirty utensils into the sink and turned to Elena. "We could've ordered something else if you don't like pizza."

"I am not hungry." She dumped the remnants of her meal into the trash can and looked at my empty plate. "You eat very much for skater."

Aubrey was behind Elena, and she gave me a look that said, *Oh, no she didn't!* I pressed my lips together and chose my words carefully.

"Do you know how many calories I burn every day?"

"I do not eat so much when I skate," she said.

Since when were salad and two slices of pizza a ginormous meal?

"I grew up in a family of Italian women. Not enjoying food is considered blasphemy." I picked up a sponge from the sink. "I hope you're not encouraging Liza to follow your eating habits."

"How I raise my daughter is not your concern."

"She'll be my stepdaughter soon, so I think it is my concern."

Whoa, where did that come from? When did I become all motherly? Aubrey was watching me with wonder as she tended to the leftover salad.

Elena slid closer to me, and being the same height, we stood eye to eye. "I do not know what idea you and Sergei have in your head, but Liza always stay with me. This is only visit, and she return to Russia with me."

"No one is saying any different. We don't have any secret plans to keep Liza here." I said that, but with the unpredictable way Sergei had been acting lately, I couldn't vouch for his thoughts on the matter.

"That is good," Elena said. "Russia is her home, and I do not want you to make her think otherwise."

"I just want her to feel comfortable here. That's it."

Elena gave me one final pointed stare before going out to

the breakfast area. Aubrey joined me in front of the sink and turned on the dishwasher.

"Didn't take long for the claws to come out, did it?" she said.

"I still can't get over the comments about what I ate. Who says something like that when you're a guest in their home?"

"It's called having no tact."

"I call it incredibly rude," I said.

"From what I've seen of Liza, her parents taught her much better manners," Aubrey said.

I rinsed the forks and handed them to Aubrey. "Thank goodness."

As we worked on the dishes, I kept glancing up to see what was happening at the table. Sergei was moving his arms like he did when he showed jumping technique to Chris and me. Liza watched him intently, and Elena stood next to her chair. Seeing the three of them together brought back that jealous pulse, throbbing harder now. No matter how many children Sergei and I would have together, I'd never be able to give him his first child.

"Em? Earth to Em?"

I looked at Aubrey, who had her hand held out to me. "You've been rinsing that plate for five minutes," she said.

"Sorry." I handed her the dish.

"I wonder if Elena was different when she was younger," Aubrey said. "She's kinda prissy. Not really Sergei's type."

"You know how little he's told me about when they dated. And after being in Moscow and seeing all the places they used to be together, I'm not sure I want to hear any more."

We finished loading the dishwasher, and Aubrey went upstairs while I moved slowly toward the threesome at the table. Elena smoothed Liza's long hair and said, "Time to ready for bed. You need good rest to skate tomorrow."

Liza inched out of Elena's touch and rose from her chair.

Sergei stood, too, looking unsure of what to do or say. He finally took the stance of resting his hand on the back of his chair.

"I'm looking forward to seeing you skate," he said. "I'll be glad to help you if you need anything. I have time between lessons."

Liza nodded with a smile. "Okay."

"Goodnight," Elena said, her eyes lingering on Sergei before she ushered Liza to the stairs.

I went over to Sergei and gave him a hug, which he returned with an even firmer hold.

"That went pretty well," he said.

I hummed in agreement. "You got Liza talking."

Sergei pulled his head back but kept his arms tight around my waist. "I can't say 'thank you' enough for everything you're doing."

I arched my neck to look straight into his eyes. "Then why don't you show me how thankful you are?"

He bent his head, and our lips met, sweet and light at first, then fuller and hungrier. Sergei's hands slid down into the back pockets of my jeans, pressing me against his body. I clung to his shoulders and stood on the toes of my flats, giving me deeper reach into his mouth. The electric heat from his lips, his breath, his touch lit me up all over.

"Excuse me."

We broke apart, and Elena took a step into the room, arms folded. Sergei turned slightly toward the sliding glass door, opposite of the stairs. He was inhaling and exhaling long and hard.

"Where do we keep laundry?" Elena asked.

"Oh, umm…" I swallowed to catch my breath. "You can just leave it in your bathroom for now. I'll get you a hamper and show you the washing machine tomorrow."

"Thank you." She hesitated a moment. "Goodnight."

I watched her leave and then curled my arms around

Sergei's neck. "I believe you owe me a few more thanks."

He splayed his fingers around my waist and kissed me again but not as deep as before. After a minute, he moved his lips to my forehead and said, "Why don't we save some for tomorrow? You must be tired."

I loosened my hold on him. He'd sure gone from hot to cold quickly. Jet lag hadn't been a concern five minutes ago when he was devouring my mouth.

"I don't think she's coming back down here," I said.

"No, that's not... I just figured you'd want to get some sleep. You've had a lot going on today."

I wasn't convinced, but getting into a big discussion was something I *was* too tired for.

"Okay." I reached up and gave Sergei a tiny kiss. "I'll walk you out."

After I saw him to the door, I returned to the kitchen for a drink of water and to shut off the lights. As I made my way up the steps, Liza emerged from the guest bedroom in her pink pajamas, her arms wrapped around a pillow and a sandy brown teddy bear. Elena was right behind her.

"Liza, you sleep in here. This is—" She saw me and stopped.

"What's going on?" I asked.

"Nothing," Elena said. "We are fine."

"I wanna sleep by myself," Liza mumbled against her pillow.

Elena glared at me wearily, and I wound my hands together, twisting my engagement ring around and around. "I wish I had another room for you, but this is the only extra bed."

"I can sleep on the sofa," Liza said.

"There is no reason. This bed is big for us both," Elena said.

"Can I sleep on the sofa?" Liza asked me.

The last thing I wanted was to get in the middle of their

mother-daughter drama, but the kid was looking at me for an answer.

"You can sleep wherever you're most comfortable. I'll get you a blanket for the couch."

I blew past them and up to the linen closet in the living room. Liza padded after me, but Elena stayed at the bottom of the stairs. Grabbing a fuzzy blue blanket from the top shelf, I unfolded it and spread it over the end of the couch.

"You're sure you want to sleep in here alone?" I asked.

Liza nodded and got settled under the blanket. Elena still hadn't made an appearance, so I guessed she was going to let Liza win this battle.

"I'll leave this on so you'll have a little light," I said, tapping the shade of the tall lamp in the corner. "If you need me, I'm on the top floor, okay?"

She nodded again. I smiled at her and then took the stairs up to my room. Once inside, I sprawled across the bed and just lay there listening to the wind swishing through the trees outside my window. My body ached with exhaustion, but somehow my brain felt wide awake.

Dragging myself up, I went through all my nightly getting-ready-for-bed rituals. As I climbed under the thick burgundy comforter, I snagged my favorite bedtime reading from the nightstand and set the book in my lap.

Titled *Lyrics*, the book contained all of Sting's and The Police's songs. I'd given it to Sergei two years ago for Christmas because we both loved Sting's music, but the book spent more time in my possession. Sergei had written notes to me next to some of the songs, and I loved reading his words before I went to sleep.

I flipped the book open to a random spot and thumbed through until I found a page with markings. The song was "I Burn For You," and Sergei had written—*The title says it all.*

I touched my lips, remembering the fire in Sergei's kiss earlier. A soft knock on the door startled me and took me away from my thoughts.

"Come in," I called.

The door opened slowly, and Liza and her teddy bear peeked inside. "Hey." I closed the book. "Do you need something?"

"There's a noise on the window. It won't stop."

"Oh, that's the big tree next to the house. The branches always hit the window when it's windy."

She stared at me, not looking appeased by my explanation. Her lack of movement from the doorway also showed her reluctance to return downstairs.

"I guess it sounds pretty scary, doesn't it?" I said.

Her head bobbed, and she clutched the bear tighter. I looked at the empty space beside me in the double bed. Elena wouldn't be happy with my idea, but I didn't want to wake her and make a big production out of this.

"Do you want to sleep in here tonight?" I asked.

Liza shut the door and was in the bed before I had time to fold down the comforter for her. "I have lots of pillows," I said, fluffing one of my extras for her.

She curled up under the covers and held her bear to her chest. Close up, I noticed his fur was pretty matted. He'd obviously been around a while.

"What's your teddy's name?" I asked.

"Peter."

"That's cool. I've heard of lots of rabbits named Peter but no bears."

"It was my dad's name. He gave him to me so I wouldn't miss him as much when he was on a business trip."

"Sounds like he's a very special bear, then."

Liza was quiet as she rubbed the brown fur with her thumb. I put my book on the nightstand and said, "I used to sleep with a teddy bear, too. His name was Ted. Not very original, I bet you're thinking, but it was for Ted Williams, who played baseball for the Red Sox. My dad's a big fan."

Liza blinked a few times. "You're really nice."

My voice stuck in my throat, and I took a swallow. "So are you. I'm glad you're here."

Her face shined with a smile, and my heart turned all gooey. *No, no, no. You can't get too attached*, I quickly reminded myself. No matter how adorable Liza was with her little Sergei replica eyes. She wasn't staying, and even if she was, she was part of a package deal that included Elena—one person I would definitely never feel attached to.

CHAPTER ELEVEN

"Liza!"

My eyes flew open at the shriek of Elena's voice. The light in my bedroom had been turned on, and Elena was flying toward the opposite side of the bed. Liza let go of her teddy bear and rubbed her eyes.

"I check on you and you are not there," Elena cried. "I think you run away."

I sat up and brushed my tangled hair away from my face. "She heard a noise and got scared, so I let her sleep here."

"You should tell me."

"It wasn't a big deal, and I didn't want to wake you. I didn't think you were going to freak out about it."

"How you feel if you wake up in strange place and cannot find your daughter?" Elena became more high-pitched with each word. "Liza, you come to me if you are scared."

Liza's face crumpled, and she jumped out of the bed with her bear and tore out of the room. I threw aside the comforter.

"Getting all worked up isn't helping," I said.

"You know because you are expert? You do not have child."

"And you've been a mother all of what, five minutes? I don't think that makes you an expert either."

Elena's dark eyes burned with simmering anger. "I take care of my daughter. She do not need you."

Was I really arguing with Elena in the middle of the night? What time was it anyway? I glanced at the clock on the nightstand, and it read four thirty. My alarm was set to ring in an hour.

"I'm not going to apologize for helping Liza," I said. "Now if you'll excuse me, I need to get back to sleep."

Elena flashed one more glare before she swished out of the room in her silky pajamas. I shut off the light, but the darkness couldn't lull me to sleep. No matter how hard I tried to drift away, Elena and Liza kept my mind buzzing.

I was still awake when the clock radio clicked on with a haunting piano tune. I lay still, listening to the piece, its melancholy notes speaking to me. As soon as it was over, I went to my laptop on the desk and pulled up the radio station's website for the playlist. The song shown for five thirty a.m. was "The Crisis."

No wonder I felt emotionally connected to it.

I noted the composer, Ennio Morricone, so I could download the piece later. In the meantime, I needed to get ready for the rink.

I didn't know what I was going to find in the living room as I descended the stairs, but Liza's blanket was neatly folded, and her pillow and bear sat on the edge of the sofa. I continued down to the kitchen, where Elena was looking in the refrigerator and Liza was perched on one of the tall stools next to the bar. Both were dressed, and Elena's make-up was impeccably done as always.

"Good morning," I said, zipping my fleece jacket.

"I look for juice for Liza," Elena said.

"It's in the door." I pointed to the carton on the bottom shelf. "We can go to the store later so you can buy whatever you need." I might be providing lodging, but feeding a family wasn't part of my budget.

Breakfast passed quietly with no mention of Elena's hysterics in my bedroom. As we were heading out, Aubrey came down in her warm-up gear, lagging behind us since the ice dancers had a later session than the pairs and freestyle skaters.

When we arrived at the rink, I set Liza up with a locker and introduced her to a couple of girls around her age. As I went through my warm-up, she hung close to my side, doing her own running and stretching. Sergei had taken a seat on the bleachers next to Elena, who was talking with animated hands. She was probably telling him about the eventful night at my house.

Liza sat with me to put on her skates, and I watched her carefully tie the laces on her shiny white boots. Her pale pink practice dress was as nice as some competition costumes. Elena had been right when she said she'd given her daughter the best of everything.

Liza fidgeted with her matching pink gloves as she surveyed the other skaters around us chatting and preparing for the session. I slipped on my blue leg warmers and said, "We have a really good group here. There are a few drama queens, but everyone gets along for the most part."

"My old rink was like that," Liza said. "We used to have so much fun."

"You must miss your friends in New York a lot."

"Me and my best friend, Hope were gonna skate a duet at our club show, but then I had to move." She looked down at her skates.

"And the rink in Moscow isn't as much fun," I guessed.

Liza shook her head.

I thought for a moment as I tugged my legwarmers over the heels of my boots. "We're having a little show here in two weeks. It's a sendoff for those of us going to Worlds, and a bunch of the kids are also skating in it. Maybe you could be part of it."

"But I'm not a member here."

"I think it would be okay," I said. "I'll talk to the people in charge."

Liza gave me a big smile, and I motioned for her to follow me to the ice for the start of the session. Hopping on behind me, she joined the crowd of skaters warming up. I ramped up speed and glided around all of them. Beside the boards, someone flipped on the sound system, and "You Get What You Give" filled the quiet rink. The music got my legs pumping harder and itching to work.

Even though Chris couldn't skate, I still had a lesson scheduled with Sergei. We could work on elements that didn't require a partner such as jumps and footwork. When I met him near the boards, his attention was over my shoulder. Turning my head, I saw Liza picking herself up from the ice.

"She fell?" I asked, grabbing my water bottle from the boards and taking a long sip.

"Double Salchow," he said.

Liza brushed off her hands and returned to doing easy crossovers. Her little legs generated more power than I'd seen in most kids her age. And her posture remained perfectly straight. I already admired the spark I saw in her movements.

"She has your speed," I said.

"And Elena's grace," Sergei added.

The perfect combination of the two of them. I shuddered and looked to the bleachers where Elena sat alone on the top row. I expected her to be watching her daughter, but her gaze was fixed on Sergei and me.

"Why don't you start with the Lutz and toe, and then I can do the throws with you," Sergei directed.

I deposited my bottle on the boards and weaved through skater traffic to set up for the triple Lutz. One after another, I popped off clean jumps. Moving on to the triple toe-double toe combination, I achieved the same results. I skated back to Sergei with Elena's eyes following me again.

Sergei gripped my hand, and we made one pass around the rink to gain speed for the throw triple Lutz. With his hands tight on my hips, we glided backward until I stabbed my right toepick into the ice and Sergei vaulted me into the air. I rotated three times and landed on my right blade, smooth and easy. Sergei nodded.

"Throw loop," he said, reaching for my hand.

I peeked at the stands. Elena's arms were now crossed and her gaze stonier. Watching Sergei and me on the ice together had obviously pricked a nerve. I didn't want to admit the small amount of satisfaction I felt.

Sergei and I practiced the two throws multiple times with success, and inspiration hit me upon my final clean landing. I circled around Sergei while I fixed my leotard's twisted shoulder straps.

"Let's run through the whole short program together," I said. "And we can do sections of the long if you're not up for doing the entire thing."

Sergei rubbed the back of his neck. "I'd prefer we just work on the elements."

"But you did run-throughs with Court last year when Mark was hurt."

"She was still learning the choreography then, so I thought it would be helpful."

Why was he fighting me? We'd never skated a run-through together, but Chris had never been sidelined for an extended period of time. My request made total sense.

"I think it would be helpful to me, too," I said. "Just doing elements isn't as good for my timing as going through them with the program."

Sergei's mouth set in a line. Was he hesitating because he didn't want to upset Elena? Whether she was feeling nostalgic over her failed career or jealous over Sergei and me skating together, neither was my problem. I had work to do on the ice.

"Please?" I asked.

He remained quiet but then unzipped his jacket. "Okay. Let me warm up a little more."

He dropped his jacket behind the boards and shot off across the ice. While he loosened his legs, I launched into my flying camel spin. After practicing the spin and my spiral, I skated over to the stereo and popped in our short program CD with "Victoria's Secret."

Sergei rejoined me, and we leisurely glided around the rink, waiting for my friend Trevor and his partner Leigh's music to end. Since they were also Sergei's students, he kept an eye on them as they worked on the new program he'd just choreographed. Chris and I were Sergei's only team going to the World Championships, so all his other pairs had new programs for next season already.

The popular Bach piece ended with a bang, and Sergei led me to center ice for our starting pose. I placed my hand on his chest and he covered it with his. The beat of his pulse throbbed against my palm, sending mine on a sprint.

We locked eyes, and a tiny shiver rolled down my spine. Skating a full program together was much different from just practicing throws and lifts.

You'd better focus and perform the elements perfectly or he's never going to do this again.

The music started, and I mentally recited my key words for the opening element, the triple twist. *Quick and tight, quick and tight.* Sergei tossed me up, and I spun three times before falling into his waiting hands. His catch wasn't as seamless as Chris's, startling me and causing me to stumble. He held onto me to keep me steady and mumbled, "Sorry" as we continued forward.

I zoomed through the triple Lutz while Sergei skipped it, not having done the jump in years. We met up with side-by-side crossovers and skated into the throw Lutz. With a solid landing, I gave Sergei a smile, and his face relaxed. He drew me into his strong arms on the entrance into the pairs spin, and tingles covered my skin. *Pretend he's Chris!*

But that was impossible to do with our noses practically bumping as we curved into the spin. I counted the revolutions in my head, focusing on the numbers instead of Sergei's breath mixing with mine and the pressure of his hands on my lower back.

Moving between the remaining elements, we became even more in sync with each other and with the music. Every look, every touch carried an emotion and played out the love story of Sergei's choreography. The additional adrenaline that coursed through me threatened to erase my well-trained muscle memory.

Sergei pressed me up into the star lift, and I noticed some of the other skaters idling and watching us, Liza included. We sped past them, and Sergei set me down, preparing for the closing seconds of the program.

In time with the final piano notes, I edged away from Sergei, and he rushed toward me, trapping me in his arms for the ending pose. I gasped at the passion with which he grabbed me. His eyes held my gaze then slowly drifted down to my mouth, and my body hummed from the fiery energy between us. I leaned into Sergei and squeezed my fingers harder around his biceps.

A few of my training mates erupted with applause and whistles, and Sergei jerked backward. He didn't say anything as he took off to cool down, leaving me alone in the middle of the ice with more than my muscles burning.

"Get a room, Em." Trevor laughed as he skated past me.

A fast-moving blur of fur behind the boards caught my eye, and I turned to see Elena hurrying to the exit. I closed my eyes, taking deep breaths.

This is too much drama.

I pushed off and followed Sergei around the rink. The

breeze cooled my flushed face and dried the sweat trickling down my breastbone. When Sergei slowed and stopped at the boards, I pulled up next to him and took a big gulp from my water bottle.

Sergei lifted his T-shirt to wipe his face, and I got a prime view of his toned stomach. I frowned to myself. I probably wouldn't get my hands on those abs much while my houseguests were in town.

"We shouldn't do any more of those," Sergei said.

"Any more of what?"

"Run-throughs."

"Why?" I hardened my voice. "Because Elena can't handle it?"

"It has nothing to do with Elena."

"Really? Then what's the reason?"

"Chris is your partner. I'm just going to throw you off, skating with you."

I shook my head. "It's more than that. I'm sure you saw Elena storm out of here."

"Forget about her."

"I wish I could, but she's in my face twenty-four seven," I spat out.

"Then why did you offer her a place to stay?"

"I had to do something before you offered to move her into your apartment."

Sergei looked at me as if I was crazy. "I wasn't going to…" Glancing at the crowd on the ice, he said, "We can't talk about this here."

I slapped the cap onto my bottle and slammed it down. "So, what do you want me to do next? More Lutzes? Footwork? Maybe I can run through the long with my invisible partner."

"That's not a bad idea," Sergei said. "I'll queue up the music. And I want you to go full-out. Put all the required feeling into it."

"It's a little hard to emotionally connect to someone who's not there."

He angled toward me, his blue eyes shining deep with purpose. "I have faith in you."

He skated toward the sound system, and I tightened my ponytail with a fierce tug. Why couldn't Sergei admit Elena had gotten into his head? Chris waved to me from behind the boards, so I raced over to him.

"I ran into Elena on my way in," he said. "She looked like she was about to cry."

I groaned. "I can't handle all this."

"What happened?"

"Em!" Sergei called from across the rink.

"Excuse me, I have to go skate with imaginary you."

Chris smirked. "He's not nearly as funny as me. Or as good-looking."

I let out a little laugh. "Or as humble."

I got into position, and when "Clair de Lune" began, I heeded Sergei's orders and emoted as if Chris was beside me, holding my hand. Sergei and I only discussed technical matters during the rest of our lesson, and at the end of the hour, I grabbed my water and hopped off the ice for a short break.

Plopping down on the bleachers, I sipped my drink and stared at the Zamboni circling the ice. Sergei stood nearby, introducing Liza to one of the freestyle coaches, but the loud hum from the ice drowned out their conversation. Elena still hadn't returned. Maybe she'd hitched a ride to the airport. A girl could dream, couldn't she?

Liza headed for the locker room, and Sergei came over to me. "Have you seen Elena?"

"I'm not her keeper," I said brusquely.

He stood with his hands on hips, staring in the direction of the door. "I need to talk to her about Liza."

"When you find her, you can let her know we won't

torture her anymore by skating together," I said, rising from my seat.

The corners of Sergei's mouth twitched downward. "Let's not make this more complicated than it already is."

"It would be less complicated if you were honest with me. You can't tell me you don't feel anything for Elena, seeing her after all this time."

He inched closer to me and spoke softer, "Em, I've told you before—my feelings for her are long gone."

"You say that, but your actions show otherwise. The way you left so quickly last night, and then today on the ice..."

"You're reading way too much into that."

"I'm not saying I think you're still in love with her, but there's something there." The Zamboni exited the ice, so I went toward the boards but then stopped and turned around. "And you need to figure it out."

CHAPTER TWELVE

AFTER A LONG MORNING OF PRACTICING solo followed by an intense workout on the elliptical machine, I retreated to the locker room, seeking an escape from Elena's constant glare. Aubrey and Marley were sitting on one of the long wooden benches, paging through fashion magazines.

"Looking for costume ideas?" I asked.

Marley lifted her head. "Zach and I are changing our free dance. I'm trying to find some color inspiration for my dress."

"What are you changing it to?" I asked.

"The soundtrack from *Movin' Out*."

"That'll be a fun program," I said, pulling on the door to my rusty blue locker. It wouldn't budge. I yanked harder, growling deep in my throat. "Stupid door," I said through gritted teeth as I frantically tugged on the handle. The loud banging echoed off the cement walls.

Aubrey jumped up. "Let me get it."

She slowly jiggled the handle up and down and pulled on it, opening the locker easily.

"Thanks." I threw my empty water bottle inside, and it hit the back wall with a thud.

"I saw you and Sergei talking earlier," Aubrey said. "You didn't look too happy."

"He insists he has zero feelings for Elena, but the way he's been acting…"

"Let's all get out of here and go to lunch. You can tell us everything that's going on."

"I was just gonna eat an energy bar. You know, since according to Elena, I pigged out last night."

Aubrey reached into my locker and handed me my purse. "We're going to lunch."

The three of us slipped our warm-up jackets over our leotards and piled into Aubrey's Jeep. With only one stop light between the rink and our favorite deli, we were seated in a booth with our salads within minutes. I shoved a forkful of romaine lettuce into my mouth and chomped on it, letting my jaws work out more of my frustration.

"What happened this morning?" Marley asked, her warm brown eyes full of concern. "Chris said Elena stormed out while you were practicing."

"Sergei and I did a run-through of the short, and I guess Elena didn't enjoy watching us skate together," I said. "You'd think ten years would be enough to get over whatever possessive feelings she had."

Marley toyed with the straw in her paper cup. "I guess it could be kinda hard seeing him skate with someone else when they were partners for so long. Didn't they team up when they were ten years old?"

"Eleven," I said. "Even so, she needs to move on. I think she made Sergei feel guilty when he shouldn't be. All he did was help me practice, and he was really into it until he realized Elena was watching."

"She's going to be at the rink every day, isn't she?" Aubrey said.

"Yes. Always in my face, always a reminder." I set down my fork and pushed away the salad. "I can't look at her without thinking about her and Sergei in that tiny bed in his parents' apartment."

"You're going to drive yourself crazy if you keep thinking about that," Aubrey said.

"I know, it's just that she was Sergei's first kiss, his first love, his first…" I swallowed hard. "Everything. And now she's here, all grown up and gorgeous, and Sergei knows what it feels like to be with her. Something he doesn't have with me," I added quietly.

"Are you regretting your decision to wait until you're married?" Marley asked.

"No, I just… I hate that Elena has that connection with him."

"Just because you haven't slept with Sergei doesn't mean you don't have as deep a connection," Marley said. "Considering how young he and Elena were when they were together, I'd say what you and Sergei have is even stronger."

"They have a kid together, though," I said. "It doesn't get much deeper than that."

The faint ring of my phone came from my purse, and I checked the number. The area code was Boston's.

"Hello, is this Emily Butler?"

"Yes, who is this?"

"My name is Barrett White with Sovereign Bank. I'm calling regarding a property on Martha's Vineyard you're renting for a week this summer."

"Yes?" I asked warily.

"The house has been foreclosed by the bank and will no longer be available for rental. I'm contacting you to discuss return of your deposit."

My hand flew to my forehead, my palm flattening against it. "How can this happen? We have a contract."

"I'm very sorry, but unfortunately the contract is void upon foreclosure. I realize it's a terrible inconvenience."

"We rented it for our honeymoon." My voice rose. "How

are we going to find something this close to summer? Most places will be booked already."

"Again, I'm incredibly sorry. I'm going to put the paperwork and your deposit in the mail to you as soon as possible. I hope you'll be able to find a new property."

After he confirmed my contact information, I clicked off the phone and sat with it in my hand, staring at it. "I don't believe this."

"Something happened to the house you rented?" Marley asked.

"It's been foreclosed by the bank and our contract is void. I knew we should've gone through an agency instead of dealing directly with the owner, but it was the perfect house! Right on the beach with that awesome deck I told you about." I pressed my fingers against my temples. "What if this is an omen? For the wedding?"

"It's not an omen. It's a crazy fluke thing," Aubrey said.

"Like running into Elena and Liza in Moscow? How many more crazy fluke things are going to happen before we get to the altar?"

Aubrey and Marley exchanged glances, and Marley said, "Nothing else will go wrong. We'll help you find a new place."

I rested my head on my hand. "Thanks. I'm going to have to scour the internet."

"What about your Aunt Debbie's summer house?" Marley asked. "I'm sure she'd let you have it for the week."

"I thought about it when we first decided to go to the Vineyard, but I don't really want to be in my aunt and uncle's bedroom for my honeymoon. I don't know... it would feel weird."

"You could always use the guest room," Aubrey said.

"I guess," I said. "That house has so many family memories, though. I really wanted some place new where I'd only have memories of Sergei and me."

"We'll find a new amazing house for you, even better than the one you had," Marley said with an encouraging smile.

I smiled weakly back at her. "You guys are the best. Thanks for getting me away from Elena for a while."

"You'll have a nice break tomorrow, too," Marley said.

"What's tomorrow?" Aubrey asked.

"Chris and I are signing autographs at a festival fundraiser thing in Boston," I said. "My mom and Aunt Deb are on the organizing committee, so they asked us to help promote it."

Aubrey dabbed at her mouth with her paper napkin. "Is Sergei going with you?"

"He was, but I'm sure now he'll want to spend the day with Liza."

"Which will mean spending the day with Elena," she said.

I nudged my salad closer to me but just stared at it. "Since she won't let Liza out of her sight, I suppose so."

The image of Elena's name carved into Sergei's windowsill flashed through my head, and I pinched the bridge of my nose. *Don't think about it.* But my mind wouldn't obey.

WHEN WE RETURNED TO the rink, the usual afternoon session of skaters covered the ice but with two additions—Sergei and Liza. Sergei had Liza's full attention as he executed a single Salchow. Watching them from the bleachers, Elena appeared much less distressed than she had earlier. She was almost smiling, something I didn't know she was capable of.

I sat on the opposite end of the stands and observed the action on the ice. Sergei beamed as Liza completed two clean double Salchows. In turn, she looked at him with wide-eyed eagerness.

When Sergei and I had talked about our future children, we'd joked that they'd either love skating or want to be as far away from the rink as possible. If they wanted to skate, we dreamed of coaching them and making it a big, fun family affair.

Sergei was getting a taste of that dream, and he couldn't appear happier. And despite the cute picture he and Liza were on the ice, I couldn't share that happiness. He was experiencing things I thought we'd first experience together.

Sergei and Liza worked on the ice until it was almost time for Courtney and Mark's lesson. I waited for Liza to make her exit before I skated out to Sergei, who still had a smile on his face.

"Looks like you had a lot of fun," I said.

"She's really talented," he said. "And I think she's like us. You know, the ice is home for her."

"With all the changes she's been through, that's probably more true now."

Sergei rested back against the boards. "Elena told me Liza slept in your room last night."

I moved next to him and poked my left toepick into the ice. "I'm sure she thinks I was trying to undermine her, but what was I supposed to do when Liza obviously didn't want to go to her?"

"I'm glad you were there for her. I told Elena that."

"That must've gone over well," I snickered.

"She's worried Liza's going to keep shutting her out. I said I'd do what I can to make sure that doesn't happen." He glanced down at the ice and shuffled his skates. "So, I was thinking maybe you shouldn't come with us to Brewster tonight."

"I'm not the problem between them," I said crisply.

"I know, but if you're there, it's easier for Liza to ignore Elena. You're kind of distracting… in many ways." He leaned toward me with a smile.

His attempt to lighten the moment didn't ease the wariness in my gut. This was exactly the scenario I'd pictured when we were in Russia—the little family going on outings together.

Turning my head, I watched Liza bypass her mother and head straight for Courtney. I supposed I could look at the one bright spot of Sergei's request. I wouldn't have to spend the evening with Elena.

CHAPTER THIRTEEN

"One more picture," Aunt Debbie said, holding up her camera and sweeping a lock of hair out of her eyes.

I slid my arm around Chris's waist, and we put on our biggest smiles. A large sign bearing our names and the Olympic rings in bright colors topped our festival booth behind us.

The fundraiser was for the ice rink in Boston's North End, the Italian neighborhood where Mom grew up. Besides our autograph table, a number of other booths circled the rink, selling a variety of food and crafts. Also mixed in were face-painting stations and games for kids. It was like a carnival without the rides.

"Do you have everything you need?" Aunt Debbie straightened the bottled water, pens, and glossy photos of Chris and me on our table.

"I'm gonna need some of that pasta I smell," Chris said.

The aroma of Uncle Joe's chicken pesto pasta had been teasing us since we'd arrived. Three booths to our left, my uncle stood with a large serving spoon in one hand and an apron tied around his hefty middle.

"I'll tell Joe to put some on the side for you and Em," Aunt Debbie said, reaching out to us. "I really appreciate you guys spending your Saturday here. I know you don't get a lot of free time."

"We're glad to help," I said.

She hugged me to her side, cozy against her cashmere sweater. "How are you doing? Your mom's kept me up to date with everything that's going on."

I wasn't surprised my aunt knew all the news since she and Mom were as close as two sisters could be, despite their personality differences. Aunt Debbie was the classic "glass half full" type, and she didn't have a snippy bone in her body.

"I'm okay." I tipped my head from side to side like a see-saw. "It's nice to have an escape from it all today."

Mom rushed up to us in a tizzy and grabbed Aunt Debbie's shoulders. "Deb, they need you at the door. Some confusion about the tickets."

My aunt left us with a parting smile, and Mom zoomed off to handle another crisis. I was about to take a seat when my great-aunt Rafi snuck up behind me and bombarded me with a smothering hug. I coughed from the lack of air and Aunt Rafi's strong citrusy perfume.

"How's my favorite skater? It was terrible you had to pull out in Russia." She released me and corralled Chris into her grasp. "Is your arm feeling better, young man?"

I stifled a laugh as Chris leaned his chin away from Aunt Rafi's poufy white hair. "It'll be ready for Worlds," he said.

"Well, I'm glad to hear that!" She turned to me. "Where's that handsome fiancé of yours?"

I looked down and twisted my diamond ring back and forth. "He had another commitment today."

How was I going to explain to the extended members of my family that Sergei suddenly had a child? It wasn't the type of thing you could mail out in an announcement.

"Oh, that's too bad," Aunt Rafi said. "I'm selling those

anise cookies he loves. You'll have to take some to him."

Hmm… I don't know if he deserves any treats right now.

"I have to get back to business, but I want an autographed picture later." She pointed at us. "Even though I already have a whole album of them!"

Chris made a half-choking, half-laughing sound as Aunt Rafi walked away. "Is that more of your family?" He jutted his head in the direction of the cookie booth. Three middle-aged women and an elderly lady were setting out little bags of goodies.

"Didn't you meet some of them at my engagement party?" I asked.

"All I remember is being hugged a lot, having my face squeezed by old ladies, and hearing lots of *Bahston* accents. I couldn't keep track of everyone."

I laughed. "That sounds like my family."

We stationed ourselves at our table with markers in hand and ribbed each other over our apparel choices. Out of all the Team USA and Olympics gear we owned, we'd both shown up in the same navy 2002 Olympics jacket.

"People will think we were dorky enough to plan our outfits," Chris complained.

I laughed loudly, so relieved to be away from Elena and her drama. I'd gone to the movies with Aubrey, Marley, and Chris the previous night while Sergei had taken Elena and Liza sightseeing. *Daredevil* hadn't been the greatest movie I'd ever seen, but Ben Affleck in a skin-tight bodysuit had briefly taken my mind off of Sergei cruising around the island with his ex.

As soon as the doors of the festival opened to the public, a line formed at our booth. Chris and I signed photos, posed for pictures, and chatted with the endless stream of people who visited us. Aunt Debbie brought us two bowls of pasta as promised, and we grabbed bites between greeting fans.

I handed over what had to be our hundredth signed

photo while I checked out the crowd waiting for us. The people near the end of the line shifted aside, and my mouth popped open. Sergei grinned at me, a sparkling light in his eyes. Both my lips and my heart smiled back.

"Sergei's here," I told Chris.

"I thought he was with Liza."

"Maybe he's planning to see her later."

We took care of the next few fans in line, bringing Sergei closer to the table. I was gearing up to give him a hug and a kiss when the crowd parted and I saw he wasn't alone. Standing at his side was Liza.

The two of them stepped up to the booth, and this time I had to force a smile. "Hey, I didn't expect to see you here."

"It sounded like a fun event, so I thought we'd surprise you," Sergei said.

"I'm definitely surprised." I kept the plastered grin on my face.

"Liza, do you want a picture?" Chris asked.

She nodded enthusiastically. "Yes, please."

After I signed my name, I stood and asked Sergei, "Can we talk for a sec?"

He glanced down at Liza, and Chris said, "She can hang out with me and keep Em's spot warm." He smiled at Liza and patted my chair.

I turned and walked as far behind the booths as I could get before meeting the stone wall. Sergei joined me with a confused look on his face.

"What's wrong?" he asked.

"You promised no more surprises."

"This is a good one, though." He took my hand and pressed it to his palm. "I know you're busy, but I wanted to see you, even if it's just for a few minutes."

"But you brought Liza."

His grip on my hand lightened while his confusion deepened. "I didn't think you'd have a problem with that.

Now, if I'd brought Elena…"

"I told you my family was going to be here. They don't know about Liza, and this isn't really the place to get into it."

Sergei rubbed his stubbly cheek. "I'm sorry. I didn't think about it."

I pulled my hand from his and tugged on my necklace. "You haven't thought about a lot of things lately."

He frowned and dipped his head before his eyes met mine again. "Do you want us to leave?"

"You just got here. What would you say to Liza?"

"I don't know. I just don't want you to be uncomfortable."

I folded my arms and peered at Liza and Chris. They were drawing on one of the glossy photos.

"How'd you get Elena to let you bring Liza all the way to Boston?" I asked. "And without her?"

"I had to do a lot of pleading, but I finally convinced her that Liza and I should have some time alone."

"Sergei!" Aunt Rafi called as she came forward with outstretched arms. "Emily said you weren't coming."

Sergei accepted her hug while I groaned inside. There was no way my family wouldn't see Sergei and Liza roaming around the festival together. And knowing how nosy they were, short answers to their certain questions wouldn't suffice.

"Had a change in plans," he said.

"You have to come by my cookie booth. I have something special for you." She squeezed his arm.

Sergei smiled. "I'll definitely stop by."

Aunt Rafi continued on to Uncle Joe's pasta station, and I looked at Sergei. "This is so awkward. What are you going to do, walk up to my family with Liza and say, 'Hey, this is my daughter that I've never mentioned'?"

Sergei took the slightest step backward and studied me. "Is it awkward because you're embarrassed I have a daughter?"

His question sliced into me and revealed hidden feelings, ones I'd buried under the frustration and jealousy I'd been battling. When it was our little secret, Sergei's past hadn't been an issue. But now that everyone was going to know about it, maybe I *was* embarrassed that my fiancé had gotten his teenage girlfriend pregnant. And I'd criticized my mother for being judgmental. I wasn't any better.

I shifted my eyes away from Sergei's stare. "What if we talk to my family before we introduce Liza so it'll be a little easier?"

I felt him continue to stare at me, probably noticing I didn't answer his question. "That sounds like a good idea," he said.

He held out his hand, and I hesitated a moment before giving him mine. We asked Liza to hang with Chris for a few more minutes and then made our way to the cookie stand. My cousins and my great-aunt Julia greeted us with tight hugs while Aunt Rafi flitted in from behind the booth. As usual, they all gave Sergei an extra bit of affection, their hands lingering on his shoulders or his biceps. I always had to stop myself from laughing at their obvious grope fest, but my current level of tension overrode any amusement.

"Sergei, I have your special bag right here." Aunt Rafi picked up a clear plastic sack, bigger than the ones up for sale, and full of white anise cookies with colored sprinkles.

"Do I get a special bag, too?" I asked.

"Of course!" She handed me one of equal size. "I put a variety of all the ones you like in there."

Sergei took a deep breath and cleared his throat. "There's actually someone I brought with me today that will enjoy these a lot, too. I want you all to meet her, but I wanted to tell you about her first."

He had the attention of all five women, and their admiring smiles had turned into quizzical stares. My face and neck started to warm, so I pulled down the zipper on my jacket.

"When I was skating in Russia years ago, my partner Elena and I had a child together. Circumstances prevented us from raising the child, but things have changed recently, and I met my daughter when Em and I were in Russia last week. She came back with us to the Cape."

The quizzical stares morphed into wide eyes. Sergei continued, "Her name is Liza, and she's almost nine years old. I'm just getting to know her, but I think she's pretty amazing. And she adores Em." He looked at me with a smile. "Who wouldn't, but... it's definitely helped her feel more comfortable here."

My family turned their eyes to me, and I forced the corners of my mouth upward. Aunt Rafi was the first to speak as the others stayed frozen. "Well, Sergei, that's wonderful you've been able to connect with her. Is she living with you now? Are you and Emily going to raise her?"

"Is her mother still in Russia?" Aunt Julia asked.

Yep, here come the questions.

Sergei explained the complex details and fielded the additional questions my family posed. Just when I thought they couldn't come up with any more, they'd ask another one such as, "So, why didn't Elena tell you she knew where Liza was all along?"

I noticed a new line forming at the autograph booth, so I touched Sergei's forearm as he concluded yet another answer. "I have to get back to Chris."

"Yeah, I need to get back to Liza."

"We're looking forward to meeting her," Aunt Rafi said.

As we left, I glanced backward and both my aunts were watching us with their thin eyebrows raised. Sergei and I squeezed through the crowd, and Liza hopped out of my chair when she saw us.

"Can I get a flower painted on my face? I saw another girl with one."

"Sure," Sergei said. "Let's go find the artist."

I sat beside Chris, and he asked, "Everything okay?"

"Yeah." I uncapped a new pen and sighed. "Just family stuff."

Between signing autographs, I kept an eye on Sergei and Liza's progress around the rink. After Liza had her cheek adorned with a large purple flower, she and Sergei approached my family. They talked for quite a while, and Sergei bought a couple of bags of cookies for Liza. Elena wasn't going to be happy when she saw all those sweets.

Sergei and Liza moved on to a game booth, and I watched Sergei become more animated with laughter as he and Liza played Ring Toss. He had a new exuberance about him, and it grew with every minute he spent with Liza. I feared it was going to crush him to say goodbye when her visit ended.

A hand clamped my shoulder, and I looked up. Aunt Rafi asked Chris, "May I borrow your seat for a moment?"

He stood and picked up his empty paper bowl. "I'm gonna get some more pasta."

Aunt Rafi sat and squinted at me with concern. "It's gotten a little messy with Sergei, hasn't it?"

"That's a good way to describe it."

"How is it having Elena staying with you? Sergei made it sound like everything was going smoothly, but I'm not buying it."

"Honestly? I think she's rude and difficult and the last person I want staying in my house. And she doesn't like me much either."

"Well, think about if you were in her shoes. She's still learning how to be a mother, and now Liza's latching on to you and Sergei. She probably feels threatened."

I snapped the cap onto my pen and clicked it off and on with my thumb as I thought about the irony of what Aunt Rafi said. I'd felt threatened by Elena since I first laid eyes on her. Maybe our feelings could somehow cancel each other out.

"How do I make Liza feel welcome while also encouraging her relationship with Elena? I feel like if I reach out to Liza even a little, Elena will get annoyed with me."

"Maybe you should have a chat with her and assure her you're not trying to come between her and her daughter." Aunt Rafi patted my hand. "I bet it will make all the difference."

I wasn't so sure about that. Nothing seemed easy when dealing with Elena, but I hoped she was right. Something had to give because I couldn't take another couple of weeks of the tension in my house.

CHAPTER FOURTEEN

CHRIS SHUFFLED THE THIN STACK OF photos on our table and counted them. "Only five left over. We were pretty popular."

I rubbed my eyes, careful not to pop out my contacts. The constant camera flashes all afternoon had me seeing spots. Only a few people remained at the festival, and the vendors had started to close up their booths.

"Can you get a ride home with Sergei?" Chris asked. "I'm going to Marley's, so your house is out of my way."

"Come on, you were going to bring me home before you knew Sergei was here. I don't want to butt in on his time with Liza."

"Liza will be ecstatic. She's your little fangirl."

"I need to squash that some." I motioned downward with my hands. "I think it's making things with Elena even harder."

"Riding an hour to the Cape won't hurt."

"And driving five miles out of your way wouldn't hurt *you*."

"Ten miles round trip," Chris clarified.

"Hey," Sergei said as he and Liza walked up. "You guys finished for the day?"

"I was just telling Em I have to meet Marley, so I thought you could give her a ride home," Chris said.

"Sure, we were just heading out."

"Emily, I can show you the cool stuff I won." Liza unzipped her purple backpack and peeked inside. "I got a skate charm and a key chain and a glitter pen…"

I shot Chris a sideways glare, and he gave me a toothy grin. "Sounds like you had a good time," he said.

"She wouldn't leave the Duck Pond game until she won that skate charm. Super competitive." Sergei smiled down at Liza then up at me. "Just like someone else I know."

I couldn't help but laugh. "And proud of it."

Chris rose and stretched his long legs. "I'm taking off. You kids have fun."

I grabbed my cookie stash and the leftover photos and joined Sergei and Liza on the other side of the table. "I have to tell my family goodbye before we go."

They followed me around the rink as I collected more hugs and kisses from my aunts, uncle, and cousins. Mom was our final stop, and while she held me in her arms she whispered, "You're too young to be a stepmother."

I pulled away and said under my breath, "Don't start, okay?"

I led Sergei and Liza out of the rink before Mom could give me one of her patented worried looks. The sun had started to dip behind the buildings, shading the sidewalk and making the late afternoon feel cooler.

"You should button your jacket, Liza," Sergei said.

Wow, he actually sounds like a dad.

Sergei clasped my hand, and I linked my fingers through his as I glanced at his profile. He was the same person… just with an additional identity. But it still seemed so weird.

"I wasn't sure if there'd be spots around here, so I parked in the Government Center garage," Sergei said.

"Oh, so you walked through the neighborhood to the

rink."

"I told Liza this is where your mom grew up."

"We heard some men talking in Italian when we were walking," Liza said.

"There are a lot of older people here who only speak Italian. My grandma spoke it whenever she didn't want me and my cousins to know what she was saying." I laughed. "We figured out after a while what the bad words probably were."

"Does she still live here?" Liza asked.

"No, she passed away when I was ten. I used to love going to her house. It was just a couple of streets over." I gestured toward the narrow cobblestone road we'd just crossed. "She taught me how to make fresh pasta when I was your age."

"I always wanted a grandma," Liza said. "My friend Hope's grandma used to babysit us, and she'd let us stay up till midnight and watch *The Tonight Show*."

Sergei and I laughed, and he said, "Well, you do have a grandmother now. My mother is very anxious to meet you."

"Is she in America?"

"No, she and my father live in Moscow."

"Oh." Liza's shoulders sagged.

"Did you have a lot of family around when you lived in New York?" I asked.

Liza shook her head. "Elena was the only one who came to visit. Oh, and Uncle Ivan came a few times, but I didn't like him."

"Why's that?" I asked.

"He didn't talk to me much when I lived here, but when I moved to Moscow, he was always telling me how much better Russia was than America. He wanted me to skate for Russia, but I don't want to. I wanna be on Team USA one day and have a jacket like that." Liza pointed to my Olympics fleece.

Sergei's forehead was pinched, and he appeared deep in

thought just like he had when he'd come up with his idea for Liza's visit. I was afraid to think what new plans might be forming in his head.

Liza skipped ahead of us and stopped in front of the wrought iron fence surrounding the Peace Garden at St. Leonard's Church. She peered through the bars. "It's so pretty in there. It's like the secret garden in the book."

I shook my head, amazed at the fleeting attention of a child. She was already distracted by the statues inside the gate.

"This is the church where Em and I are getting married," Sergei said.

"Really?" Liza gaped at us.

I stepped up to the fence and looked up at the large brick church. "I went to mass here every Sunday with my family before I moved to the Cape."

"Let's go inside," Liza said, heading for the gate.

I checked my watch. "Vigil mass is going on right now, so we can't go inside, but we can walk through the garden."

We wandered down the path, and Liza gazed at the statues of Jesus and the Virgin Mary surrounded by flowers that had bloomed early. She twirled to face me with excitement in her eyes. "What does your dress look like? Does it have one of those long skirts?"

"It does. I actually have my final fitting on Monday to try it on and see if it needs any more work."

"I wanna see it! Can I go with you?"

Squash the fangirl, Em. I paused with my mouth half open. "The seamstress is here in Boston, so it's not going to be a quick trip. But if the dress fits, I'll be bringing it home, so you can see it then."

"I'm guessing I won't get a peek." Sergei smiled and circled his arm around my waist.

"You guess right. The first time you'll see the dress is when I walk through those doors." I pointed my thumb toward the church.

"Will I be able to come back for the wedding?" Liza asked.

Both Sergei and I shifted our weight, and Sergei's arm tensed. We hadn't broached the topic of Liza and the wedding yet. I figured he wanted to give Liza a positive answer, but would he do it without talking to me first?

"I'd love to have you there," Sergei said. "We'll have to see how your summer plans look."

He didn't make any promises. That was a start.

Liza chewed on her lip as she looked wistfully at the church. I scrambled to think of a diversion, something to take advantage of Liza's short attention span.

"Hey, I asked about you skating in the sendoff show, and if you have a program ready, you're in," I said.

The brightness returned to Liza's eyes. "I can do my free skate from last year. It's Chopin."

Sergei brushed his lips against my hair. "Thanks for doing that."

"Since Chris and I can't skate, she can take our spot."

"You and Sergei should skate together in the show," Liza said. "You looked awesome at practice yesterday."

"That wouldn't be a good idea," Sergei said.

I stiffened as I remembered Sergei fleeing from me on the ice. Could he dismiss Liza's thought any quicker? I tipped my head to look up at him. "Because you'd be 'throwing me off'?" I made air quotes.

"That and I haven't skated in front of an audience in ten years."

"You'd be great," Liza said.

Sergei might give in to Liza on a lot of things, but there was no way he was agreeing to this. I slipped away from him and took a few steps down the path.

"I have another idea," Sergei said. "Why don't you skate a solo number, Em?"

I wrinkled my forehead. "Why would I do that?"

"I think it would be good for you. Your confidence has grown so much since you switched to pairs, but this could give you even more, to know you can go out there on your own and perform."

"The last time I was on the ice alone was 1999 Sectionals where I fell three times and wanted to dig a hole in the ice and crawl into it."

Sergei came over and stood in front of me. "That was the old Emily, the one who skated in fear. You're so far past that now. And there won't be any judges watching."

"You should do it!" Liza bounced up and down.

Sergei was being awfully persistent even though he knew how much performance anxiety had hampered my singles career.

"You're really pushing this," I said.

"Because as scary as it sounds to you right now, I think it will make you feel amazing."

"I don't have a program."

"You're always telling me about the programs you choreograph in your head," Sergei said. "I bet you could put something together in a week."

I hugged my arms over my chest and looked between Sergei and Liza's enthusiastic smiles. "I'll think about it."

We exited the garden and took a right onto Hanover Street. As we passed the rows of Italian shops and restaurants, Liza tried to pronounce the names on all the signs. My mind wandered to the jukebox in my head as I thought of a list of songs I could use for a program. If I agreed to skate.

At the end of Hanover, we left the quaint North End and entered a mess of construction for Boston's "Big Dig." On the way to the garage, Elena called Sergei's phone, and Sergei told her we were about to leave the city. I was thankful he didn't mention I was with Liza and him. No need to give Elena an hour to get riled up over me spending time with Liza.

We weren't far into the ride home when I glanced at the

back seat and discovered Liza had fallen asleep. Her head was cocked to one side, her little pink mouth slightly open.

"She wore herself out today," I said with a quiet laugh.

"I think she had a lot of fun." Sergei kept his voice low. "She's getting more and more comfortable around me, which is all I hoped for."

"You have a way of putting people at ease. You do it with all your students."

Sergei peeked at the rearview mirror and scratched his chin. "I didn't know what to say when Liza asked about the wedding."

"I appreciate that you didn't give her a definite answer without talking to me."

"Are you okay with her being there?"

"Definitely. She's your daughter." I shook my head a little, still unaccustomed to the sound of those words. "But I don't want Elena there."

Sergei stayed quiet until he sent a quick look my way. "She's not a bad person, Em."

"I didn't say she is. I just said I don't want her at our wedding. I don't think she'd want to be there anyway."

Sergei fiddled with the heater, and we rode for at least a mile before he spoke again. "I wish there wasn't so much tension between you."

"She's just so... I don't know... cold? Has she always been like that?"

"She's always been guarded with most people because of her father. He put a lot of fear in her, told her not to trust anyone." Sergei's eyes remained glued to the highway. "I was the only person she really let in."

Literally and figuratively. I cringed at the thought and squirmed against my seat belt. Before unwanted images could invade my mind, I steered the conversation back to Liza.

"I think the fact Elena grew up without a mother shows in how she interacts with Liza. I feel like she needs a softer approach, but there's no way I'm telling her that. She'd probably yell at me again about how I'm not a mother and I should mind my business."

"You might not be a mother now, but you're going to be a great one someday." Sergei reached over and massaged my shoulder.

I smiled at him. "You seem to be catching on to this 'dad' thing pretty quickly."

"Liza's making it easy so far." Sergei hesitated before he continued, "This was a lot of fun tonight—the three of us hanging out together."

I nodded. "Yeah, it was."

Sergei rubbed the steering wheel as he appeared to be gathering his thoughts again. Finally, he asked, "What if we could do it more often?"

"I thought you wanted me to let Liza have more time with Elena?"

"I didn't mean these next few weeks. I meant further in the future."

I sat up straighter, fully alert with both curiosity and concern. "I'm not sure I'm following."

"Liza thinks of the States as her home, and it kills me to think of her being miserable in Russia. So, I wanted to see how you'd feel about Liza and Elena moving here."

It was a good thing I wasn't driving because we would've ended up careening into the woods. After the initial numbness left my body, I turned to face Sergei as far as my seat belt would allow.

"There's no way Elena will agree to that," I said.

"I was going to start working the idea in slowly with her. She has to see how happy Liza is here."

"When you say move *here*, do you mean here as in this country or here as in Cape Cod?"

"Well, ideally, Cape Cod, so I can see Liza often."

I rotated in the seat again and propped my elbow against

the window, resting my chin on my hand as I stared at the darkening trees. I felt like the Titanic was sinking in my stomach. Mom had said this would happen. It had only taken three days for Sergei to come up with a grand plan.

"I just can't see Elena moving here. Didn't you say she never wanted to leave Russia?" I realized my tone had grown louder and I quickly hushed myself, not wanting to wake Liza in the middle of the discussion.

"It can't be all about what she wants anymore. She needs to think about what's best for Liza. And with her inheritance from her father, she has the means to live anywhere."

I pushed my hair away from my face and held it there. Suddenly, the heater felt more suffocating than cozy.

"Are you thinking of trying to get some kind of partial custody?" I asked.

"I haven't thought about any of the legal stuff. I just want Liza to be somewhere close, where we don't have to cross the ocean to see each other."

I turned to the backseat to confirm that Liza was still asleep. Her head had slipped even further to one side, and her raven hair fell across her cheek. She looked so sweet and peaceful. Then Mom's last words to me popped into my head — *You're too young to be a stepmother.*

Shifting forward in the leather seat, I asked, "Do you realize how much this would change our lives?"

"I know it's asking a lot, and I've asked for more understanding from you this past week than a man should ever ask from his fiancé… but I feel like I have to try to do this for Liza or I'm going to regret it forever."

"I don't know how I'm supposed to respond to this, though. If I say I'm not on board, then you're going to resent me for keeping Liza away from you."

Sergei looked at me and said softly, "Not if you tell me the reasons why you're not on board."

"I'm not saying I'm not. I'm just saying hypothetically. I

honestly don't know what I feel, and I don't think I'm going to be able to process it in a one-hour car ride."

He nodded slightly. "It's a lot to think about. We can talk more later."

I leaned my head back against the seat and shut my eyes but opened them when Sergei's hand closed around my knee.

"No matter what changes might happen..." He glanced back and forth between me and the road. "Nothing will ever change how much I love you and how much I want our future together to be everything we dreamed of."

I looked into his deep blue eyes and didn't doubt his love for a second. But the future he mentioned was the potential problem. My dreams didn't include an instant child in our lives, and not only would Liza be around but also the oh-so-pleasant Elena. Those were compromises I wasn't sure I was ready to make.

CHAPTER FIFTEEN

Upon arriving home, I blew past Elena in the living room and headed up the stairs, letting Sergei deal with her. She looked surprised and, as expected, annoyed to see me with Sergei and Liza.

Inside my bedroom, I stripped off my jacket and tossed it and the bag of cookies onto the bed. Disbelief over Sergei's big plans had built up inside me during the ride home until I could barely breathe. I'd thought Sergei might want Liza to spend summers with us, maybe extended holidays, but he wanted to make her part of our daily lives. He wanted to make *Elena* part of our daily lives.

I sat at my small desk in the corner and unlatched the window next to it. The breeze helped return some of the air to my lungs. Slowly and methodically, I breathed in and out as visions of my future with Sergei played in my mind. Our time as newlyweds would be disrupted as we helped Elena and Liza get settled on the Cape, and Elena would always be at the rink, battling us over every issue with Liza. It would be like marrying three people instead of one.

Needing a distraction, I woke my laptop with a tap of the

mouse and found an email from Marley. It contained the address and phone number for a vacation house on Martha's Vineyard recommended by her aunt. Under the information, Marley's note read—*It's available the week of your honeymoon!* I quickly grabbed my cell phone from my jacket. I needed all the good news I could get.

A call to the owner revealed the house in Chilmark had its own private beach and spectacular views from the master bedroom. I wanted to inspect the place in person, so the owner and I planned to meet at the house the following weekend. I was ending the call when Sergei knocked on my half-open door.

I jumped up and showed him the phone. "We might have a new place for the honeymoon."

"That's great." Sergei smiled and came over to me. "Do you have pictures?"

"No, but you could go with me to see it next Saturday. We can stay at Aunt Deb's and go to the cliffs in the morning." Could he hear the hope in my voice? It had been so long since we'd had quality time together.

Sergei's face turned apologetic. "I promised Liza I'd take her whale-watching next Saturday."

His answer popped my balloon of hope with a loud bang. "Of course," I said quietly.

"It might be our last weekend together for a long time... depending on what happens..."

"I'm not ready to discuss that right now." I set the phone on the desk and went to the dresser.

"You always do this, Em," Sergei said with gentle frustration. "You hold everything inside instead of talking about it."

"Says the man who still barely speaks about his past."

"I've opened up more to you than I have to anyone."

I stared at my jewelry box before removing my earrings and inserting them into the velvet slats. Sergei moved beside me and rubbed my neck. "You can tell me whatever you're feeling."

I felt like I was smothering again. I wanted to lock my door, take a long shower, listen to incredibly loud music, and think about why I'd ever suggested going to that rink in Moscow. I couldn't have a thoughtful conversation at the moment, not with the frustration and disappointment currently choking me.

"I just want to be alone."

I opened the middle drawer of the dresser, forcing Sergei to take a step back. Pulling out a T-shirt and a pair of gray sweats, I walked past Sergei to the window and opened it wider.

"Em, we need to—"

"I said not now, okay?"

Sergei came slowly toward me and cradled my face in his hands, following with a kiss on my forehead. We stood with his head bent over mine and my arms locked around my pajamas, neither of us moving or saying a word. The warmth of his touch relaxed my body but not the jumble of thoughts buzzing inside me.

Sergei finally lowered his hands to his sides and said softly, "I'll call you later."

I shut the door behind him and trudged to the computer. I needed the loud music before the shower. Something in which I could lose myself and imagine I was skating to.

The first song listed in my music folder was "The Crisis," the piece I'd heard and downloaded the previous day. I clicked on it and turned up the volume, and a program came to life in my mind. I saw myself alone in the spotlight, gliding in a spiral on a deep inside edge then opening my arms to the sky. The melancholy music carried me along, creating the movements for me. It was the perfect piece for me to express my tangled emotions.

You can do this. You can skate to this at the show.

I pressed repeat on the player and swiveled the volume knob on the speakers even higher. With my eyes closed, I began to walk through choreography in the space between my bed and the dresser. The knocking on my door didn't resonate with me until it turned into loud banging. *That better be Aubrey.*

I paused the music and swung open the door. My nerves clenched. It wasn't Aubrey.

"Liza tell me something." Elena entered my room, not bothering to wait for an invitation. "She say she go to your wedding."

I put my hands on my hips. "Sergei said he'd like to have her there, but he didn't make any promises."

"You should not speak about it with her until you speak to me."

"We passed the church where the wedding's going to be, so Sergei just happened to mention it. There was no premeditated discussion."

The big word prompted the stare from Elena that usually meant she couldn't translate. She took a moment to reply, "Liza have summer training she cannot miss. She already miss time with her coach as she is here."

"I don't think missing skating is the reason you don't want her to attend the wedding."

"The more she is here, the more she want to stay, and she belong in Russia with me." Elena patted her chest. "You do not need her here. You have everything. You have career, you have family, you have marriage soon. Liza is all I have."

Her emotional outburst blew around me like a windstorm. Before I could respond, she added, "You cannot turn her against me."

"I'm not doing that." I placed my hand over my heart. "I would never do that."

"Sergei say he want to help me be closer to Liza, but I think what he want most is Liza to stay here."

"He wants you both to stay here," I said.

As soon I spoke, I clamped my lips together. Sergei wouldn't have to slowly approach the idea with Elena now.

"To live here?" Elena gaped at me.

"I told Sergei you'd never agree to it."

Elena's expression changed from surprised to one of consideration, and my stomach began a slow descent. *Stop talking. Just stop talking.*

"I do not know how I leave Moscow. I know nothing here." Elena sounded unsure yet contemplative at the same time.

What was I supposed to say? I didn't want to sound encouraging, but if I seemed too opposed to the idea, Elena might be more interested.

"It could be difficult," I said, trying to keep my tone casual.

Elena's gaze wandered to the photo of Sergei and me on the dresser—the one of us at the cliffs. She studied it intently, just as she had the first time she'd seen it. Turning to me, she said, "I speak with Sergei about this."

She left the room, and I stared at the door, numb and unable to move. Once Elena told Sergei I'd relayed his idea to her, he might think that was my way of endorsing it. Somehow, I kept getting in my own way, sabotaging my chance at a peaceful existence. First, I'd taken Sergei to the rink in Moscow, then I'd invited Elena and Liza into my house, and now I'd inadvertently invited them into the rest of my life.

I made my feet move toward the desk, where I restarted the music. Sinking onto the bed, I curled into a ball and closed my eyes, letting "The Crisis" surround me.

TWO NIGHTS LATER, I traveled Highway Three to Boston again, that time alone as I headed to my wedding dress fitting. The CD player in my car blared U2's "Ultraviolet," and I found myself continually ramping up the volume to drown out the persistent worries in my head.

When I'd told Sergei I spilled his idea to Elena, he asked me again how I felt about Elena and Liza moving to the Cape. I still didn't give him an answer and I continued to evade him. If I avoided the problem, maybe it would miraculously go away.

The deeper I ventured into Boston's rush hour traffic, the tighter I gripped the steering wheel. The honking horns, the drivers weaving between lanes, the pedestrians straying outside the crosswalks—they all served to tense my body even more. After circling Boylston Street three times, I jerked my sedan into a parking spot near the shop and ran up to the second floor.

Mom was already in the workroom, chatting with Louann, the seamstress. Louann had sewn every skating costume I'd ever worn, so when I'd decided to design my wedding dress, she was the first person I called. We'd worked on the design together, as we did on my costumes, and she'd created my vision exactly.

I pecked Mom's cheek and hugged Louann. "Sorry I'm late."

"It's okay," Louann said. "Gave your mom and I a chance to catch up."

Her sympathetic smile told me Mom had shared the Liza news. It wasn't a topic I wanted to discuss, so I quickly asked, "Is the dress in the changing room?"

Louann pushed aside the green curtain that covered the doorway behind her. "It's all ready for you."

I went inside the small room and pulled the curtain shut. The ivory satin dress hung on the wall. The first time I'd tried on the gown, we all ended up in a mess of tears—me, Mom, Aunt Debbie... even Aubrey, who was the least sentimental person I knew.

Stripping out of my clothes, I stepped into the dress and

peeked around the curtain. "Mom, can you help me?"

She maneuvered around the dress's long train as her fingers carefully made their way up the long row of delicate buttons. When she finished, Mom held my skirt and we moved out into the shop and in front of the huge mirror on the far wall.

My chest tightened as I stared at my reflection. Louann's final alterations made the dress fit my petite curves perfectly. I ran my hand across the off-the-shoulder neckline and down the draped bodice to the A-line skirt, sliding my fingertips along the cool, silky material. I hadn't wanted any frills on the dress, so the gown had a simple yet elegant look with only a touch of beading. It was everything I'd dreamed, just like I'd thought my life with Sergei would be. The tightness in my chest rose to my throat, creating a painful lump.

"It's so beautiful," Mom said. "I know I say that every time I see it, but it's true."

I nodded and attempted to speak, but no words came. Only tears. I tried to breathe them back with quick gasps, but I couldn't stop them as they seeped from my eyes.

Mom brushed my hair away from my face. "Sweetie, those don't look like happy tears."

Through the mist, I watched Louann's reflection quietly retreat to the other side of the room. I swiped at my tears before they could drip from my cheeks.

"I don't wanna mess up the dress," I choked.

Mom grabbed a tissue from the box on Louann's worktable and blotted my face. I felt like I was ten years old again, crying after a horrible competition and letting Mom dry my eyes.

"Is this about Liza?" Mom asked.

I gently took the tissue from her and blew my nose. The teary image staring at me in the mirror wasn't how I wanted to see myself in my wedding dress. I turned away and looked down at the flowing yards of ivory satin.

"Sergei wants Elena and Liza to move here permanently," I said quietly.

Mom smoothed my hair again. "And that's not what you want."

"I don't know if I'm ready to share him," I sniffled. "I thought it'd be years before we'd have a kid."

Mom lifted my chin, and I faced the deep concern in her brown eyes. "If you need more time, if you're not sure this wedding is what you want, we can—"

"I just want things to be normal again," I cried.

Mom clasped her hands around mine. "We'll let Louann look at the dress, and then we'll go home and talk, okay?"

I gave her a shaky nod, and she beckoned Louann to rejoin us. Mom stepped aside but kept a close eye on me as Louann slipped on her reading glasses and examined every inch of the gown. When she was satisfied with the fit, I changed out of the dress with Mom's assistance and Louann packed it into a large white garment bag.

Mom rode to Brookline with me since she'd taken the T to the shop from the university. I pulled into the driveway of the house where I'd grown up and felt a warm, comforting feeling. A night at home might be the perfect tonic for me.

We entered the kitchen through the side door, and a peppy Big Band tune greeted us from the front of the house.

"Dad must be hard at work," I said. Whenever my father prepared lectures for his Twentieth Century History class, he listened to music from the applicable decade.

"I have to put the lasagna in the oven." Mom aimed for the refrigerator. "Can you tell Dad he has about an hour until dinner?"

I started through the living room to Dad's office but stopped when I saw the boxes of wedding invitations stacked next to the bookshelves. Two hundred blank envelopes waited to be addressed and stamped. Sitting beside the invitations were thank you cards embossed with *Emily and Sergei* in silver script. The cards were so white, so clean. So deceivingly perfect.

I made a swift turn toward the small office off the foyer and poked my head around the doorway. "Hey, Dad."

He looked up from the fat textbook he was reading, and his pale blue eyes lit up. "Hey, I was hoping you'd come to dinner."

I met him behind his large mahogany desk and soaked in his extra-long hug. When we broke apart, I leaned against the desk. "Mom said dinner's in an hour."

"How's the dress looking?" he asked.

"It's done. Louann did an amazing job."

Dad patted my hand. "I don't know how I'm going to walk you down the aisle without getting emotional."

The upbeat tune on the stereo faded away, and "I'll Be Seeing You" began. The slow romantic song was one of my favorites from the era, but as I listened to the lyrics now, they reminded me of Sergei and Elena, seeing each other in those familiar places in Moscow. Tears welled in my eyes, and I dipped my head.

"I, umm, I'll let you get back to work," I croaked, scooting away from the desk.

"Shoot, I didn't mean to make you cry," Dad said.

"It's just been one of those nights. Emotional bride-to-be, you know?" I pretended to laugh it off and then snuck out before Dad could question me.

In the kitchen, Mom was crushing cloves of garlic on her butcher block chopping board. I climbed onto the stool next to the island and watched her rub the garlic over slices of ciabatta bread. So many times I'd sat in that seat while Mom cooked and dished out advice. But this might be one time my problems were beyond solving.

"Have you told Sergei your concerns about Liza and Elena moving here?" Mom asked.

I traced my finger between the squares of the tile counter.

"No."

"You need to talk about this with him."

"I know, but when I think about my concerns, they just sound so selfish. Is being afraid of all the changes or wanting Sergei all to myself really a valid reason to keep Liza away from him?"

Mom wiped her hands on a dishrag "Any hesitation, any doubts you might have, you can't ignore them. You have to be honest with him."

"I don't know what to tell him. I mean, if Sergei *didn't* want his daughter in his life, he wouldn't be a man I'd want to marry. But he's so consumed with being a father to Liza that sometimes I wonder…" I stopped tracing and rested my head on my hand. "He says he still wants a future with me, but he has other priorities now, and I can't shake the feeling that I'm not one of his top ones."

"How does Elena play into this?" Mom asked. "Do you think there's anything unresolved between her and Sergei?"

"I think he still feels the need to take care of her. Old habits die hard," I muttered.

"He probably feels guilty that he couldn't take care of her when she needed him the most," Mom said.

I raised my head to look at Mom as a sobering thought accosted me. What if this was about more than Sergei making up for lost time with Liza? What if it was also Sergei's chance to have the life with Elena that was denied by her father? I'd thought I was Sergei's destiny and his mistakes had served a purpose—to lead him to me. But maybe fate had a different plan all along.

CHAPTER SIXTEEN

THE ICE LAY BEFORE ME LIKE a blank canvas, ready for me to create the program I'd been imagining the past few days. Skating around my training mates, I stopped at the center of the rink and waited for my CD to begin playing. I'd finished my usual routine for the day but had stayed on the ice to work on the show program. Liza was also still practicing, and Sergei watched us both from behind the boards.

Every time I listened to the music, I found more nuances to explore. I flew across the ice, putting together the steps I'd envisioned and adding small movements to accentuate the highs and lows of the piece. Everything was so natural and easy, and I felt an overwhelming sense of freedom, like I was opening up and letting go of every emotion inside me.

As the music ended, I released a long breath and stayed in my final pose. My skin tingled with invigoration. I hadn't expected to be so energized, so inspired. The only question was if I'd feel the same once the spotlight came on.

I cooled down and skated over to Sergei, whose eyes followed me with an admiring glow.

"That was beautiful. What's the music?"

"'The Crisis,'" I stated in a clear voice.

He turned pensive as he appeared to recognize the meaning behind my song choice. Sliding back into a slow smile, he said, "You're going to be the highlight of the show."

"If I don't have a panic attack before I skate."

"You won't." Sergei leaned forward on the boards and gave me one of his pep-talk stares that always grabbed my attention. "You'll be strong and confident and ready to show everyone this amazing program."

I smiled, feeling more excited about debuting my creation. Not wanting to leave the ice just yet, I set off on another round of easy stroking. Liza crossed over from the opposite side of the rink and fell in step with me.

"I love your program," she said. "You have some really cool moves."

"I thought I'd play around with some things I don't get to do with Chris."

"Can you teach me how to do that spiral when you're in a split?"

"The Charlotte? Sure. Can you do a back spiral well?"

"Uh-huh," Liza answered quickly and bobbed her head up and down.

"Well, you balance your weight the same, on the ball of your foot, and you have to make sure your balance doesn't shift forward when you move into the split position."

"Got it."

I performed the move slowly and explained each step before I let her try the split while stationary. When she'd demonstrated her ability to balance, I gave her the okay to try the move in motion.

Liza was off and gliding before I could say another word. I chased after her and circled around as she worked up speed and skated in reverse into a regular back spiral, extending her left leg above her hip. She leaned forward and lifted her leg higher, stretching almost into a complete split. I raised my hands to applaud but froze when Liza's momentum took her too far forward. Her stomach struck the ice first, followed by her chin. She lay sprawled on the cold surface, gasping for air.

My heart leapt into my throat, and I sprinted over to Liza like a speed skater, kicking up a shower of ice when I braked beside her. Kneeling next to Liza's head, I slid my hand under her chin, and warm, sticky liquid touched my cold fingers. She was bleeding.

I put my other hand on her back as her breathing slowly returned to a normal pace. "Is anything besides your chin hurt?"

She gave me a slight head shake. Meanwhile, Sergei had made a quick shuffle across the ice in his loafers. He squatted on Liza's other side and caressed her hair.

"Can you sit up?" he asked, taking one of her tiny hands.

I kept my fingers cupped under Liza's chin as she rose to her knees, while Sergei reached inside his jacket pocket and extracted a packet of tissues. I pressed one to Liza's wound and she winced.

"Let's see how bad the cut is." Sergei peeked under the tissue as Liza tilted her head back, revealing a ragged gash. "Doesn't look too bad. Might need just a few stitches."

I recognized the tone of voice he used. It was his I'm-worried-but-I'm-not-going-to-let-the-kid-know tone that he used when one of his students took a bad spill. And in this instance, he sounded like he was trying extra hard to cover up his emotions.

"Liza!" Elena ran up to the boards, out of breath. "I watch upstairs. You are hurt?"

"I'm okay," she said in a small, shaky voice but her eyes watered with tears.

Elena walked along the boards and reached out to Liza as soon as we stepped off the ice. "So much blood," she cried, nudging herself between Liza and me.

"She'll probably need just a couple of stitches," Sergei

said.

Elena zeroed her eyes on me. "Why you teach her that move? She have trouble with back spiral."

I glanced at Liza, and she looked down at the concrete floor. "I asked her if she could do it well, and she said yes."

"And you do not make her show you? Of course she tell you yes. She want to do everything you do."

The freedom I'd enjoyed on the ice minutes earlier evaporated, and all the negative feelings twisted together again in my stomach. I backed further away from Elena, seeking space to breathe.

"It was an accident," Sergei said.

"Accident which should not happen," Elena snapped.

Liza sniffled as she kept her head down. Sergei pulled out a fresh tissue and held it to Liza's chin while he glared at Elena. "We should get to the hospital. Em, can you handle Court and Mark's lesson?"

"Sure," I mumbled.

The three of them left the rink, and I dropped onto the first row of bleachers. With my head bent, I heard the click-clack of Courtney's skate guards before I saw her.

"Is Liza okay?"

She sat next to me, and I straightened up. My eyes drifted to the spot on the ice where Liza had fallen. "She might need stitches."

"Ick." Courtney leaned over to retie her laces. "Are you still gonna have her birthday party tomorrow?"

"I would think so. Of course, her mother might have other ideas," I muttered.

"I got her this really cute beach bag," Courtney rattled on. "Since she'll probably be here for summer."

I jerked my head to face her. "Where'd you hear that?"

Courtney hesitated at the sharp tone of my question. "Liza said she heard Elena and Sergei talking about it. She said Sergei wants her and Elena to move here."

Oh, man. Liza wasn't supposed to hear that conversation. "I don't think Elena's made a decision yet."

"Well, I got the feeling Liza thinks it's happening for sure," Courtney said.

I looked at my palms and realized they still held traces of blood. After a quick search for my skate guards, I excused myself and walked carefully in my boots to the restroom.

While washing my hands, I glanced at myself in the mirror and sighed. I was so tired of seeing the weary, worried look in my eyes.

A piece of Sergei's heart belonged to Liza now, and he wasn't going to let Elena keep her in Russia without a fight. If I kept focusing on the negatives of the situation, I'd just make myself unhappier. I had to believe that Sergei and I would come through this stronger, just like we had after every storm we weathered. There were two options before me—I could continue to stress over the changes in my life or I could accept them and try to be the best stepmom possible.

The hot water stung my skin, and I rubbed my hands together, scrubbing them clean. It was time for a fresh outlook.

I PLACED MY PHONE in my purse and turned to Aubrey. "Liza had to get five stitches, and she also has a mild concussion."

"Oh, no." Aubrey pulled open the door to the Cape Cod Mall. "I thought she just cut her chin."

"Her head started hurting, so they checked it out." My shoulders slumped as I followed Aubrey inside. "I never should've tried to teach her that move."

"She said she could do the spiral."

"I know, but..." I stopped at the entrance to the department store. "I shouldn't have taken her word for it."

"You didn't do anything wrong. Don't let Elena get into your head."

"I just feel so bad. Now Liza has to stay off the ice for a week, and she won't be able to practice for the show."

"Then we'll have to make her party extra fun." Aubrey linked her arm through mine. "First on the list—some fabulous gifts."

We snaked through the store to the children's section and flipped through the racks of tiny T-shirts, skirts, and dresses. Aubrey eyed a purple ruffled skirt. "What's her favorite color?"

"Pink," I said, swiveling toward the display of bathing suits. "Courtney said she bought Liza a beach bag. What if I got her a suit? She could use it if she's here this summer."

"Is that definitely happening?"

I picked up a one-piece with three red hearts sewn together on the front. Running my fingers over the glittery design, I said, "It would mean the world to Sergei, so I've decided I'm going to try to make the best of the situation."

"I doubt Elena will have the same attitude," Aubrey said. "She's all about the drama."

"Is she? I hadn't noticed," I said dryly.

"Sergei owes you the most spectacular present ever. Something very sparkly."

I didn't want anything sparkly. I wanted normalcy. *Remember your new attitude—adapt to the changes.*

I turned back to the racks and held up a pink polka-dotted bikini. "How cute is this?"

"Oh, you have to get that." Aubrey grinned with approval. "And we can find some pink sunglasses to match."

I laughed. "She'll be a little fashionista."

After we found a pair of sunglasses and had the two items gift-wrapped, we swung by the bookstore and picked up a couple of new mysteries I thought Liza might like. Sergei's SUV was parked at my house when Aubrey and I returned, but only Liza was in the living room, reclined on the sofa and watching a cartoon on TV.

Aubrey reached for my shopping bags. "I'll take these upstairs."

"How're you feeling?" I sat beside Liza. "Sergei said you have a concussion."

"My headache's better." She lowered her gaze to the blanket covering her legs. "I'm sorry I messed up."

"You don't have to apologize. I wish you would've told me you weren't totally comfortable with the spiral."

"I can do it!" She lifted her head. "I was just going too fast."

I spread my arm across the back of the couch and gave Liza a smile. "It's okay if you're still working on it. Once it gets really strong, I can show you the Charlotte again."

Liza bit her lip and slid her knees up to her chest. "Elena said I can't ask you for help with skating anymore."

Heat tinged my face. Elena's reaction wasn't shocking, but it still disappointed me. A snarky response sat on the end of my tongue, and I ground my teeth together. I couldn't say anything to Liza. *Make the best of the situation,* I reminded myself.

"Maybe she'll change her mind. She was just really scared when you got hurt." I looked toward the stairs. "Do you know where she and Sergei are?"

"They went upstairs. They said they'd be back in a minute."

Elena was probably trashing my coaching ability to Sergei. I stood and straightened the folds of Liza's blanket. "Do you need anything? More juice?" I pointed to the half-empty glass on the coffee table.

"I'm okay."

On my way up the stairs, I continued to remind myself to keep cool and collected. Then I reached the top floor and saw Sergei and Elena outside on the terrace. I squeezed my fingers around the handle of the glass door but didn't move. It was bad enough seeing them alone in a special spot of Sergei's and mine, but they were also standing closer together than necessary. Elena's face was tilted upward as she listened to Sergei speak. He had her rapt attention.

I shoved the door open, and Sergei and Elena both turned in my direction. With a purposeful stride, I went toward Sergei, curled my arm around his waist, and planted a kiss near the corner of his mouth.

"Liza seems good," I said, keeping my eyes on him.

"Yeah, she—"

"A hurt chin and concussion is not good," Elena said, cutting off Sergei.

I couldn't look at her because if I did, I was only going to say something that would play into her drama.

Sergei cleared his throat. "She handled everything so well. The doctor said she was an excellent patient."

"Emily, I make clear to Liza you not teach her anything at rink ever again," Elena said.

Slowly, I cast my eyes on her. "She told me. I'm sorry to hear that."

"Can you go down and check on her?" Sergei asked Elena.

She left without another word, and when Sergei and I were alone, I moved away from his side to the edge of the terrace. "You don't agree with her, do you? About me helping Liza?"

"No, absolutely not. I trust you with Liza on the ice any time."

"Did you tell Elena that? Is that what you were talking about?"

Sergei joined me along the patio railing. "She knows how I feel."

I shifted to face the bay. The fading daylight made the water a dark shade of blue, and gray clouds blocked any shine from the moon. That time of year, the beach sat silent and untouched—no evening barbecues or couples spread out on blankets. I liked the quietness. I longed for more of it.

Turning to Sergei, I said, "I'm trying my hardest to make this work."

He eased me into his arms and rested his forehead against mine. "I know, and I love you so much for it."

I pulled Sergei closer, pressing my cheek to his chest. He wrapped his arms snug around me, and I held on tight to the moment of peaceful solitude. Lately, those moments were too few and too far between.

CHAPTER SEVENTEEN

I TIED THE LAST OF THE pink balloons to the bannister and scooted down the stairs. The sweet, sugary smell of birthday cake overpowered the kitchen and adjacent den. Elena fussed with the favors on the table, rearranging the miniature gift bags I'd set out earlier. Of course, she wanted them her way.

I opened a pack of napkins that matched the pink and white cake and placed them on the table in the middle of Elena's shuffling. She stopped maneuvering for a moment and said, "Thank you for giving Liza's party here."

Since she'd spoken only a few words to me since Liza's accident, Elena's cordial tone shocked me. "You're welcome," I sputtered.

Elena stepped back from the table and appraised the new setup. "She not have good birthday last year. My cousins pass away one week before."

"Oh, wow," I whispered. "I didn't realize it happened so close to her birthday."

"I want this to be happy night for her."

"Definitely." I nodded. Were we actually having a civil conversation? I should try to engage Elena further and warm the Arctic air between us.

"Liza seems to be very resilient," I said. "You obviously did a great job helping her deal with her grief."

Elena smoothed a tiny wrinkle in the paper tablecloth. "She cry every night for months and months. I do not know what I do for her. She love to read, so I buy her *The Secret Garden* book and we read together every night. It help take her mind away, and she finally sleep better."

I felt a hint of warmth as Elena spoke softly and not in the rigid manner I'd grown accustomed to hearing. I had to latch onto it and keep her talking.

"I read that book when I was young," I said. "Since the little girl in the story lost her parents, too, I can see why Liza would feel connected to it."

"I read it with her to help her see life get better. I think she understand."

Sergei and Liza came down from the living room, breaking up the strangely thoughtful chat. Elena took to fussing with Liza's hair while Liza chattered about her party guests. Her normally long, straight locks had been curled into bouncy waves, held away from her face with a pale pink headband. She was fidgeting with excitement, and I thought about how awful her last birthday must've been. I hoped the fun she'd have today would make those memories fade.

"Emily, can you take photo of three of us and cake?" Elena asked as she retrieved her camera from the bar.

I swallowed the sourness in my throat. *You have to get used to this.* With a smile, I accepted the camera from Elena.

Sergei brushed his hand over the small of my back and took a few uncertain steps to the table. Liza and Elena also moved into place behind the cake with Liza awkwardly positioning herself between her parents.

I raised the small digital camera and framed the three of them on the screen. Now all smiling, they looked like the perfect family—two gorgeous parents and their beautiful daughter who'd inherited their most striking features.

My finger shook as I snapped the photo, creating the family's first portrait. I quickly handed the camera to Elena, and Liza asked, "Can I get one with Emily?"

Elena's smile disappeared, but she complied. The doorbell rang, and Sergei jogged up the stairs while Liza and I posed with one arm around each other. Sergei made several trips to the door during the next twenty minutes as the guests arrived—a few girls who'd befriended Liza at the rink plus Courtney, Chris, and Marley. A pile of colorful gift bags and shiny wrapped boxes formed in the corner of the den.

Liza and the other girls sat on the rug in the den with jewelry-making kits, crafting necklaces and bracelets, while my friends and I gathered in the kitchen. Elena hovered near the girls, and Sergei kept busy in the den, fixing a problem with his camera.

Chris grabbed a carrot stick from the snack tray on the bar and bumped my arm. "When are we gonna play Pin the Tail on the Donkey or Red Light/Green Light?"

I laughed. "Liza's nine, not five."

"That jewelry kit looks like fun," Marley said. "I need to get one of those."

"You can squeeze in there with the kids if you want." I smiled.

"I might do that." She laughed and hopped off her stool.

Chris stole Marley's seat and rested his elbow on the bar. "So, you're gonna be a stepmom to a teenager in a few years."

On my opposite side, Aubrey said, "You can be a cool stepmom, like Julia Roberts in that movie with Susan Sarandon."

"Considering how uncool I was as a teenager, I don't know how useful I'll be in giving advice," I said.

"With the tight leash Elena has Liza on, I doubt she'll be dating before she's eighteen. You may not need to worry about boy problems," Aubrey said.

My head hurt thinking about the moody pre-adolescent years to come. Liza might start tugging hard against Elena's tight leash. I'd seen kids at the rink turn from sweet little girls to bratty pre-teens in a flash. I rubbed my neck, forcing my thoughts back to the present. There was enough to worry about in the immediate future without stressing over events years down the road.

We continued to snack and watch the girls entertain themselves until Elena announced it was time for Liza to open the gifts. Soon, instead of being surrounded by beads and baubles, Liza was elbow-deep in tissue paper and discarded wrapping.

With two presents left in the stack, Liza opened the small box from Sergei and gasped at the silver charm bracelet inside. It held one dangling aquamarine jewel, Liza's birthstone.

"I thought you could put your skate charm from the festival on it, too," Sergei said.

"Thank you," Liza said, still wide-eyed.

The last gift in the pile was mine, and Liza grinned when she read the card. She tore away the paper and squealed as she lifted the bathing suit from the box. "I've never had a bikini!"

Elena had stooped behind Liza to pick up the mess, and her mouth set into a stern line, a look I'd seen from Mom when she didn't approve of something. I couldn't imagine what Elena's issue was unless she was just annoyed Liza loved my present.

All the girls admired the suit as Liza slipped on the pink sunglasses. She shot me a big smile, and Sergei snapped a photo with his camera.

After everyone stuffed themselves with cake—everyone except those of us training for Worlds—the guests cleared out, and I started cleaning the kitchen. Liza ran upstairs and returned with her skate charm, which she hooked onto the bracelet. Elena helped her clasp it around her wrist, and Liza bounced over to Sergei, who bent to get a closer look.

"It's so pretty," she said.

"It'll be our special bracelet," Sergei said. "Every time we do something fun together, we'll add another charm."

Liza blinked a few times and then put her arms around Sergei's shoulders. My heart turned to mush as Sergei's eyes glistened. He shut them and embraced Liza harder.

When they broke apart, Sergei said, "We'll have to find a charm for our whale-watching trip tomorrow."

I put my head down to resume wiping the counter, and Elena quietly slipped into the kitchen. "May we speak in living room?"

Is this going to be about the look she gave me earlier? I ditched the paper towel into the trash can and trailed Elena up the stairs. She stood in the center of the room with her arms folded.

"Liza is too young to wear bikini. It is not appropriate for girl her age."

A combination of humiliation and anger burned my scalp. I should've been accustomed to Elena's lectures, but they still scratched at every one of my nerves.

"They sell them in the children's department," I said.

"It does not mean it is okay." Elena let out long breath through her nose. "You are young. You do not know what is good for child."

I crossed my arms, mimicking her stance. "Nothing I do is going to meet your approval, is it?"

"I know what is best for Liza, and I do not want you to teach her different."

"Would you prefer I ignore her and have her think I don't care at all?"

"I prefer you not..." Elena's forehead creased as she stammered to find the right word. "Influence her."

"Because I'm such a horrible role model?" I snapped, my voice rising.

"Because you are young and not ready to be mother."

I threw my hands up in the air. "I don't expect to be Mother of the Year! I'm learning as I go here, and you're not making it any easier."

Elena further stiffened her rigid posture. "No one make anything easy for me."

"So, I shouldn't expect you to lighten up on me any time soon. Is that what you're saying?"

"I worry only about Liza."

The glacial air had returned, chilling me down to my core. Elena and I remained locked in a reciprocal glare until I turned toward the stairs.

"I'm done with this," I muttered.

I clomped down to the kitchen, where I snatched the dirty serving platter and threw it into the sink. The clang of metal on stainless steel caused Sergei and Liza to look up from the books they were examining.

"Sorry," I said.

Sergei's eyes lingered on me with concern, and I let my hair fall around my face as I bent to wash the tray. Elena returned and asked Liza to bring the rest of her gifts into the guest bedroom, so Sergei came into the kitchen and stood against the sink with me.

"What happened?" he asked.

I sloshed soap and water over the tray and scrubbed a spot that had been on the silver for years. "Just another lecture from Elena. I don't know why it even bothers me anymore," I said through gritted teeth.

"What was she lecturing you about?"

"My gift was apparently inappropriate for a nine-year-old."

"What?" He sounded just as surprised as I'd been.

I lifted my head, tossing my hair away from my face. "It's always going to be something. I thought when Elena and I talked earlier that maybe we'd had a little breakthrough, but we're right back where we've always been."

Sergei passed his hand over his mouth and chin. "I'll talk to her."

"No!" I said more forcefully than I'd intended. "It's not going to change anything, so just… don't bring it up."

"I want to do something…" he said.

I shut off the water and stared up at Sergei. "There's one thing you could do. Come with me to the Vineyard tomorrow. Let's get away from all this for a day."

The conflict in his eyes didn't give me much confidence in a positive response, so I inched closer to him and put a soapy hand on his forearm. "Please?"

He looked too pained to answer. Finally, he said, "Liza's so excited about tomorrow. I'd hate to disappoint her."

I turned back to the sink. "But you'll disappoint me."

"Em, come on. That's not fair."

"None of this is fair," I said.

He was quiet, and I clenched the dishrag, whitening my knuckles. I started scrubbing again and Sergei stopped me, his hand on mine.

"Come back to my apartment with me. We can be alone for the rest of the night."

Sergei stroked my skin under the warm water, and part of me ached for more of his silky touch. The other part of me stomped those stirrings, not wanting to give in so easily. The stubborn side won.

"I have to get up early for the ferry," I said, pulling my hand away.

Sergei stayed at my side, watching me rinse dishes but not saying anything. When I didn't speak either, he slowly retreated from the kitchen, not even giving me a goodnight kiss.

I wrung out my frustration with the towel and slumped over the counter. Making a bad situation worse had become my new specialty.

CHAPTER EIGHTEEN

THE IGNITION CLICKED AND LIGHTS ON the dashboard flashed, but the engine made no sound. I turned the key again and again, willing my car to start. Nothing. I slunk down in the driver's seat and groaned. *Can't anything be easy?*

I glanced at my watch. I had to get to the ferry in Woods Hole, and the village on the southwest tip of the Cape was a fifty-minute drive from Hyannis. Jumping out of the car, I ran into the house and up to Aubrey's room, which was still dark.

I shook Aubrey's shoulder and tugged on her comforter. "Hey, wake up."

She peeled open her eyes and squinted at the sunlight from the hallway. "What?"

"Can I borrow your car? I think my battery's dead."

"I need my car," she mumbled.

"Please. I don't have time to call AAA. I can't miss the ferry."

She sighed and smashed her face to her pillow. "Okay. Key's on the dresser."

"Thank you, thank you!"

I snatched the key and raced outside. A few light

raindrops dotted the windshield of Aubrey's Jeep as I sped out of the parking lot.

Gray skies made the ferry ride from Woods Hole to Vineyard Haven even gloomier than I felt, and the normally bright and sparkling harbor looked cold and bleak. I raised my eyes to the sky, wondering if the weather was another bad sign. I'd become obsessed with omens lately.

The large boat docked, and I gunned the Jeep away from the coast and west toward Chilmark. Since I knew the town well from my summers at Aunt Debbie and Uncle Joe's house, I easily located the rental property on Stonewall Pond. The two-story home sat on a bluff, set back from the road and secluded from the neighboring properties. As my feet hit the rocky driveway, a middle-aged man greeted me from the open front door.

"Found the place okay?"

"Yes, very easy." I arched my neck to look up at the second-story deck. "The house is beautiful."

"Thank you." He extended his hand. "Corbin Davis. Good to meet you."

I returned his handshake and followed him into the airy living room. Corbin pointed out the updated entertainment system and brand-new white furniture before leading me to the kitchen. Stainless steel appliances gleamed between the maple cabinets and granite countertops.

"This is a great kitchen." I palmed the smooth granite on the island. "I love to cook, so this will be perfect."

"You're gonna cook on your honeymoon? Your fiancé is a lucky man."

I don't think he feels so lucky after my behavior last night. Even though I believed my annoyance with Sergei was justified, I hated how selfish I'd sounded.

Corbin directed me to the dining area, which looked out onto the garden. Blue hydrangeas and pink hyacinth colored the landscape, and the ocean rolled in the distance.

"Can't beat having breakfast here every morning." He tapped the solid wood table. "I'll show you the bedrooms and then we can head out to the beach."

The loud jangle of a phone sounded, and Corbin reached into his shirt pocket. Peering at the screen, he said, "It's my wife. Why don't you get a start on the upstairs tour and I'll meet you in a minute."

I ascended the narrow staircase from the kitchen to the second floor and bypassed two small bedrooms, aiming for the one at the end of the hall. I walked through the doorway, and my mouth fell open.

Floor-to-ceiling windows and a pair of open glass doors comprised one entire wall. The ocean breeze streamed through the opening and filled the room with a cool freshness. The spectacular views Corbin had mentioned on the phone extended before me.

I went over to the queen-sized bed and ran my hand along the pristine white duvet and the fluffy pillows. As the breeze tickled my face, I pictured Sergei and I wrapped around each other, the summer wind dancing over our bodies. Heat bloomed deep inside me and rose to my face. Sergei and I had waited so long to be together that sometimes I felt the time would never come. That feeling had been especially prevalent the past few weeks.

I turned left into the bathroom and gaped again. A huge window over the garden tub provided more amazing views. Besides the bathtub, there was also a large shower with multiple top-of-the-line shower heads. My mind wandered to another fantasy similar to the one I'd had in the bedroom. I touched my flushed cheek and left the spacious bathroom behind.

Corbin resurfaced and showed me the private beach as promised. I couldn't believe the place was even nicer than the original home Sergei and I had rented. A good omen, finally? I signed the necessary paperwork and wrote a check for the deposit, knowing Sergei would love the house, too. I just wished he was there to see it.

The dreary, rainy day didn't give me a lot of options for activities, so I stocked up on food at Alley's General Store in nearby West Tisbury and settled in at Aunt Debbie's house for the day. If the rain didn't stop, I wouldn't be able to go to the cliffs at sunrise, which was disappointing. The beautiful clay cliffs at Gay Head were a place where the rest of the world didn't seem to exist. I'd looked forward all week to visiting the serene spot.

At only midday I changed into my pajamas, an old T-shirt and a pair of gym shorts, and lounged on the couch with the reading material I'd brought with me—*The Notebook* and Sergei's *Lyrics* book. I opened *Lyrics* first and selected a random page. The song listed was "Fields of Gold," and Sergei had written—*With you in my life, I feel like I'm walking through fields of gold every moment of every day.*

The more notes from Sergei I read, the more I wanted to talk to him. A little rain wouldn't have cancelled his trip with Liza, so I waited until early evening to call him. I called three times, getting his voice mail on each attempt. A burst of excitement hit me. What if Sergei was on his way to the Vineyard? What if he was coming to see me?

Don't get your hopes up. He's probably still with Liza. I shuddered. *Or Elena.*

I'd packed my DVD of Season One of *Due South*, so I popped it into the DVD player to pass the time. I selected the "Victoria's Secret" episode and poured a glass of wine. Aunt Debbie wouldn't mind that I borrowed a bottle from her stash.

As I watched the show, I remembered the day Sergei had showed Chris and me his choreography inspired by the episode. I loved his work and the emotion he put into it, and I'd shared my admiration with him.

"I think you have a special talent for creating romantic programs," I said, leaning into Sergei. *"You have sexy in your soul."*

He smiled and brought his mouth close to mine. "My muse has a lot to do with that."

The doorbell shook me from my memories, and my heart rate accelerated. It had to be Sergei! I leapt from the couch and stuck my head between the curtains on the front window. With no lights in the living room except the glow from the TV, I could clearly see the dark street. No cars. I ran to the door and looked through the peephole, and my heart plummeted. My visitor was the long-time neighbor, Mrs. Bloom.

I opened the door, and the elderly lady smiled with relief under her umbrella. "Oh, Emily, I'm glad it's you. I didn't recognize the Jeep, so I wanted to make sure everything was okay over here."

"That's my friend's car. Mine wouldn't start this morning." I rubbed my arms as moist, chilly air seeped into the foyer.

"Well, it's good to see you. Come by if you need anything."

"Thanks," I said as Mrs. Bloom started across the lawn. I was about to close the door when headlights burned through the darkness and a taxi rolled to a stop in front of the house. I held my breath, waiting for the passenger to emerge. This couldn't be another disappointment, could it?

The back door of the cab opened, and my emotional yo-yo took an upward swing.

Sergei!

He hurried through the heavy drops to the porch and stood across the threshold, his chest rising and falling with hesitant breaths. He stared at me with his hypnotizing eyes, and I gazed back at him, open-mouthed.

"You came," I uttered.

Sergei stepped closer. "I needed to see—"

I grabbed a fistful of his damp T-shirt and pulled him toward me, pressing my mouth to his. He took a second to react and then used his body to steer me further inside, shutting the door behind him.

I circled my arms around Sergei's neck as he brought me flush against him, our lips not leaving each other. He smelled like a rainy night in the woods, and I wanted to kiss him until I was drunk from the scent.

We had to come up for air, but Sergei continued to brush soft kisses on my forehead, my nose, and my cheeks as we caught our breath. When I could speak once more, I whispered, "Come sit."

I slid my hands down his contoured muscles, clutching his shirt once again. We walked as one entity to the sofa and sat as close as we could get without me being on Sergei's lap. I didn't care why he'd come. I just wanted to enjoy the fact he was there.

Sergei noticed the show playing on TV and gave me a slow smile. "Getting inspired for Worlds?"

"Well, since someone won't skate with me, I had to look for inspiration elsewhere."

"Do you want to know the real reason why I can't skate with you?"

I tensed, hoping the explanation wouldn't involve Elena. I needed an Elena-free night.

Sergei fingered a long strand that had escaped from my big hair clip. Tucking it behind my ear, he said, "I can't handle it."

I tilted my head to one side. "I don't understand."

"You know how hard I work to keep things professional between us at the rink. When we skated together that day, it took every ounce of willpower I had not to kiss you." Sergei's eyes kept mine captive as he continued, "Skating with you was the biggest rush. I wanted to stay on the ice with you forever."

My tension melted away along with the rest of me. "Why didn't you tell me before?"

"I need you to only think of Chris as your partner, and I

have to make sure that bond is as strong as it can be. I was afraid if I told you how I felt, your focus wouldn't be on Chris."

"Because I'd be thinking about skating with you?" I asked with a little smile.

"I don't mean it to sound like I have some big ego." Sergei laughed. "That's not where I'm coming from."

I tenderly squeezed his bicep. "I know what you mean. And I love you for being such a thoughtful coach."

"So, you won't bug me anymore to practice with you? It kills me to have to say no."

"No, I won't tempt you."

Sergei caressed my cheek with his thumb and slowly slid his hand to the nape of my neck. The light from the TV flickered across his face, illuminating the desire in his eyes.

"You have no idea the effect you have on me," he said.

With gentle pressure he brought my head toward his and kissed me, the tip of his tongue teasing mine and making me tingle all over. I curled my hand behind his neck and leaned deeper into him.

My hair spilled over my shoulders as Sergei removed my clip. His fingers tangled among the waves, sending more sparks through me. He angled me down onto my back, and I closed my eyes as he kissed his way down my throat and the deep V of my neckline. The well-worn cotton of my shirt was merely a formality between my body and Sergei's searing touch.

His lips met my heartbeat, and I drew in a quick breath. I nudged up his T-shirt and ran my hands above the waistband of his jeans, needing to feel his skin. It had been too long—far, far too long—since we'd been this close.

I splayed my fingers across Sergei's back, and he lifted up slightly to look at me. Not saying a word, he lowered himself over me again, his muscles rippling under my palms.

Our heated kisses grew more urgent, our bodies more

entwined, and I felt myself becoming further lost in the moment, carried along by the waves of passion. We were quickly headed to a point we knew very well, where one of us needed to slow things down. As difficult as it was, I forced myself to take a breath.

"I have to tell you about the house I saw today," I said as Sergei's mouth temporarily left mine.

Sergei bumped my nose with his. "We have all night to talk about it."

"I know, but I thought you might be interested in one particular feature."

"What's that?" he asked as he nuzzled my neck.

"The master bathroom has a very roomy shower," I said, trailing my fingertips down to his waist.

He raised his head and gave me a crooked grin. "Is that right?"

"I may have had a little fantasy when I saw it."

"Not my sweet, innocent Emily?"

"You don't know the thoughts that go on up here." I pointed to my temple.

"I'm intrigued," Sergei said, returning his lips to mine.

A buzzing sensation trilled against my thigh, and after a moment I realized the source.

"You're vibrating," I said.

"What?"

I laughed. "Your phone."

"Forget about it," he said and kissed me.

Seconds after the phone ceased moving, the noise began again. I concentrated on the heat from Sergei's kiss, trying not to think about the caller, because I knew who it probably was.

When the vibration stopped and started a third time, I dug into Sergei's jeans pocket. A low groan caught in his throat as I captured the phone and pulled it out. The name on the screen was no surprise.

I pressed the green button and answered, "Hello, Elena."

"What…. Sergei say you are away," she sputtered.

"He surprised me on the Vineyard."

"May I speak with him?"

I bit down on my lip and handed the phone to Sergei. "I don't know what she wants."

Sergei sat up, and I turned to face the TV. Victoria and Fraser were locked in a steamy kiss as Sarah McLachlan's "Possession" played in the background. *That's what Sergei and I should be doing right now.*

"She didn't mention a sore throat when I was with her," Sergei said into the phone. "If she doesn't have fever, it's probably just a cold."

I picked up my empty glass from the coffee table and went into the kitchen. The dream world I'd been in since Sergei arrived rapidly disintegrated around me. I boosted myself up onto the island and poured a fresh serving of the sweet red wine. With the kitchen open to the living room, I could hear most of Sergei's side of the conversation, and I gathered Elena wanted him to get something for Liza.

I tried to tune out Sergei's voice as I watched the rain form squiggly patterns on the window above the sink. If Elena stuck around the Cape, this call was only the beginning of many disruptions to come. She'd constantly be in my face, either criticizing me or seeking Sergei's assistance. We wouldn't have a moment of peace. And I wasn't sure if I had the patience to put up with all the problems.

My fingers drummed on the granite. The wine wasn't doing its job of relaxing me. The longer the phone call lasted, the hotter I boiled inside.

I was on a second glass when Sergei entered the kitchen. He eased himself between my knees and set his hand on my thigh.

"Sorry about that," he said, stroking my leg.

"Is Liza okay?" I asked in a strained voice.

"Yeah, she'll be fine. Elena wanted…" He cleared his

throat. "Never mind. We can pretend we weren't interrupted."

He leaned in to kiss me, and I twisted my head. "Don't."

I pushed against his stomach so I could have room to jump down from the island. Taking a few steps away from Sergei, I said, "This is how it's always going to be. Elena's always going to need you for something. You can't expect to move her and Liza here and not have it majorly disrupt our lives."

He closed the gap between us. "It's going to take some adjusting—"

"It's gonna take *a lot* of adjusting. And Elena will make things difficult every chance she can get."

"We can all talk about that and try to come to some understanding."

"Talking isn't going to change the fact that she'll be around *all the time.* She's going to need help living in a new country, and who do you think she'll call every time she's in need?"

"Once she gets settled, things will be more normal."

"No, they won't! Normal is gone, and it's not coming back with Elena and Liza here."

Sergei gave me a long stare. "Do you want them to stay in Russia?"

There was hesitation in his question as if he feared my answer. My throat ached from a sudden swell of tears, and I realized I had to say everything I was feeling. It was time to be completely honest even if I caused pain in the process.

"I know how deeply you want Liza here, and that's why I feel terrible for having these thoughts," I cried. "But I like having you all to myself. I couldn't wait to be married and to do everything together. Just you and me. And now everything's going to be different."

"Are you asking me to make a choice? I don't..." Sergei's face wrinkled with hurt and confusion.

"No," I said quickly and shook my head. "That's not

what I want. I just... I'm trying to deal with this and I don't know how." I walked away from Sergei and covered my face. "Maybe Elena's right. Maybe I am too young for this. I'm scared that everything's changing so much, and it's not just having Elena around. I have no idea how to be a mother..."

"I have no idea how to be father," Sergei said. "We can figure it out together."

I turned to face him but didn't respond because I couldn't shake my fear. Sergei's eyes drooped, and a chill iced over me. The last time he'd looked at me that way was when I left him after he lied to me about his past.

He swallowed hard. "I told you once there's nothing we can't handle together. Do you remember that?"

I nodded weakly as my chin trembled harder. He'd said it after the Olympics when I wondered if we could make a marriage work while training for another run at the Games.

"You don't believe that anymore?" he asked.

I wanted to so, so badly. Why couldn't I do it? Tears leaked from my eyes and down my cheeks, and I tasted their salt as I parted my lips to speak.

"I'm trying," I said hoarsely. "I really am."

"You have to trust in me. In us." Sergei came to me and took my face in his hands. "You have to believe we can get through any challenge."

"I guess I thought after all we went through to be together, there wouldn't be any more challenges so soon."

He brushed at my tears with his thumbs. "If I didn't feel in my bones that getting Liza out of Russia is the best thing for her, I wouldn't be doing this. I know there's going to be a few ups and downs, but we can handle them."

He held my watery gaze, searching my eyes for a reaction. "Are you ready to go through them with me?" he asked.

My first instinct wasn't to scream yes, and that scared me. A tiny voice of doubt nagged at me, reminding me how trying the ups and downs could be. How would I know for sure if I was ready? How would I know if I could handle the challenge?

Without giving a verbal reply, I wrapped my arms around Sergei and let him swallow me in an embrace. *You just need time*, I repeated over and over. The answers would come.

CHAPTER NINETEEN

THE NEXT WEEK I BURIED MYSELF in preparations for Worlds and the send-off show. We were leaving for Washington D.C. in two days, and I still had errands to run before the trip, including picking up my new long program dress at Louann's.

"Can I go with Emily to the costume shop tomorrow?" Liza asked Elena as we rode to the rink for the show.

Elena rubbed her temples and then turned to look at Liza in the back seat. "It is too far from here."

"Please? I really want to see all the costumes."

I merged the car onto Route Six and gave Elena a sideways glance. She wasn't going to cave to Liza's pleading. Perhaps I could take the opportunity to offer an olive branch. My relationship with Elena wasn't going to improve if I didn't make an effort.

"Why don't we all go?" I suggested. "You haven't seen Boston, and the shop is in the heart of the city."

Elena switched to massaging her forehead. "If I feel good tomorrow. I have sinus headache all today."

"You might've caught Liza's cold," I said.

"So we're going?" Liza asked in a high-pitched voice.

"We see in morning," Elena replied.

Liza started to babble about a purple costume she'd worn when she was six, and I was happy to listen to her rambling. With each mile we traveled, my stomach grew tighter with nerves. My moment in the spotlight was fast approaching, and I prayed I wouldn't humiliate myself.

We arrived at the rink, and I dressed in the bathroom before gathering with the other skaters in the locker room. I opened the door to peek at the crowd and saw the bleachers filling quickly. I recognized a lot of the faces—parents of club members, adult skaters, kids from the Basic Skills classes—and they were all expecting me to skate like a national champion. An Olympic silver medalist. But I'd earned those achievements with Chris, not on my own, and my last memory of skating alone had given me nightmares for years.

My palms began to glisten with sweat. *Breathe, Em,* I commanded, but I couldn't stop the trembling in my knees. Liza paced beside me, and I knew I should say something to reassure her, but I didn't have much to offer in my current state.

"Feeling good?" I asked.

She tugged on the edges of her sparkly pink sleeves and didn't make eye contact with me. "Uh-huh."

She'd missed a lot of practice time and had been weakened by her cold, so she had to be worried about her readiness. I bent down and hugged her, hoping she couldn't feel my body shaking with anxiety.

"Just have fun out there," I said. It wasn't profound, but it was the best I could do at the moment.

The show director stuck his head into the locker room, and everyone put more urgency into their warm-up. When the lights in the rink lowered, applause rang out from the crowd, and I followed my fellow skaters rinkside. Liza was one of the first performers on the program, so I found a spot in the corner to watch while I continued stretching.

Peering through the darkness, I spotted Sergei sitting with Elena. He'd given me a pep talk after my last practice that afternoon, but I was blanking on what he'd said. The image of me falling on jump after jump kept getting in the way. It was an ugly movie stuck on repeat in my head.

The emcee introduced Liza as a special guest, and she glided out to a warm ovation. I bounced up and down to get loose and to shake out the nerves I felt for her, too. She'd talked about the show constantly the past week. This was her Olympics.

Liza started with some easy moves-in-the-field, building up speed for her first jump. The Chopin piece increased in tempo, and Liza pushed off her left blade for the double Salchow. I gasped as she tilted in the air and came down with her feet crossed. She tumbled to the ice, and the audience clapped to encourage her, but her dazed eyes showed her loss of focus. On the next three jumps she either stumbled or fell, and I had to watch the rest of the program between my fingers.

I felt heavy with sadness as Liza bowed and skated to the boards. She kept her head down the entire way. As soon as she stepped off the ice, Elena and Sergei steered her to the side, and Elena wrapped her in a hug. Sergei stood behind Liza, rubbing her back as she sniffed back tears.

I should've encouraged her more before she skated. After all, it had been my idea to put her in the show.

I swallowed the huge lump in my throat and squeezed my eyes shut. I had to block everything out and set my mind in a good place, but now I had the images of Liza's stumbles in addition to my past mistakes burned into my brain.

As I walked in circles, visualizing my program, Liza disappeared into the locker room, and Sergei and Elena returned to their seats. I turned away from the bleachers to stare at the concrete wall. If I didn't see the crowd, my pulse might simmer down.

No luck.

My heart only beat faster, throbbing in my chest so hard I thought my arteries would burst. I had to get to Sergei. He would know the perfect thing to say to calm me.

I whirled around and started for the bleachers, but Sergei and Elena were gone. I spun my head in all directions. Where could they be? Rushing to the locker room, I pushed open the door and found only skaters inside. Liza was sitting with Courtney and didn't notice my entrance.

Trevor saw me dashing around the rink and said, "You're up next, Em."

Where is Sergei? I made one more frantic scan of the crowd and then stopped to take a deep breath. I had to trust my years of training.

Thunderous applause, the loudest of the night, welcomed me to the ice upon my introduction. My knees were still wobbling, and I reminded myself I could skip my three planned jumps. Only Sergei and my training mates would know I watered down the program.

Coward.

"The Crisis" began, ending my internal debate. I closed my eyes for a moment, picturing myself in a bubble with just the music and me inside. That technique had helped at the Olympics when I suffered from an anxiety attack. *Just me and the music.*

With deep, long crossovers around the ice I approached my first jump, the triple Lutz. Should I try it? What should I do?

Go for it!

That was the last thought I had before I turned and vaulted myself into the air. The spotlight blurred around me as I rotated, and I opened up my arms for the landing. My right blade hit the ice with a scratchy thud, jerking me forward, and a streak of fear took hold of me.

I'm gonna fall!

Straining all my core muscles to remain upright, I stretched out my hand and touched the ice to steady myself. The shock of cold to my fingertips gave me an extra shot of awareness. My leg stopped shaking, and I exhaled as I stood up straight.

I did it!

I forced my excitement down by imagining myself in the bubble again, allowing the music to guide me. The piano notes resonated deep inside me, drawing out all the frustration and unhappiness I'd been experiencing. Every movement brought more of my pent-up feelings to the surface, and as I completed my second successful jump, tears collected in my eyes. There was no stopping the flow of emotion now. I coasted into a back spiral and the Charlotte, and as I moved into the upside-down split position, I blinked and two teardrops fell onto the ice.

I finished the program in a haze, weeping through my final jump and the closing choreography. The audience's cheers made me cry even harder, and I was a blubbering mess when I left the ice. The performance had forced me to open up, flooding forth all my emotions, and I couldn't plug the busted dam. I hurried toward the locker room, but a hand touched my shoulder from behind.

"Em!" Sergei circled in front of me.

I wiped my face and cried, "Where were you?"

"When?"

"Before I skated. Where were you? I looked for you and couldn't find you."

"Elena was feeling dizzy, so I walked with her outside."

My hands clenched at my sides. Elena. *Always* Elena. "Did you even see me skate?"

"Of course. I saw the whole thing. You were amazing."

"I was freaking out before I went on. I needed you and you weren't there. You knew I was going to be a nervous wreck."

"But you skated great. You didn't need me." Sergei squeezed my shoulders. "You did it all on your own just like I knew you could. I'm so proud of you."

I swiped at a runaway tear and stared up at him. Indeed, I had found strength without his help. I'd teetered on the edge of disaster and pulled myself up. Was that another sign Elena needed him more than I did?

"I have to get changed," I said and slipped away from Sergei, taking long breaths to compose myself.

When I reached the locker room, Liza noticed me, unlike earlier. She paused while untying her skate laces, and she watched me with her puffy eyes as I walked across the room and sat beside her.

"You were so good." She cocked her head to one side. "Why were you crying?"

I gave her a little smile. "Skating by myself... it made me pretty emotional."

Liza loosened her laces and tugged off one of her boots. "I wish I could've skated as great as you did."

"We all have rough performances sometimes. I've sure had plenty of them. You just have to learn from it and then put it behind you."

"But I wanted to show everyone what I could do. I wanted Sergei to be proud of me," she said quietly.

Her disappointment brought fresh tears to my eyes. It was sweet how much she already looked up to Sergei, and I could identify with her wanting to impress him.

"He's proud of you for just getting out there and trying your best."

"He told me that, but... he's such a good coach, and all his students are so good."

"He's so happy you're here that it doesn't matter how you skate. I mean, he wants you to do well, but how you perform doesn't make him any less excited or proud to be your father."

Liza chewed on her lip. "I hope I don't have to go back to Russia. I asked Elena if we were staying, and she said she hasn't decided. I don't wanna leave you and Sergei."

My heart swelled, and a stronger rush of tears choked me. No matter what hang-ups I had about the situation, I couldn't deny that Liza belonged here. I had to find a way to get over my fears because having Liza and Elena with us permanently really did make sense. I put my arm around Liza's shoulders and hugged her to my side.

"We don't want you to leave either."

"MY HEAD IS SO heavy," Elena said, sinking deeper under her blanket. "I not go to Boston today."

Judging from the congestion in her voice, Elena had definitely caught Liza's cold. "What about Liza?" I asked. "We won't be gone long. I just have to pick up a few things from my parents' house after Louann's."

"No, she not go."

"Sergei's at the rink, so she doesn't have anything else to do today. You could rest while she's gone."

"Please, please, please?" Liza snuck into the doorway with her hands clasped together.

Elena rubbed her throat and closed her eyes. I wasn't sure if she was dismissing us by going to sleep. Liza rested her bandaged chin on her hands and stared at the bed. I turned to leave, but Elena slowly opened her eyes.

"Okay," she said.

Liza hopped up and down, and I nodded thanks to Elena. "We'll be back around lunch."

"Liza, you have my phone number in your backpack?" Elena asked. "You use Emily's phone to call if you need me."

I resisted the urge to roll my eyes. We were going to Boston, not the other side of the country.

Liza grabbed her bag, and we were soon on our way with the rest of the morning commuters. I felt excited to have some time with Liza without Elena judging my every move. We spent the entire car ride talking about Liza's favorite books, and I got to reminisce about the ones I'd read as a kid. I promised to give her some of my old books from my parents' house when we stopped there.

We reached Brookline mid-morning and parked in my parents' empty driveway. "Your mom and dad aren't home?" Liza asked.

"They have early classes on Fridays. Don't worry, I have a key." I smiled. "Let's get to Louann's first and then we'll go in the house when we come back."

Finding a parking spot in downtown Boston would've been impossible that time of day, so I'd opted to take the T. It would also give me a chance to show Liza more of the city.

We walked along the tree-shaded sidewalk, and Liza gazed at the Victorian style homes on both sides of the street. "This reminds me of my neighborhood in New York. Did Elena tell you we're gonna go visit my friends at my old rink after Worlds?"

"No, she didn't." I assumed Sergei hadn't been told yet either. "That's really cool."

"I can't wait to see my friend, Hope. I miss her *so* much. And my coach said she'll give me a few lessons while I'm there."

"I bet everyone's going to be so excited to see you."

"I'm excited to see *them!*" Liza did a little skip.

We turned from the residential area onto the commercial block, and I told Liza how my friends and I would ride our bikes to all the shops.

She pointed at Brookline Booksmith. "Ooh, we have to go in there!"

I grinned. "My favorite spot of all. We can stop for a minute on our way back."

I stayed close to Liza's side as we crossed busy Beacon Street and waited on the median at the Coolidge Corner T stop. We'd missed most of the crowd leaving for work, so only a few people stood with us. Liza continued to look all around at the stores and restaurants, and she curved her neck up toward the big clock above the corner drugstore.

"That's pretty," she said.

"Yeah, the building looks like something you'd see in Germany."

"I remember when you and Chris skated in Germany two years ago. You won gold."

I tapped the top of her head with my finger. "You have a good memory."

The Green Line C train approached from the right and rumbled to a stop, and I dropped in the exact change for the fare. Twenty minutes later we were at the Boylston station and after a quick walk, Louann's shop.

While I put on my new dress to make sure the final adjustments worked, Louann let Liza try on a few of the off-the-rack costumes. Liza and I both twirled in front of the big mirror, making skating poses and giggling, and I thought about Aubrey saying, "You could be the cool stepmom." Was I capable of being more than that?

My cell phone rang, and when I saw the caller, I dampened my laughter before answering.

"Hi, Elena."

"I want to check if Liza is okay," she croaked.

"She's great. We should be leaving the shop in a few minutes."

I shook my head as Elena said a few words and then ended the call. Liza picked up another costume she wanted to try on, but I didn't want to dawdle much longer at Louann's if we were going to browse the bookstore. I asked Liza to change into her clothes, and she gave me a frown but complied.

Sunny Boston Common and the picturesque Public

Garden called to me from across Boylston Street, and I wished I had more time to take Liza on a stroll. But Elena would probably call again if we ran just a few minutes behind schedule. I led Liza into the train station, and we rode the escalator down to the underground platform.

A train was waiting on the tracks, and Liza jumped from the last step of the escalator. "Let's catch it before it leaves!" she said, running toward the open doors.

"Liza, wait!" I cried as I noticed the digital sign on the train read *D—Riverside*. It wasn't the C line we needed.

Liza kept running and I took off after her, but two people cut in front of me, blocking my path. As I dodged them, I watched Liza hop onto the subway and turn around to look for me.

And then the doors closed.

CHAPTER TWENTY

No! No! No!

I lurched forward and banged on the door with my fist, but the train pulled away with Liza inside watching me with terror in her eyes.

No!

I fumbled with my costume bag and stumbled away from the track as the train disappeared into the dark tunnel. I'd experienced sickening fear at competitions, but nothing like this. My entire body clenched, paralyzed by cold horror. A few people on the platform gave me understanding looks, and I couldn't do anything except stare at them as my mind raced.

What should I do? Call the police? Get on the next train and hope Liza's waiting at the next stop?

The second option sounded the best. Liza was a smart kid. She'd know to exit the train and wait for me... right?

I squeezed the cross on my necklace as I bobbed up and down and gazed down the tunnel for the next train. What was taking so long? Minute after minute ticked by with nothing but eerie silence from the track.

The subsequent squealing of metal on metal was the most

beautiful sound I'd ever heard. A gust of air blew into the station along with the train, and I boarded the moment the doors opened, staying close to the doorway. I needed Liza to see me right away.

I prayed every second of the ride and used my shaky hands to grip the handrail, bracing myself for the stop. *Please, God, let Liza be there.*

We emerged from the darkness and into the station, and I darted my eyes across the platform, yearning to see a little girl with a purple backpack. My stomach plummeted as only adult faces watched the train screech to a stop.

I pressed my palm to my sweaty forehead. *What do I do now? Stay on the train? No, this is the B line!*

I rushed through the doors and into the dank station. Would Liza have gone up to the street? *No, no, you're not thinking clearly.*

I stood on the mostly empty platform with my hand on my head, forcing myself to focus while my pulse sprinted faster and faster. I had to call the transit police. They could start looking out for Liza at all the D line stops.

Another train roared into the station, and the *D* on the digital sign made me pause with my fingers around my phone. I could board and look for Liza myself. But what if she was in trouble? Fear tightened its hold on me, and I shuddered.

My phone showed no bars. I pounded it against my palm, trying to shake a connection into it. When my throat began to ache with tears, I took a few deep breaths and made a quick decision. I ran to the train and hurried inside to the front.

"Excuse me!" I rushed up to the conductor. "Can you call the police? My fiancé's daughter got separated from me and she's on another train."

The man turned his weathered face toward me. "Which one is she on?"

"The last D that left Boylston."

He adjusted his glasses and picked up his radio. "I need a description."

"Nine years old, black hair, blue eyes, umm... umm... carrying a purple backpack."

"Name?" he asked as he pressed a button on the radio.

"Liza. Liza Overett."

The driver called in the information along with my name and cell number as he guided the train out of the station. I tapped my foot, hoping for immediate confirmation of the search effort.

"They put out an alert," he said.

"Thank you," I said and slid over to a window seat to keep watch for Liza.

We traveled underground through three stations before rising to street level. I squinted at the sunshine and looked down at the phone still in my hand. Four bars showed now. *I should've given Liza my number.* Then she'd have it with her when the police found her. And I'd thought Elena was ridiculous for giving Liza hers.

Elena.

When she found out about this, she was never going to let me take Liza anywhere ever again. And maybe I didn't deserve the chance. Why hadn't I held her hand? Tears stung my eyes, and I hugged the garment bag to my chest. Liza was probably so scared. I *had* to get to her.

My phone rang, and I jumped at the sound. I stopped breathing when I saw the caller.

Sergei.

I stared at the phone, unable to bring myself to answer. How would I tell him I'd lost his daughter? After the ringing stopped, the message notification chimed. I dialed my voicemail and listened to Sergei's happy voice.

Hey, I hope you and Liza are having a great time. If anyone can make her smile after her rough night, it's you. Call me later and we can make a plan for dinner. I love you.

I disconnected and struggled to keep my face from crumpling. *You have to hold it together.*

The train seemed to be moving slower than any subway I'd ever ridden in my life. I wanted to get out and run the rest of the way. If Liza wasn't at any of the stops, had she gone all the way to the end of the line in Riverside? Hadn't the driver of her train been alerted? Why hadn't the police found her yet?

My eyes hurt from straining to scour each stop through the window. Thirty minutes had gone by. We were getting farther away from the city, and I had no idea if I was even getting closer to Liza. Every minute that passed made me feel more ill. So many people rode the T, including some who might prey on a lost little girl. The thought of someone approaching Liza, wanting to harm her… I shivered again and rocked back and forth in my seat. *God, please watch over her. Please keep her safe.*

My ringtone sounded, zapping me with a ray of hope, and the Boston area code on the screen further raised my excitement. I slapped the phone to my ear and answered in a rush.

"Emily Butler?" the man asked.

"Yes!"

"This is Officer Ben Cager with the MBTA Police. We found Liza."

The heaviness sitting on my chest lifted and released a flood of tears. I threw my head back and looked up at the roof, silently sending a long stream of thanks to God.

The officer explained Liza was with him at the Packards Corner Station on the B line. The D train she'd originally boarded had to be taken out of service at Kenmore, so she'd transferred to the B train, thinking it would take her to Brookline. If I'd stayed on the first train I tried, I would've caught up to her!

I realized I needed to get off the T before I ended up deeper in the suburbs. At the next stop, I hopped off and arranged to meet Officer Cager and Liza two stops back. While I waited for the next inbound train, the policeman would drive Liza to Beaconsfield Station.

When I reached Beaconsfield, I ran up the steep stairs to the street and breathlessly swerved my head in both directions. An officer stepped out of a blue and white police car and opened the rear door, and I sprinted toward him as Liza slid out of the back seat.

"Liza!" I dropped the garment bag onto the ground and pulled Liza into my arms.

She sobbed quietly on my shoulder, and I started weeping again. Never had I been so happy and relieved to see someone. I ran a soothing hand over Liza's silky hair while keeping one arm clamped firmly around her back. I didn't want to let her go.

Liza clung to my neck and gasped through her sobs. "I'm so sorry."

"It's okay," I choked out and rubbed her back. "I'm just so glad you're safe."

I had to speak to the officer, so I stood up straight but kept my arms around Liza's shoulders. She locked her grip around my waist.

"Thank you so much for finding her," I said.

"She's a brave little girl." The young man smiled. "She didn't cry until I called her mother."

Part of the heavy weight returned to my chest, and I gulped. "You talked to Elena?"

"When Liza said she'd been with her father's fiancé, I asked if she had her dad's phone number so I could confirm. She didn't, but she had her mother's."

"Elena must've been hysterical."

"She was very upset." Officer Cager's smile turned sympathetic. "I let her talk to Liza, so she could hear that she's fine."

That wasn't going to lessen Elena's fury with me. I could

already hear her screaming at me that I wasn't capable of taking care of a child.

"I can give you a ride so you don't have to get back on the T," Officer Cager said.

"That would be great," I said. "Thank you."

I picked up my wrinkled bag and climbed into the backseat of the police car with Liza. After I gave the officer my parents' address, I turned to Liza whose sobs had simmered to sniffles.

"I got on the next train after yours because I thought you might get off at the next stop and wait for me," I said.

"I remembered the big clock from the stop by your house, so I was gonna go there and wait for you, but then this lady with a baby sat next to me on the train, and she asked if I was by myself." Liza wiped her nose with the back of her hand. "My mom always told me not to talk to strangers, but if I got lost I should ask another mommy for help, so I told the lady we lost each other and I was gonna meet you at the stop with the pretty clock and the building that looks like it's in Germany, and she said I was on the wrong train."

I smiled. "That's good advice your mom gave you. And that lady was very nice to help you."

"She told the driver I was lost, and he said the police were looking for me, and then Officer Cager came to the train and got me."

"Sounds like he was right and you were very brave." I squeezed her arm. "Next time we're in the city, though, we're gonna hold hands and stay together, no matter what, okay?" *If there is a next time.*

Liza nodded briskly.

"I was really, really scared when I didn't know where you were. You promise you won't ever run off again?"

Her little head didn't stop bobbing. "I promise."

I gave her a hug, and she looked up at me with her big wet eyes. "I'm sorry I scared you."

I hugged her again. Was this what being a parent felt like? I couldn't have been any more terrified if Liza was my own child. Somehow, I didn't think Elena would agree that I could identify with a parent's feelings.

Officer Cager dropped us off at the house, and I quickly grabbed the items Mom had bought for me for the Worlds trip. My old books I wanted to find for Liza would have to wait. As much as I dreaded facing Elena, we needed to get home.

My phone rang shortly into the ride, and I took a breath before answering Sergei's call.

"Hey, I'm sorry I hadn't called you back yet," I said. "I'm guessing you heard from Elena."

"Is Liza okay?" His voice resonated deep with concern.

"Yeah, she's fine. We're on our way back now."

"What exactly happened? Elena didn't go into much detail."

I recounted the harrowing incident from beginning to end, and Sergei said, "I wish I could thank the woman who helped her. You must've been going crazy when Liza was missing."

The memory of my crippling fear washed over me, and my skin grew cold. "It was a horrible feeling."

"I'm sorry you had to go through that," Sergei said.

I let out a tiny laugh. No way was Elena going to feel sorry for me. I didn't want to say that out loud with Liza listening from the backseat.

"I'm sorry I didn't do something to prevent the situation," I said.

"Kids do careless things. I don't have much experience being a father, but as a coach I've been around enough kids to know we can't stop every bad thing from happening."

"I know, but if I would've just held her hand…"

"The important thing is Liza's okay. That's all that matters now."

He was so understanding. He reminded me a lot of my

dad in that way, and it was one of the reasons I knew he'd be a great father.

We talked for a few more minutes before I hung up and turned on one of the classical discs in my CD player. Soft piano concertos and string symphonies flowed into the car. Calming music was what I needed to prepare for Hurricane Elena.

"LIZA!" ELENA CRIED HOARSELY from my front stoop. She embraced her daughter before she could walk through the door.

I moved past them into the foyer and set my things down on the stairs. Sergei took me into his arms, and I rested my weary head against his chest. I could've stayed there all day, but I let him go so he could welcome Liza inside. He gave her a long hug and made her promise not to have any more train adventures.

"Liza, you rest in bedroom and I stay few minutes with Sergei and Emily," Elena said. "Then we finish to pack for tomorrow."

Liza went into the guest bedroom, and Elena pulled the door shut. I trudged up the steps to the living room and sank into my favorite chair. It was old and soft and big enough for me to curl up and sleep in, which sounded so appealing after the morning I'd had. But I couldn't relax with Elena stalking toward me.

"Do you know how it feel when police call you and ask if you are Liza's mother?" she shouted as loud as she could with her strained voice. "To have moment when you do not know if she is hurt or worse?"

"Elena, stop." Sergei stood next to her. "I told you this wasn't Em's fault."

"She let Liza run onto train. She should watch her close in

place like that."

"I'm sorry," I burst in. "I wish I would've done something diff—"

"You are sorry." Elena's shouting lowered. "Sorry do no good if Liza hurt or lost forever."

I shrank against the chair and dipped my head. I couldn't allow myself to cry. I had to stay calm, but all the emotions of the day were spinning inside me, ready to explode.

"Liza is fine," Sergei said.

"But someone could take her. She is alone in big city with bad people and—"

"It was my fault!" Liza cried.

We all looked toward the stairs. None of us had noticed that Liza had appeared.

"Liza, go back to rest," Elena commanded.

"I'm the one who ran onto the train!" she exclaimed through her tears.

"Please go downstairs," Elena said with more force.

Liza stared at us a moment and then ran down the stairs, slamming the bedroom door behind her. I covered my mouth to muffle a cry, but I couldn't halt the tears from moistening my eyes.

Sergei pinched the bridge of his nose and exhaled a loud breath. "Lena, can we please just move on from this? It's done, and it's not going to happen again."

"No, it not happen again because Liza not see Emily again," Elena said. "Ever."

I lowered my hand but was unable to speak. Sergei glared at Elena with confusion. "We're getting married. Liza's going to have to see Emily."

"I do not trust her. I do not want her with my daughter."

"*Our* daughter," Sergei corrected her.

"I know what is best for her. I should not bring her here. We have good life in Russia, and we stay there, and you not see Liza because I do not want her with Emily."

I found my voice and asked weakly, "What are you..."

"What are you saying?" Sergei finished for me. "That since I'll be married to Emily, you're going to keep Liza away from me?"

Elena wouldn't look at me. She replied with a simple and powerful, "Yes."

I bent over at the waist and put my head in my hands as I quivered with sobs. This was whirling so far out of control. *What have I done? That stupid, stupid train!*

"You're being completely unreasonable," Sergei said in a hard tone. "As Liza's father I have the right to see her. I'll get a lawyer if I have to."

I raised my head to see Elena crossing her arms and shooting a dark look at Sergei. "You do not fight me. I have money and best lawyer. You do not win."

"You sound like your father."

Elena narrowed her eyes. "I protect my child."

She marched out of the room, and Sergei slowly dropped onto the couch. He sat pale and dazed with his hands in a steeple position.

"She'll back down once she cools off," he said.

I looked at the stairs. Elena had left, but her anger still hovered all around me like an ominous cloud. The storm had definitely not passed.

"I don't know about that," I said in a rough whisper.

"She's not thinking right now," Sergei insisted.

I shook my head as another batch of tears choked me. "I'm so sorry. This is all because of me..."

"Listen to me." Sergei jumped up and came over to kneel in front of me. He put both hands on my face. "You didn't do anything wrong, and I'm not losing Liza. I'll talk to her when we get to D.C. and she's had time to realize she's overreacting."

It sounded so easy, but I didn't have half the faith Sergei had. Elena hadn't wanted me around Liza before, and the incident in Boston just confirmed her opinion of me. I closed my eyes, not wanting to look at Sergei. This was really happening. He could lose Liza because of me. He could lose his daughter because of *me*.

CHAPTER TWENTY-ONE

I REMOVED THE WORLD CHAMPIONSHIPS CREDENTIAL badge from around my neck and looked at my photo. I wore a forced smile just like the one I'd been giving everyone since I'd arrived in Washington D.C.

A large and enthusiastic crowd had gathered to watch the practices at the MCI Center. I stood at the entrance to the ice and scanned the arena, searching the many faces for Elena and Liza. Because they were staying at a different hotel, I hadn't seen them since we'd parted ways at the airport the previous day. Liza hadn't spoken to me during the trip from the Cape to D.C., and she wouldn't even make eye contact with me. She probably hated me for being the reason she couldn't stay in the U.S.

Sergei walked out from the backstage tunnel and stood beside me at the boards. I handed him my badge, and he looped it around his neck for safe-keeping while Chris and I practiced.

"Did you try calling Elena again?" I asked.

"Goes straight to voicemail," he muttered before taking a sip of his coffee.

"I can't wait to get on the ice," Chris said as he flanked my other side.

I kept my head down, trying to push away all thoughts of Elena and Liza. I had to get into my competitive zone. Even with Chris's injury, we were still the favorites to win, and the chance to compete for a world championship on home soil didn't come around often. We had a golden opportunity before us, and I couldn't let my personal issues get in the way.

"Do you remember how to skate?" I asked Chris as I stood tall and rolled my neck.

"Ha. Very funny."

The announcer declared the start of our practice session, so Chris and I led the three other couples in our group onto the ice. I took off at full speed, working my blades over the ice and getting a feel for the rink, but my movements lacked their usual energy. My legs felt like fifty-pound weights, and my knees didn't have the softness I needed. Not sleeping much the past two nights and picking at my meals likely hadn't helped.

Chris fell in step with me and took my hand, and we did crossovers in tandem, warming up for the difficult elements to come. As we turned the corner of the rink, two figures in the stands walking down the aisle caught my eye. Elena and Liza! Chris released my hand and skated ahead of me, and I twisted my neck to look behind me at the seats.

"Em!"

I turned in the direction of Chris's voice just in time to see the German national champions barreling backward toward me. I gasped and ducked out of the way, dodging them at the last moment. They stared me down as they returned to their exercises, and Chris skated over and reached for my hand.

"Something interesting in the stands?" he asked.

"Huh? Oh, I saw Elena and Liza."

"Is Elena still avoiding Sergei?"

"Yeah." I glanced again at the spot where Elena and Liza

had found seats. Liza was finally looking at me, and I wanted to wave but was afraid she wouldn't return my gesture. I set my gaze straight ahead. "I shouldn't be thinking about this right now."

Chris nodded and squeezed my hand. "Let's work."

We'd practiced the triple twist and the lifts on the floor backstage, so we knew Chris had enough strength in his shoulder to handle those elements. Sergei had told us before the session not to push too hard in our on-ice work. We glided over to him for more detailed instruction, and he was staring into the crowd. He'd spotted Elena and Liza, too.

He set his attention on us, but his eyes didn't hold the clarity and focus they normally had when he addressed us. He made his instructions brief, and Chris and I left him to run through sections of our short program. It had to kill Sergei to see Liza and not be able to go to her. And I was the reason.

The heaviness in my heart sapped even more of my energy, and as we practiced our jumping passes, I stumbled through most of them. I couldn't get enough spring in my legs. Chris was having more success, and he'd been off the ice for weeks. My frustration level built, which only threw me off more.

Sergei fed me technique reminders every time I circled back to him at the boards, but as soon as I skated away from him, he looked at the stands again. His distracted behavior was distracting me, and I almost had another collision, that time with Claire and Brandon, our American teammates.

At the end of the forty-minute session, Sergei handed our credentials to Chris and me. "I'm going to try to catch Elena on the concourse. I saw her and Liza headed up there."

He hurried backstage, and Chris put his arm around me, guiding me toward the locker rooms. Away from the media, skater, and coach traffic, he cornered me against the wall and rested his hands on my shoulders.

"You're all over the place, Em."

"I'll pull it together for the short tomorrow. I promise."

"Sergei's the one who helps you focus, and his head's not exactly in the game either."

"Well, I learned I don't necessarily need his help to be successful, so..."

Chris studied me, and I fidgeted under his unwavering stare. The situation felt very familiar, and I flashed back to Worlds two years prior when Chris had discovered I was secretly dating Sergei. He'd spent the whole event giving me weird looks like he was trying to figure me out. He was giving me one of those looks now.

"I'm ready to compete," I said, but I didn't feel the fire inside. Where was the hunger, the desire to be the best? I had to find it before the competition. At the moment I was full of only sadness and guilt, and I had no clue how to get rid of those feelings.

SERGEI WASN'T ABLE TO catch up to Elena, and when the next evening came, he still hadn't talked to her. There was something more pressing that required attention, however—the short program. I paced around Sergei backstage, alternately fiddling with my curly up-do and the short hem of my shiny black dress. I'd been shaky on my jumps again at practice that morning. My legs just wouldn't cooperate, and my confidence had taken another hit.

I flexed my knees and jiggled all my limbs, but I couldn't shake the tightness. I'd been wound into one huge knot that I wasn't able to loosen.

"Em." Sergei grasped both of my hands. "Remember—let your body take over, and it'll stop your mind from getting in the way."

That was one of Sergei's famous lines which all his students could recite. The problem was my body knew what to do but couldn't execute it. I didn't have the energy. Sergei looked tired, too. Still incredibly handsome in his gray suit, but tired. His bright eyes became dimmer every day he was away from Liza.

The time to skate neared, so Chris and I inched toward the tunnel with Sergei at our side. Chris set his arm across my shoulders and said in my ear, "We're gonna fight through this. Give it all you have."

I nodded and said a few prayers while we waited our turn to skate. Not prayers for victory but prayers for strength.

When we received the call to the ice, the building erupted with cheers, and I tried to channel the crowd's energy into my bones. The audience waved American flags of all sizes and banners with our names in red, white, and blue. Somewhere among the spectators sat Elena and Liza.

Don't think about them. Focus, focus, focus!

The cheers diminished to complete silence as Chris and I locked into our starting pose. I zoned in on Chris's face and said one last prayer.

We began the program and knocked out the triple twist before I had a chance to think too much. But I had time to worry about the looming side-by-side triple Lutzes and whether my muscle memory would fail me.

I picked hard into the ice, giving myself extra spring but throwing off my timing. Panic and adrenaline battled each other inside me as I came down with a backward lean. My body was tilted so much I couldn't stay upright. It all happened in a matter of seconds, but it felt like slow motion as I crashed to the ice.

Now cold and wet, I scrambled to my feet and rushed back in step with Chris. He gave my hand a firm squeeze, his way of telling me to shake off the mistake.

We moved through the elements and the choreography I loved so much, but I wasn't enjoying it. I didn't feel the connection to the music as I had every other time I'd performed the program. A mountain of suffocating negative emotions had buried my passion.

Chris pressed me up into the star lift, and his injured arm trembled as his hand gripped my hip. I summoned all the strength I could find to hold myself up, using his shoulder as support. We couldn't afford another error in the program. When we completed the element with a clean exit, Chris exhaled an audible breath and gave me a little nod.

At the end of the performance, the crowd gave us a roaring ovation despite my mistake. Chris hugged me and said, "We got through it."

We met Sergei at the boards, and he embraced both of us before we all sat in the kiss and cry. Sergei slipped his hand around my waist and kissed the top of my head, and tears pricked my eyes. He could've directed his anger at Elena toward me since I was the cause of her decision, but he hadn't. He was as loving as always.

The scores appeared on the monitor, and the audience responded with muted applause. With more than ten teams left to skate, we were in third place. We had to hope none of those couples bumped us down in the standings. Sergei walked between Chris and me and gave us a reminder as we went backstage.

"Top three means you still control your own destiny."

Chris and I knew all the particulars—as long as we won the free skate, we'd win gold. I just didn't know if I had a golden performance in me. I needed to dig deeper than I ever had.

After I changed out of my costume and finished my press obligations, I took the elevator up to the concourse to find my parents. Fans easily spotted me with my Team USA jacket and rolling bag, so I was stopped several times for autographs and photos. Everyone said such nice things, and I spent a minute chatting with each person. I'd given enough quotes to the media over the years to know how to sound poised even when

I was torn apart inside.

I continued toward the section where my parents had said to meet them but stopped short when I saw a familiar purple backpack in the concessions line.

Should I try to talk to Elena? She wouldn't make a scene in public, so maybe she'd listen to me. Or I might make things worse if I confronted her before Sergei did.

While I stared at the backs of Elena's and Liza's heads, Liza turned and discovered me. She gazed at me a few moments and then quickly ducked her chin.

She really does hate me.

I bit the inside of my lip to stave off more tears. I definitely couldn't talk to Elena now. Who knew the emotional blabber I'd start spewing. I had to let Sergei take care of it, and I had to have faith Elena would change her mind.

CHAPTER TWENTY-TWO

"Sweetie, you've barely touched your dinner." Mom eyed me with concern across the table. "You need to eat."

I nudged my grilled chicken with my fork. With the free skate in twenty-four hours, I should be fueling my body for the event, but my appetite had been missing since the train took off with Liza.

"My stomach will feel a lot better if Sergei finally talks to Elena tonight and gets everything straightened out."

"I can't believe she won't answer his calls," Mom said. "It's ridiculous he has to camp out in her hotel lobby to track her down."

Dad sipped his wine and shook his head. "Elena has to realize she's hurting Liza by doing this. The child's already lost two parents and now she's losing another."

I picked up my cell phone from the table and looked at the screen even though there had been no ring or message notice. Sergei had said he'd call as soon he had news.

"Maybe I should speak to Elena. Mother to mother," Mom said.

"I don't think that's a good idea," I said. "If she gets

snippy with you, then you're going to get snippy with her, and it'll just blow up into a bigger mess."

"But I understand the feeling of wanting to protect your daughter. Not a day goes by that I don't worry about you."

"I really think Sergei's the only one who could get through to her." Admitting that fact made my meal look even less appealing. I set my fork down and pushed away my plate. "I'm gonna go up to my room and watch a movie or something. I need a distraction."

"Why don't you take your dinner to go?" Dad suggested.

I rubbed my stomach as I rose from the table. "I can't eat, Dad."

He stood along with me and gave me a warm hug. "We just want you to keep your strength up."

"I'll be okay," I said.

Over Dad's shoulder, Mom's brow wrinkled deeper. I picked up my purse and went around the table to kiss her cheek. "I'll see you at practice tomorrow."

"I hope you get good news from Sergei," she said.

I snaked through the busy hotel restaurant, waving at skater acquaintances from around the world. Normally, I lived for competitions like this—the sport's biggest names all gathered in one spot, the large crowds, the pomp and circumstance. I'd get so fired up just from the atmosphere. But I hadn't felt any of that excitement since being in D.C. Everything around me existed in a dulled haze.

Inside my room, I flipped on the TV and scrolled through the movie listing. The U.S. Skating Federation gave its Olympic medalists the perk of single rooms at competitions, so I had the space all to myself. I selected the movie *Center Stage*, which I owned on DVD and had watched at least fifty times, but it was light and fun, and I was in the mood for something familiar.

Even with the distraction of the movie, I peeked at my cell phone every ten minutes. It was getting late, and Elena and Liza should've returned to their hotel from the day's events at the MCI Center. An extended conversation between Sergei and Elena could be a good sign... if that's what was taking so long.

A weak knock took my eyes off the phone. I got up from the bed and hustled to open the door. Sergei stood with his hand resting against the frame and his head down. The tiny bit of dinner I'd eaten turned in my stomach. I reached for Sergei's free hand, and he lifted his head to look at me. The dim light remaining in his eyes had completely faded.

I led Sergei inside and clutched his hand harder as we sat on the end of the bed. "She didn't change her mind," I guessed quietly.

"No." He stared at the TV with a blank expression. "After they visit New York, they're going to Russia and never coming back."

Another wave of guilt churned a bigger hole in my gut. I circled my arms around Sergei's shoulders. "I'm so sorry."

"She said I'd have to fight her to get visitation. In Russian court, where I'm sure her father had connections she can use to her advantage."

I pressed my face to his sweater. I couldn't look at him. All this agony was my fault.

"I just can't believe it," Sergei said, wavering between anger and hurt. "I had the miracle of finding Liza, which I never dreamed could happen, and now I might never see her again. We were really starting to connect. I think she was starting to understand how much I love her and..."

His voice broke and so did my heart. I held him tighter, and he muffled his cries against my hair. The anguish in his tears further splintered my soul, and my attempts to say, "I'm sorry" came out fractured and unintelligible. I started to pull back so I could speak more clearly, but Sergei locked his arms around me as he continued to shake with emotion. Feeling his despair, I fought my own tears. *He shouldn't have to go through this.*

We stayed in that spot, holding each other and not saying a word until Sergei slowly pulled away and rubbed his hand over his face.

"I should let you get to sleep," he said hoarsely. "I'm not doing a good job of preparing you for tomorrow."

"Don't worry about me. You're dealing with so much..."

"I can't let you and Chris down. I feel so helpless as far as Liza is concerned, but I can actually help you and Chris get through tomorrow." Sergei kissed my forehead and swallowed me in an embrace. "I know it's easier to say than to do, but promise me you'll get some rest."

Why is he being so good to me? He must still be in shock. Soon he won't be able to look at me without thinking how I ruined his chance to be a father to Liza.

Sergei left, and I got ready for bed, but sleep evaded me again. My thoughts weren't dominated by my usual pre-competition worries, though. Only thoughts of Liza and trains and Elena and regrets kept me staring at the dark ceiling. I'd been looking for signs that a life with Sergei was still my future, my destiny, but so many things had happened to make me believe otherwise.

I pulled the blanket up to my chin and clamped my eyes shut. If I could just sleep, I wouldn't have to face those thoughts. I wouldn't have to face the growing reality that Sergei and I weren't meant to be.

SKATING LAST AT A competition was both a blessing and a nerve-wracking pain, and I felt more of the latter as Chris and I awaited our turn in the free skate. As the last pair, we wouldn't have to worry about the judges "saving room" in the scores for other teams, but waiting all night to perform gave me more time to think. On a normal occasion that was bad news; on this night, with so many things besides skating on my mind, it was a surefire disaster.

Sergei hovered nearby backstage, close enough to give an encouraging smile and snippets of instruction but far enough not to make me feel smothered. Our eyes connected, and he gave me one of those comforting smiles, but all I could think about was him crying over Liza. I'd never heard him break down like that, and it was one of the most gut-wrenching sounds I could imagine.

I turned away from Sergei to watch Chris miming our choreography. He stopped and held up one hand for a high five. I complied, and he clasped our fingers together.

"We're strong enough to do this," he said.

I'd been telling myself that all day, but I was running on just caffeine from three cups of coffee, the only thing I could stomach. My strength would have to come from determination, and I didn't know if I had enough to carry me through. The haze surrounding me had grown thicker and darker. I couldn't see past it, and I was scared how numb I felt going into the most important performance of the season.

Chris resumed acting out our program, and every so often he touched his shoulder, which wasn't part of the choreography. I wondered if his arm hurt more than he'd told us. He was broken physically, and I was broken mentally. We were quite the pair.

Sergei patted Chris's back and smiled but didn't say anything. He had to be worried about Chris's fitness level, too. We hadn't done a full run-through of our long program since before we went to Russia. Four minutes of jumping, throwing, and lifting were an eternity for someone not in top physical condition.

Chris and I handed Sergei our team jackets and walked toward the ice just as the Canadian champions finished their program. The crowd exploded with applause, telling me Madeline and Damien had skated lights-out. They were the leaders after the short program, so we'd have to be perfect to beat them.

Do I have it in me?

I looked flawless on the outside—brand new elegant teal dress, impeccable makeup, and my hair in a tight bun. My appearance had gold medal written all over it. But on the inside, I couldn't escape the guilt and the doubts that made me feel so far from perfect.

The announcer bellowed Madeline and Damien's scores as Chris and I circled the ice to keep our legs warm. 5.8's and 5.9's. There was room for us. Chris took my hand, and we skated over to Sergei at the boards for his final words. The crowd had calmed during our warm-up but was now in a full frenzy, so loud I had to lean toward Sergei to hear him speak.

"Take this energy and use it." He set his eyes first on Chris and then on me. "Live inside the program. Feel it. Breathe it. Own it."

I nodded sharply and maintained focus on Sergei's face, seeking the comfort he always gave me, but again the memory of his tears bombarded me. I quickly shifted my gaze downward.

Skating! A world championship! Staying on your feet! That's what matters right now!

Chris led me to center ice, and I made sure not to look at Sergei behind the boards. When the soft notes of "Clair de Lune" began, I visualized the bubble and squeezed Chris's hand as my lifeline.

We sailed through the triple twist, garnering a roar from the crowd, and then separated to prepare for the side-by-side triple Lutzes. *Your body knows what to do. Let your body take over.*

Chris and I picked into the ice simultaneously, and I pulled my arms in tight to rotate. I opened up for the landing, and my blade made solid contact with the ice. Next to me, Chris held the same position—arms outstretched, free leg extended—the perfect jump exit.

You got lucky. Can you do it again?

Why was I being so negative? I reminded myself to think positively, but I didn't have much time before the next two elements, the throw triple Lutz followed by the star lift. Chris grasped my hips and propelled me into the air, and three revolutions later, I landed clean again on one foot.

This is going too well.

I chided myself once more for being pessimistic as Chris pressed me up into the lift with ease. The audience's cheers grew louder with each completed element, but they sounded muffled to me, as if I was disconnected from my surroundings.

After we executed our spins and another lift, we transitioned into crossovers to set up for our second set of side-by-side jumps, the triple toe loop-double toe loop combination. I took a breath, and my lungs burned in response.

No! It's too soon to be tired. We're only halfway done!

I tried to dig my blades harder into the ice, but my legs felt rubbery. I couldn't generate much speed. How was I going to get through the combination?

I jabbed my toepick into the ice and knew I was off center the moment I went airborne. My crossed feet hit the ice, and I couldn't untangle them. I crashed hard as Chris completed the second jump.

Perfect is gone.

Catching up to Chris, I attempted to inhale deeper, but the weight on my chest wouldn't allow it. Another throw jump and our final lift lay ahead. I had to slow my pace to get more air.

Chris didn't seem to mind the reduced speed as I heard him taking quick breaths beside me. He was losing steam, too.

This is not good.

We glided into the throw triple loop, and Chris muscled up to give me enough height. My right foot came down, and I struggled to hold myself steady on the landing, but my leg had no strength. Dread filled my veins right before I slipped down onto the ice.

I rose to my feet and hurried to dry my hands on my skirt. Chris was waiting for me, and we needed to set up for the lasso lift. He grabbed both my hands and swung me up above his head, but his right arm started to bend under my weight. I gritted my teeth while searching for the core strength to stay upright.

My vision was blurry, and my body wasn't responding. I collapsed onto Chris's shoulders and clung to him to keep from dropping onto the ice, but the damage had been done. An aborted lift on top of my two falls certified the program as a total catastrophe.

When the music ended, I hunched over to let the blood rush to my head. Chris also bent at the waist. We slowly stood up at the same time and hugged as the crowd gave us a heartier ovation than we deserved.

"I thought I had the lift," Chris said.

I looked at him with wide eyes. "Don't even... you did everything you could. I should've held it."

We took our bows and skated over to Sergei, who embraced Chris first and rubbed his bad shoulder.

"I'm so proud of you," he said. "I know how hard that must've been."

Sergei turned to me but stayed quiet as he brought me into his arms. I thought he might chastise me for not fighting harder, but he was probably waiting until we went backstage.

We sat in the kiss and cry, and I held my head in my hands. I couldn't watch the scores. It was bad enough hearing them announced. The numbers were the lowest we'd received since our first competition as a new team. The announcer concluded the marks and stated, "They are in sixth place."

I dipped my head further and covered my face. We weren't going to win a medal of any color. Olympic silver medalists. World medalists. Three time national champions.

Buried in sixth place. Another huge bad sign.

We shuffled backstage, and Sergei motioned us close to him. "You guys will come back from this. You WILL be world champions."

Chris nodded, looking too tired to reply. He walked toward the media, and Sergei moved in front of me, blocking me from the press.

"You usually fight for those landings." He didn't speak with a stern or accusatory tone but a concerned one.

"You're not angry with me?"

"I've put you through so much lately. I can't be angry when I didn't have you ready for this competition."

How had we reached this point? All we were doing was hurting each other. My actions had caused him devastation, and his problems had made me lose touch with my skating, something I never thought would happen. How much lower were we going to drag one another?

"I need to catch up with Chris," I whispered.

Chris and I quickly talked our way through the interviews so we could change and meet our respective families outside. Mom and Dad hugged me, and I remained numb, not shedding any tears. I was akin to an emotional zombie. My parents offered to treat Sergei and me to drinks, but I didn't feel like sitting in the bar where everyone would give me looks of pity.

When we returned to the hotel, Sergei walked with me to my door, and I paused with my key in hand.

"I'd kinda rather be alone right now," I said.

Sergei caressed my cheek. "I'm afraid if I leave you alone, you're just going to beat yourself up about tonight."

He had no idea how much I'd been beating myself up over other things. My performance was just another item to add to the list.

"Maybe I can finally sleep," I said.

"I can stay with you until you fall asleep."

I inched away from Sergei toward the door. "It's okay. You don't need to. I should really be alone."

I shoved the key in the card reader and turned the handle, and Sergei trailed me into the doorway. As I faced him, he leaned in and gave me a tender kiss, and for the first time that night, I wanted to cry.

"Goodnight," I mumbled, closing the door before the tears completely choked me.

I stumbled forward and crumpled at the foot of the bed. Sobs racked my body and stole my breath. When my gasps subsided, I brought the back of my hand to my mouth and pressed my diamond ring to my lips, just as Sergei had done when he proposed. Tears came again, faster and harder, and I hugged my knees to my chest.

There was only one way to fix the mess that our lives had become. I had to accept it. I just didn't know if I could go through with it.

CHAPTER TWENTY-THREE

THE NEXT FEW DAYS IN D.C. felt like the longest of my life. The pairs event had ended, but the ice dance competition had just begun, so I stayed to support Aubrey and her partner Nick. With so many people around, it wasn't the time or place to talk to Sergei about our future. I decided to wait until we returned home, which gave me an agonizing four days to think about the conversation and the choice I was making.

We flew home on Sunday evening, and Sergei went to his apartment to unpack and repack. He was leaving the next day to teach a pairs camp in Chicago, so I had a small window of time to talk to him. I paced up and down in my bedroom, visualizing what I'd say as if it was one of my programs. The difference was my programs didn't make me feel as if I was dying inside.

I stopped pacing and sat on the bed, facing my open closet. On the end of the rack hung the white garment bag containing my wedding dress. So many times I'd imagined walking down the aisle toward Sergei's beaming smile. He'd take my hand, and I'd see in his eyes how much he loved me. Neither of us would have to say a word, and the moment would be perfect.

Tears seeped into my throat, and I jumped up and shut the closet door, pressing my forehead against it. *You have to do this.*

Before I could change my mind, I grabbed my purse and car keys and jogged downstairs to Aubrey's room. She stood in the middle of multiple suitcases and mounds of clothes, preparing for a Hawaiian vacation with her parents.

"I'm going to Sergei's," I said, barely stopping as I passed the room.

I made the five-minute drive to Sergei's apartment but didn't leave my car. I sat in the parking lot, staring at the smattering of lights in the harbor across the street. Sergei and I had spent countless evenings strolling along the dock and dreaming of our future—the waterfront house we'd eventually buy, the children we'd raise, the coaching dynasty we'd become together.

None of our plans would happen now.

About to succumb to overwhelming emotion, I bolted from the car and took deep breaths as I climbed the stairs to the second floor walkway. Outside Sergei's door, I raised my hand three times to knock before finally following through.

Sergei answered and opened the door wide. "I was getting ready to call you to see if I should pick something up for dinner."

I drifted into the small living room and stopped beside the coffee table. A picture I'd taken of Sergei helping Liza at the rink lay next to a stack of paperbacks. I picked up the photo and looked at their happy faces.

Quickly setting it down, I said, "We have to talk."

Sergei approached me, and I slid backward to put more space between us. "What's wrong?"

I brought my eyes to his and parted my lips to speak, but my voice vanished. Sergei came closer and peered down at me. "What is it?"

I touched my engagement ring and inched it toward my knuckle. My pulse raced, and my hands shook. If I didn't say what I had to say soon, I was going to crumble into a heap.

"I can't let you lose Liza," I said. "She needs you, and you need her. I believe there's a reason you found her, and it wasn't to have just three weeks together."

"Have you thought of a way to get Elena to change her mind?" Sergei asked.

I bit hard on my lip, but my chin was trembling too much to hold steady. Tears pooled in my eyes, and I looked down at the carpet, fighting the devastating ache in my chest. With a swift tug, I pulled the ring from my finger and swallowed the cries that needed to escape.

"Em, what are you..." Sergei asked in shock.

I held the ring out to him. "It's the only way to fix this."

"No." Sergei cradled my face in his hands. "You're talking crazy. This isn't the answer."

I took one of his hands and tried to put the ring into his palm. He jerked away and set his jaw. "I'm not taking it. You're not thinking clearly."

"You have to take it. You have to let me do this." My voice cracked with tears. "I can't be the reason you lose your daughter."

"You're not! Elena made that decision."

"But if I wasn't in the picture, you'd be able to see Liza."

"I want you in the picture! We can fight Elena. There are other ways—"

"She's going to make it impossible for you to win. You could be fighting for years."

"So it'll be hard," Sergei said. "We can get through it together."

"It's not just..." I swiped at my cheeks. "Too many things have happened. There've been too many signs telling me this is the right thing to do."

Sergei's brow wrinkled into a sharp V. "What signs?"

My head hurt from crying, and I couldn't think. I pressed my hand to my forehead. "I don't know. Elena coming back into your life, the way I skated at Worlds..."

"I don't want Elena," Sergei said firmly. "And Worlds wasn't a sign. It was just a tough competition."

"No, it was more than that. I was so out of it. I didn't feel anything on the ice, and it was because of what was going on with us. Our relationship has always given me strength, but now... everything is so screwed up."

"Then let's talk about it and figure out how to make it better." Sergei reached for my shoulders, and I scooted away from him.

"This is the only way to make it better." Another cry stifled my breath. "We can't be together."

Sergei stared at me. His eyes darkened with tears, showing his transition from confusion to cold realization. "I'm not letting you walk away from me."

I gulped and turned so I wasn't facing him. It would be so easy to throw myself around him, to kiss his lips, and to take back everything I'd said. But we'd still be in the same hurtful place, where I was buried under guilt and Sergei was missing out on more years of Liza's life. I squeezed the ring and then placed it on top of the photo of Sergei and Liza.

"Don't." Sergei pleaded. "Don't do this."

"I have to," I whispered through fresh tears.

I hurried toward the door, but Sergei shot in front of me and caged me inside his strong arms.

"You can't leave me," he said, his voice panicked and breaking.

Needles of pain stabbed me all over, and I couldn't hold back my deep sobs any longer. I used my arms as a shield against Sergei's chest, forcing myself not to sink into him.

"Please don't leave me," he said, repeating it again and again as he kissed my hair and then my face and my neck. "I love you so much."

His lips were so soft, his breath so warm, his words so passionate. My body weakened and "I love you, too" sat on the tip of my tongue, but I held it inside. I clenched my hands into fists and pushed as hard as I could against Sergei's T-shirt, releasing myself from his embrace.

"I have to go," I cried and grabbed the door knob.

"Em!" Sergei tried to shut the door, but I yanked hard.

I rushed outside, sprinting down to the parking lot with Sergei on my heels. He continued to beg me to stay, choking on his pleas. I sobbed harder, and my hand shook so violently that I struggled to put the key into the ignition. I slammed the gas pedal all the way down Ocean Street and arrived home in a blur.

Inside the townhouse, I pounded up the stairs and closed myself in my dark bedroom. Crawling onto the bed, I latched onto a pillow and wept into it, shedding more tears than I thought possible.

The faint noise of the doorbell sounded, and I inhaled sharply.

Sergei had followed me.

I couldn't see him. I didn't have any strength left to stand my ground.

Another chime rang, and I realized Aubrey might answer it. I leapt from the bed and raced into the stairwell. Aubrey had just emerged from her room, clad in a robe and a towel over her hair.

"Don't answer that!" I yelled over the railing.

She looked up with startled eyes. "I thought you were at Sergei's."

"I was, but—"

"Em!" Sergei called jand banged on the door. "Please let me in!"

"What is going on?" Aubrey glanced from me to the stairs below her.

I ran down to her, and her eyes grew bigger. "Em, you're

a mess. What happened?"

"We have to talk!" Sergei bellowed.

"He can't come in." I shook my head vehemently.

Aubrey grasped my arms. "What did he do to you?"

"Nothing! It was me. I did something."

"Emily, please!" Sergei's cries grew more excruciating to hear.

I covered my ears, and Aubrey said, "The neighbors are gonna call the cops if he doesn't stop."

I backed into the wall and sank down to the carpet. "Can you make him leave?"

Aubrey watched me with confusion for another moment and then headed downstairs. I listened as the door opened, but the voices were too low. Aubrey returned a few minutes later and sat beside me.

"Sergei said you called off the wedding?"

I looked at my hand, and the naked spot on my ring finger glared at me. I shoved my hand under my thigh and nodded slowly. "I had to."

"Because of Liza?"

"I can't live with myself, knowing I'm keeping Sergei from her. So much has happened. We just don't make sense together anymore." I pulled my knees up to my chest and rested my head on them.

"You're letting yourself get too caught up in emotion, especially coming off the craziness at Worlds. You need time to think—"

I lifted my head. "It's all I've thought about for a week."

Aubrey studied me again. "What you need is a vacation, a place to go and clear your mind and maybe see things from a different perspective. If I can get you a ticket on our flight, you should come to Hawaii with me. I'll pay for it."

"I can't go to Hawaii," I said numbly. "There's somewhere else I have to go."

"Where?"

"New York. I have to make sure Elena knows I'm out of Sergei's life. I don't want her to have any hesitation in changing her plans. She needs to hear it from me."

"You won't be completely out of Sergei's life, though. He's still your coach."

I'd thought so much about breaking the engagement that I hadn't figured out how to handle the skating part of my relationship with Sergei. I could only focus on one life-changing decision at a time.

"Maybe not," I said.

"You're not quitting?" Aubrey gasped.

"No, but Chris will be out for months after his surgery. I can coach myself until he's back and then maybe things will be easier..."

"I still think you should get away somewhere to try to make sense of all this. And not to New York."

"I've made up my mind," I said, rising to my feet.

Aubrey stood and cinched the sash on her robe. "Why don't you ask Marley to go with you? You shouldn't drive alone when you're so upset."

"She'll just try to talk me out of it the whole way."

"That would be good."

"No, it wouldn't! Do you know how hard it was for me to do this?" I teetered on the verge of breaking down again. "I can't look back now."

Aubrey hugged me. "I'm sorry. I can't even imagine what you're feeling. If you need me when I'm away, call me anytime, any hour."

I squeezed her tight and waited until I regained composure to let her go. "I'm gonna leave early in the morning and try to find Elena at Liza's old rink. They were planning to go there."

"I hope you tell her off. At least give yourself that satisfaction."

"I don't feel like arguing." I massaged my temples. "I just

want to say my piece and talk to Liza if I can."

Aubrey put her arms around me again and made me promise to drive safely but to also rethink my decision. I could only agree to the first of her requests.

When I returned to my room, I clicked on the lamp, and the light glowed over the *Lyrics* book on my nightstand. My fingers skimmed the gold cover as I yearned to read the loving notes Sergei had written.

I curled up on the bed and stared at the book. Reading it would make me feel worse, but I couldn't refrain from picking it up and opening to the first page.

I made my way through the beautiful notes, searching for breath between my tears. Would I ever love anyone as much as I loved Sergei? It seemed impossible. He was so deeply embedded in my heart and in my soul. I let out a strangled cry and smashed my face to the pillow. *What have I done?*

Spent with tears but unable to put down the book, I continued to read until I reached the page with the song "If You Love Somebody Set Them Free." Sergei hadn't written anything next to its lyrics. I never thought we'd have use for that song.

As I read the words, an idea came to me, and I dug for a pen in the nightstand. Taking a deep breath, I wrote next to the lyrics—*I need you to understand why I'm letting you go. I love you so much, and I want you to be happy, and I don't think you can be truly happy without Liza in your life. We each have a different path now. I have to set you free.*

I wiped the moisture from my eyes and searched in the drawer for a bookmark Sergei had given me. A photo of a bright red sunrise over the ocean covered the glossy paper. I slipped the marker next to the page with my note and slowly closed the book.

The night brought little sleep, so in the morning I brewed a large cup of coffee to take on the road with me. The sky had just started to wake as I climbed into my car with the coffee and the *Lyrics* book. I had one stop to make before I headed south toward New York.

Sergei's parking lot was quiet with just a few birds welcoming the morning. I left my car door ajar to avoid making any noise and then crept up the steps. Stopping at Sergei's apartment, I stooped and placed the book against the door.

This was the right thing to do. I had to keep believing that.

CHAPTER TWENTY-FOUR

FOUR HOURS OF LONELY INTERSTATE GAVE me plenty of time to relive the torturous scene from Sergei's apartment. My phone rang nonstop with calls from Sergei once he woke, but I didn't answer and I deleted his messages without listening. Hearing his voice would only make me break down, and my red eyes couldn't handle any more tears.

Sergei's calls stopped around the time his flight to Chicago was scheduled to leave. When my phone shrilled a bit later, the caller was someone else I wanted to avoid. My mother.

My parents would be supportive of my decision once I explained my feelings, but I still felt as if I was letting them down. I'd failed at the relationship that I'd fought so hard to make Mom accept. She'd been right from the beginning—Sergei and I were doomed. Our break-up just happened for different reasons than she'd predicted.

Then there was all the money my parents had spent on the wedding. I knew they'd tell me not to worry about it, but so many items had been bought, so many nonrefundable deposits paid. And my dress. My beautiful dress. I sighed and dabbed at the corners of my eyes. What was I going to do with it? I couldn't even think about marrying someone other than Sergei, but if it happened, I could never wear that gown. I didn't think I could even stand to look at it again.

I reached Westchester County before noon and glanced at the directions I'd printed. A tree-lined, four-lane road took me to the rink, where I parked and followed inside two teen girls wearing matching skating club jackets.

A few skaters dotted the spacious and brightly lit lobby, and a couple of the girls gave me second looks. I turned toward the row of large windows, and in her long fur coat, Elena stood out among the adults watching the action on the ice. Beyond the glass, Liza skated alongside a smiling, middle-aged woman.

Seeing Elena burned my sadness into steaming anger. Heat flushed my face and rose to my scalp. There were so many things I wanted to shout at her. Aubrey's idea of telling her off didn't sound so bad.

I brushed the front of my jacket and exhaled a slow breath. Getting into a screaming match wasn't the answer. I had to confront Elena with poise while letting her know how difficult she'd made life for Sergei. With my shoulders straight and my head held high, I marched over to the windows.

"Elena," I said.

She flipped around and gaped at me. "Emily. Why are you here?"

"You'll want to hear what I have to say."

The other skating moms watched us with interest, and Elena's eyes darted back and forth from them to me.

"We talk outside," she said.

We exited through the double doors, and Elena stood beside one of the benches along the sidewalk. She closed her coat and crossed her arms. "You are here for Sergei. You ask me to let him see Liza."

"Yes." I hesitated, knowing that once I told Elena the

news, it would be official. Moistening my suddenly dry lips, I said, "I broke off our engagement, so there's no reason to keep Liza away from Sergei now. I won't be with him anymore."

She arched her eyebrows. "You cancel wedding?"

My blood pressure ticked higher. Why was Elena acting so surprised, as if this wasn't her master plan to split up Sergei and me?

"It's what you wanted, isn't it?" I snapped, my poise slipping away. "To get me out of the way so you can have Sergei?"

"Sergei… he never be with me again," she said matter-of-factly but with a hint of sadness.

I angled my head to the side, unsure if I understood Elena correctly. I hoped Sergei would never reunite with her, but I was shocked to hear her dismiss the possibility.

"You sound very certain of that," I said.

"I see how he look at you when you skate together for practice. He never look at me that way when we skate as pair."

She'd stunned me again. I had no idea how to respond, and I fumbled with my words. "Sergei loved you. You had a child together…"

"He love me different way. I depend on him, and he protect me. If we had chance to be together when we are young, we are happy but not now. I see how it is different with you."

"So, you know how much Sergei loves me, but you're still doing everything you can to keep us apart," I seethed.

"This is about Liza and what is best for her, not about you and Sergei."

I let out a harsh laugh. "I don't believe that at all. Why don't you admit that you can't stand seeing us together?"

Elena pinched her lips into a line and inhaled loudly. "Yes. It is hard to watch you with Sergei, to see your life, your career. You skate for world championship, for Olympic medal. You have everything I have if my father not take it from me.

And now you give up Sergei so easy."

"Easy?" I cried. "There's nothing easy about this. Walking away from Sergei when he begged me to stay was the hardest thing I've done in my life. But he's miserable without Liza. There's a hole in his heart I can't fill, and I had to make things right."

I caught my breath and added, "You should be thankful for what you do have. Don't you realize how lucky you are to have Liza back?"

"Of course I realize. Liza is my life. She is only child I have ever." Elena's voice heightened and shook.

I examined her, again questioning our language differences. "Why do you think that? You're young—"

"I cannot have more children. It is why my husband divorce me." Elena's dark eyes glistened. "So, yes, I hold onto Liza tight. I cannot lose her."

My mouth stayed open as I processed Elena's admission. It explained her fierce protectiveness, but it didn't give her the right to take away others' chances at happiness.

"I'm sorry," I stammered. "I understand how that would make you more protective of Liza, but—"

"You do not understand how I feel. I cannot let Liza be with you. You do not show care with her, and she is not safe."

"For crying out loud! You act like I've tried to physically harm her or something. I've made a few mistakes, but—"

"Emily!" a small voice exclaimed.

I twirled, and Liza hurried toward me in her skating dress and sneakers, her long ponytail flying behind her. "Hope said you were here! You came to see me? Where's Sergei?"

I hastily put on a smile. "He's teaching at a camp in Chicago. I know he'd rather be here, though."

"I thought you were mad at me for causing so much trouble," she said.

"No! Not at all." I reached down and hugged her. "I thought you were upset with *me*."

"Why?"

I leaned back but kept hold of her shoulders. "It's not important. I'm just really happy to see you."

"How long are you staying?"

"I have to drive home soon," I said, standing up straight. "I just came for a quick visit and to talk to Elen—your mother."

"My mother's dead," Liza said quietly.

"Liza!" Elena's pale face turned even whiter.

Despite all the anguish Elena had caused me, I couldn't help but feel sorry for her, especially since I knew now just how precious her daughter was to her.

"May I talk to Liza alone for a few minutes?" I asked.

Elena eyed me warily but agreed. I walked Liza over to a bench on the other side of the entrance, and she smoothed her short skirt as she sat beside me.

"Elena loves you very much," I said. "She's taken such good care of you since your parents died."

Liza looked down and picked at her knit gloves. "I know. It's just not fair that she wouldn't let me see you and Sergei."

"I think she realizes that keeping you from Sergei was a mistake, and that's going to change very soon." *Because I haven't given up the love of my life for nothing.*

"Are we leaving Russia for good?" Her head popped up, showing the hope on her face.

"We haven't talked about it yet, but I think you and Sergei will be able to spend lots of time together from now on."

Liza grinned. "I need to show him my double Axel. I landed it for the first time today!"

"That's awesome! He's going to be so excited for you."

"Can you come in and meet my coach and my friends? I told them all about you."

My heart plunged. I couldn't bring myself to tell her I'd broken up with Sergei and this might be the last time we'd talk. She'd have too many questions, and the answers would all make Elena look bad. There was no point in weakening their already fragile relationship.

"I don't have much time." I gave Liza an apologetic face. "I have to get on the road after I talk to Elena."

"It'll just be a few minutes."

I looked into her pleading eyes and saw Sergei's matching baby blues imploring me not to leave him. I cleared the lump from my throat and nodded weakly. "I'll try."

I rose from the bench, and Liza followed my lead. When we reached Elena, Liza paused and shuffled her feet. "I'm sorry about what I said."

A tiny smile graced Elena's lips. She kissed the top of Liza's head. "You are best daughter in world."

Liza returned her smile and then scooted inside. Elena stared at me, unblinking. "You have chance to turn her against me, and you not do it."

I held her gaze. "I guess that's the difference between you and me. I would never come between you and someone you love."

Elena quickly averted her eyes downward and jangled her bracelets. The tension in the air grew denser the longer she remained silent. When she spoke, she still didn't look at me.

"Sergei must be very upset you call off wedding."

Upset? The image of Sergei's distraught tears and the sound of his desperate pleas would stay with me forever. I started to tremble with more frustration.

"He's devastated," I said.

Elena clanged her bracelets together until I wanted to rip them off her wrist. I wrung my hands and waited for her to say something. Did she finally understand the consequences of her demands? Was she going to concede and tell me to go back to Sergei?

"I speak to him about visit with Liza and to make permanent arrangement," she said.

"Good," I said. "That will make him incredibly happy."

And what about me and your daughter? Any second thoughts there? Clang, clang, clang went the jewelry with more silence from Elena. She gazed at the rink and said, "I should return to Liza."

The morning was sunny and the model of a spring day, but a heavy chill draped over me. Elena wasn't going to budge. Not even after she'd seen my good intentions toward her relationship with Liza. I was an idiot for having even a sliver of hope.

"Can you tell Liza I had to leave?" I asked. Sergei or Elena would have to explain the break-up. I wasn't going to lie to her.

Tears barged into my throat, and I didn't stick around for Elena's reply. I found my way back to the interstate, continually blotting my eyes to see the road clearly.

I'd driven to New York with zero expectations, and then Elena had to go and act human for a few moments, making me think I'd been wrong about all the bad omens. I pounded the steering wheel with my fist, stinging my hand until it was numb. Nothing had changed, and nothing was ever going to change.

CHAPTER TWENTY-FIVE

I walked into the rink with tentative steps, keeping my focus on the concrete floor and then on the locker room to my left. Sergei was due back from Chicago, and I wanted to avoid him as long as possible. If not for Courtney and Mark's lesson, I would've stayed away from the rink. I'd evaded all my friends the past three days, saying I was decompressing from Worlds. I needed a week to get over my crying fits, and then I'd start telling my family and friends about the cancelled wedding.

I ducked into the locker room and stayed there even after I put on my skates. Kids came in and out, but I kept my head down, retying my laces over and over. When I couldn't stall any longer, I crept to the door while donning my gloves. I had to keep my bare ring finger hidden. Courtney noticed everything.

My favorite aria from *Samson and Delilah* played on the sound system, but I didn't sing along as I usually did. Every muscle in my body was tense with the anticipation of seeing Sergei. He wasn't on the ice or at the boards, but he had to be somewhere in the building. I stood next to the boards and bounced lightly from heel to heel as I watched Courtney and Mark warm up.

Courtney saluted me as she skated toward my corner, and I was about to wave when I heard my name behind me. The voice froze me and sent a shockwave to my pulse.

Sergei came up beside me, but I didn't look at him. His mere presence was more overwhelming that I could've imagined. All my instincts went haywire, crossing each other and pulling me apart inside. The strongest instinct tugged on me to move closer to Sergei, but I stood my ground and hugged my arms over my chest.

Afraid Sergei might bring up a painful topic of conversation, I quickly asked, "How was the camp?"

He didn't reply, and I didn't have to look at him to know he was staring at me. I could feel the intensity in his eyes. My cheeks flamed despite the cold air surrounding me.

"Are you really making small talk?" he asked.

Before I could respond, he went on, "Did you get my messages?"

It would only hurt him more to tell him I'd deleted them all on sight. I stepped back from the boards and said, "We should just stick to work."

Sergei glanced up at the big clock on the far wall. "For the next hour, I'll do that. But there are some things we need to talk about after."

Why couldn't he accept our fate? There was nothing we could do to change the situation, and talking about it wouldn't make either of us feel better.

I took the ice and dove into the lesson, keeping a constant eye on the kids and not letting my mind stray. Sergei gave me a pained look as Courtney and Mark skated away from us, and I hastily turned my head. *You did the right thing. You have to keep remembering that.*

When Courtney had trouble with a section of footwork, I happily spent half of the hour going over each rocker and counter with her. If I could have a detailed task like that to concentrate on every minute of every day, I'd be set.

The clock's hands moved too quickly, and Sergei trailed me off the ice at the end of the session. I headed for the locker room, and Sergei rushed to my side.

"Meet me in the ballet studio in a few minutes. You're not running out of here without talking to me."

During the lesson, I'd contemplated doing just that. I was trying to make a little progress every day in moving on with my life, and dredging up all the pain wasn't part of my plan.

I pushed open the heavy locker room door with my fists and sat on one of the benches facing the lockers as I untied my laces. When I didn't hear Sergei move, I said, "You don't have to stand there and watch me. I'm not gonna leave."

A few moments passed before the door squeaked, signaling Sergei's departure. I dropped my head into my hands. Was there any chance Sergei just wanted to tell me that he and Elena had worked out an arrangement? Maybe he wanted to thank me for talking to her? Not likely, considering how edgy he'd sounded.

With my skates traded for sneakers, I walked past the ice to the studio at the rear of the rink. Sergei stood with his back to me and his hands gripping the barre. He looked up into the mirror and held my gaze as I entered the room. Away from the cool of the ice and under the spotlight of Sergei's strong stare, I grew uncomfortably warm. I dropped my purse next to the door and unzipped my fleece jacket while Sergei turned to face me.

"Elena told me you went to New York. I wish you hadn't done that."

"She agreed to let you see Liza, didn't she?"

He set his hands on his hips. "I didn't want it to happen this way."

"It was the only way," I insisted.

"No, Em. It didn't have to be like this." He came toward

me, his eyes afire. "How could you leave me without fighting for us?"

He was questioning me just as Elena had. Why did everyone think I'd made this decision easily? Did I have to throw myself on the ground and wail to the heavens to show them how gutted I felt?

"I told you why I did it," I said, hearing myself grow louder. "Elena is never changing her mind, and neither of us could be happy the way things were."

"And we're happy now?" he exclaimed.

No! I shouted inside, but there was no point in feeding Sergei's denial. I shuffled backward and calmed my voice. "It's going to take time, but we have to move on."

Sergei shook his head as he advanced nearer. "I can *never* move on from you."

His words slammed into my heart, filling me with more sadness and double the anger. What good was saying things like that? Unless a miracle happened, he couldn't have both Liza and me in his life.

"It'll get easier…" I stammered.

"No, it won't. You can't throw away our entire future and tell me I'll get over it. Deep down, I don't think you believe what you're saying either."

I pressed my fingers to my temples. "Stop making this harder than it is. I told you we don't make sense together—"

Sergei surged forward. He slid his hands inside my jacket and grasped my waist, pinning me against him. "Does this feel like it's not meant to be?"

"Sergei, stop," I demanded.

My body was wrought with confusion. I tensed upon Sergei's touch, ready to reject him, but then I found myself leaning into his familiar muscles, so hard and strong. *Don't do it….*

I tried to wiggle away from him, but he hugged me tighter. "How about this?" He softened his voice.

I pushed on his biceps, fighting more with myself than with Sergei, struggling to believe I was right and he wasn't. But the longer he held me, the less certain I became.

Sergei brought his head down to mine, and I stayed completely still. His mouth was so close I could drink in his breath. How could he torture me like this? I wanted to yell at him, but all I could manage was a whispered, "Don't."

He continued not to listen, running his hands over my back with long, slow caresses. I couldn't think anymore. I could just feel, and all my instincts pointed in one direction. I relaxed into Sergei's arms, giving up the fight.

His lips brushed over mine, and I couldn't deny his kiss. Everything around us disappeared, and we were on an island where nothing would tear us apart. I crushed my mouth to Sergei's, taking in as much of him as I could. I had to hold onto him and make this last.

It's not real, the nagging little voice in my head reminded me. *It can't last.*

I tried not to hear it, but the voice grew louder, taunting me until I wanted to scream. It didn't matter how connected I still felt to Sergei or how much passion we shared in our kiss. We didn't have a future, and being together like this would just make it harder to let go.

I shoved Sergei's chest, but he pulled me back against him.

"We can't do this!" I cried.

"I'm never going to stop loving you," he said, closing in for another kiss.

"You have to!" I jerked my head away and gasped when I saw Elena standing in the doorway.

I pushed loose from Sergei's embrace and sputtered, "This isn't... we're not together. What I told you in New York is the truth."

Elena's eyes swept back and forth from me to Sergei. She looked flustered, and I worried when the surprise wore off she'd be annoyed.

Sergei rubbed his hand over his mouth and cleared his throat. "I didn't think you were coming here before you left for Moscow."

"Liza want to see you, so we hire driver. I tell her we return to America soon, but she beg me." Elena glanced at the door. "She is with Courtney."

"Thank you for bringing her," Sergei said.

I didn't trust Elena not to whisk Liza away from Sergei again. I had to assure her she'd walked in on a mistake. But I was shaking so much on the inside that I didn't know if I could even talk.

"Sergei and I really are through." I spoke slowly and firmly to steady myself. "I'm not with him now, and I'm never going to be with him again. I think he understands that now."

I looked at Sergei, and he gave me a long stare filled with more frustration than acceptance. "I'm going to see Liza," he said and left the room.

I picked up my purse and aimed for the door, too, but Elena said, "Emily, may we speak?"

Turning around, I rested my back against the wall. I was still reeling from being in Sergei's arms. Now I had that memory fresh in my mind, making me ache deeper.

"You and Sergei argue," Elena said. "He is angry."

"How much did you hear?"

"I hear most." She peeked at the mirror and then dipped her head. "It make me remember so many years ago when I tell Sergei I cannot marry him."

"Your father didn't give you a choice."

Elena raised her eyes to mine. "And I do not give you one."

So, she was suddenly aware of how much her actions resembled her father's. I was curious how she would justify it.

"No, you didn't," I said, losing patience.

Elena fiddled with the sash of her trench coat. With her

bright red lips pinched together, I couldn't tell if she was irritated or regretful.

She paced to the middle of the room, her heels clapping noisily on the wood floor. "When I bring Liza here, and I see how she take to you and Sergei, I fear I lose her. I lose everything once, and it cannot happen again. Without Liza, I am alone."

"I told you many times Sergei and I would never have taken Liza from you."

"I cannot trust that. All I see is Liza admire you, and she want to leave me." Elena's voice cracked. "I see only way to stop this is to make you and Sergei part."

"Leaving me with nothing," I stated. "Just like you ten years ago."

My stomach turned, and I shut my eyes, letting Elena's admission sink in. The mistakes I'd made with Liza... those weren't the reason Elena had acted the way she did. She'd used them as excuses to mask her other fears. When I looked at Elena, she lowered her head again.

"So, all along it hasn't really been about protecting Liza," I said. "It's been about protecting yourself."

"You must understand," Elena said shakily. "I try to be near to Liza, but she keep distant from me. When we are in Russia, I do not know how to make her happy, and I feel she never see me as her mother. This make me so hurt..."

She held her fist to her mouth and then pulled it away, clenching her hand tighter. "I should not lose so many years with her. If my father not send her away, she do not see me as cousin only. But I cannot change this... I can change only now, and I try to keep my daughter close. This is all I want... you must see."

And I did see it through the desperation in her eyes. As messed up as the situation was, I did understand. But I couldn't take any more of it—the anguish, the pleas, the despair. I was talked out, and I just wanted to be away from

Elena.

"I do see. And I don't think there's much more to say."

I left Elena staring into the mirror, and I hurried out the side exit to avoid Sergei and Liza. Outside in the misty drizzle, I walked slowly to my car, thinking about my conversation with Elena as I trudged through shallow puddles. The chill of the rain on my face made me more alert, more aware of what I'd just heard.

When Elena's father had ripped Sergei and Liza from her, he'd done irreparable damage. Even with Liza back in her life, Elena lived in fear that she would lose her daughter again. Add to that the fact she couldn't have more children, and her tight hold on Liza made further sense.

I climbed into my car and leaned back against the headrest. If I'd experienced the heartache Elena had… if I'd been raised by a man like Ivan, who taught Elena not to trust anyone… would I have behaved the same way she had?

The door of the rink opened, and Sergei, Elena, and Liza appeared on the steps. I slunk down in my seat and watched through the rain-spotted windshield as Sergei helped Liza raise the hood on her raincoat. She said something and giggled, and Sergei smiled and put his arm around her.

I closed my eyes and swallowed hard. Sergei was where he needed to be.

CHAPTER TWENTY-SIX

I PULLED THE FOUR CHEESE BAKED macaroni out of the oven and set it on a trivet to cool. All weekend I'd channeled my emotions into kneading fresh pasta and cooking dishes for Chris. He was undergoing surgery the next morning, and I'd promised to make his favorite meals to put in his freezer. His mom was coming from Baltimore to stay with him for a few weeks, but I knew from his horror stories about her cooking that he didn't want her feeding him.

Removing my oven mitts, I started for the sink but stopped when the doorbell rang. A mixture of dread and excitement twisted my insides. I hadn't heard from Sergei since we'd argued at the rink. I couldn't handle fighting with him again, but I couldn't deny how much I wanted to see him.

I walked deliberately up to the foyer and checked the window beside the door. Chris stood on the mat. My shoulders dropped with both relief and disappointment.

I opened the door with a smile. "Hey, I was going to bring all the food over to your place."

"My mom just got in, and I wanted to talk to you without her around."

Chris wore his serious face, which I didn't see often. *Did he find out about Sergei and me?* I'd been waiting to tell him after his surgery.

Leading him down to the kitchen, I asked, "What's up?"

He shoved his hands in the pockets of his hoodie and leaned against the door frame. "Is there something you need to tell me?"

I played with my necklace, and before I could reply, Chris added, "About us moving to New York?"

"What?"

"I was reading the message boards on Figure Skating Central, looking for any off-season gossip, and someone posted that they saw Sergei at Liza's old rink today. He was taking a tour and asking about the facilities and the coaches. They said it sounded like he wants to set up camp there."

I couldn't speak, and my limbs went numb. *Sergei's leaving the Cape?*

"I guess Elena gave in? She and Liza are moving to New York?" Chris asked. When I didn't answer, his eyebrows bent. "You knew he was there, didn't you?"

I slowly shook my head, the only part of my body I could move. "I haven't talked to him much lately," I said quietly. "I broke up with him."

It was Chris's turn to be speechless. He sputtered, and I spilled everything that had happened.

"So, I'm not sure Sergei's plans include you and me moving to New York with him," I finished.

"Em..." Chris came over and hugged me. "I'm so sorry. Why didn't you tell me?"

"I didn't want to stress you out before your surgery. I knew you'd worry about how it would affect our training. I thought it might be okay once things settled down, but if Sergei's going to New York..."

Chris stepped back and rested against the counter. "Do you really think he's gonna leave us? What about all his other teams?"

"I… I don't know." My voice became faint. "Maybe Elena doesn't want him coaching us or maybe he wants to get away from me."

"I just don't think he'd give up the chance to coach us to an Olympic gold medal," Chris said. "Not after all the work we've done together."

"Sometimes we have to make tough decisions." My eyes clouded, and I grabbed a napkin.

Chris looped his arm around my shoulders and squeezed me to his side. "We don't know for sure what his plans are. You know how many ridiculous rumors there are on the internet. Remember when somebody posted that you and I were dating?"

I laughed through my tears. "Yeah, talk about crazy."

"It'd be like dating my sister. Ugh." Chris made a face.

I leaned my head into the crook of his arm and dabbed at my eyes. "The message boards will be on fire when people find out Sergei and I split up. There'll be rumors flying all over the place about why it happened."

"Just keep your head down and skate. That's all you can do. And the second I get cleared by the doc, I'll be back out there with you, whether it's here or New York or Alaska."

I smiled. "Marley might be a little upset if you moved to Alaska."

Chris hesitated and ran his fingers through his hair. "She might be going away to train somewhere else, too."

"What? She hasn't said anything to me."

"It probably won't happen for a while. She and Zach haven't made any plans yet. They've just been talking because they feel like their coaches are always gonna favor Aubrey and Nick. Don't say anything to anyone."

"I won't." I patted Chris's back. "We're just two sad sacks of bad news, aren't we?"

He snorted. "I'm getting out of here. Hanging out with

my mom has to be more fun than this."

"Hey, be nice or I'm keeping all this food for myself."

Chris dashed to the refrigerator and started snatching the plastic containers of pasta I'd assembled. I laughed at the large stack in his arms. "Hold on, I'll get some bags. And I still have to divvy up this macaroni."

When we'd packed his backseat with the meals, Chris gave me a long hug. "You should come have dinner with me and my mom. We have enough food."

"I've been sampling my cooking all day, so I'll probably skip dinner. Thanks for the offer, though." I kissed his cheek. "I'll see you at the hospital tomorrow."

"I'll be the one giddy on pain meds." He smiled.

As he drove away, I stood on the doorstep and breathed in the cool breeze caressing my face. The feeling reminded me of the rush of air hitting my skin when I skated. I needed that sensation now more than ever.

Glancing at my watch, I hurried inside, changed into leggings and a long-sleeved T-shirt, and grabbed my skate bag. The evening public session at the rink was starting soon, and it was usually pretty empty. I'd have the ice mostly to myself. My training mates wouldn't be around, and Sergei was in New York so no chance of running into him.

I couldn't get to the rink fast enough. As expected, only two adults occupied the ice, giving me plenty of space to skate as freely as I wanted. I stretched for a few minutes, bouncing to the pop music on the sound system, and then tied the laces on my boots in record time.

I joined the skaters and took long strokes, enjoying the deepness of my edges and the feeling of being one with the ice. The cold air swept over me, and I smiled as goose bumps tickled my neck. Around and around the rink I glided, trying to keep all focus on my body and my skates, but the familiar fresh smell of the ice and the sound of my swooshing blades brought visions of Sergei calling out instructions to me.

I might never see him standing by those boards again. He could be completely out of my life.

My pace slowed as the dose of reality stole my energy. I drifted toward the boards and gazed around. I couldn't imagine the place without Sergei. His smiling face had been the first one I'd seen when I walked into the building four years ago. He'd helped make the rink home for me.

I rubbed my hands over my face and through my hair. *Keep skating. Just keep moving forward.* I made a few swifter strokes, but each scratch of my blades felt like a slice into my heart. I couldn't escape the memories of Sergei all over the ice—him teaching me, encouraging me. Loving me.

I glided numbly around the rink, sinking further into the past and losing the will to continue forward. Then a very familiar song came on the stereo, and my skates skidded to an abrupt stop.

"When We Dance" by Sting.

Sergei had used the lyrics as part of his marriage proposal. Of all the songs he and I had put on the rink's playlist, why did that one have to play right now?

I stared down at the ice and saw Sergei on one knee on my snow-covered terrace, a sparkling diamond in his hand. The world had stopped at that moment, and I'd thought that night was the beginning of a lifetime of happiness.

I gasped with a soft cry, and my head shot up. I had to get off the ice before I lost all composure. I scrambled to the bleachers and untied my skates in a frenzy, wishing I could close my ears and not hear Sting singing to his prospective wife.

When I was alone in my car, I gave in to my sobs and wondered how I ever could've doubted my future with Sergei. I would've gladly dealt with Elena if it meant having Sergei back, and I would've worked to be the best stepmother to Liza I could be.

I swiped at my eyes as I thought of the little chats Liza

and I had every morning at the rink. I hadn't expected to form a bond with her so quickly, but she was such a special girl with Sergei's sweet soul, and I wished we could've grown even closer. I probably would've made more mistakes while learning how to be a mom, but it would've been worth it to have Liza as my stepdaughter.

All the things I'd feared—sharing Sergei, dealing with Elena, being a parent to Liza—those were manageable issues. A life without Sergei... I had no idea how to manage that.

When is this hollow feeling in my soul going to disappear? Maybe it was better if Sergei did leave town. If I had to see him every day, I would never heal.

By the end of the drive home, I'd cried myself out but knew it wouldn't take much to set me off again. I was a time bomb of tears, and as I drove into my parking lot, I saw something that reignited my fuse.

Sergei's SUV.

He wasn't in the car, so I assumed he'd used his spare key. I hadn't thought of asking for it in the chaos of breaking up with him.

I plucked a tissue from my bag to wipe my face and then checked my appearance in the rearview mirror. My eyes were red and swollen, but there was no way to hide them. What were the odds I'd get through this conversation without crying again, anyway?

I slowly made my way into the quiet house. No movement came from the kitchen, and the living room sat empty. I turned up the stairs, my heart wrenching with each step. Sergei had to be on the terrace, the place that had just haunted my memories.

Pausing on the top floor landing, I squeezed the banister and moved forward to the open glass door. Sergei looked up at me from the patio table, and the lantern light beamed over his face. A world of anxiousness filled his eyes.

Sergei stood as I stepped onto the creaky wooden

floorboards. "I wouldn't have used my key, but I didn't know if you'd let me in."

I walked over to the railing and gazed at the moonlit bay. "I can't go through a repeat of our last conversation."

"I have to ask you something, and I need you to tell me the truth."

I turned to Sergei, and he took two tense steps forward. "Do you really believe everything you said about us not making sense and not belonging together?"

No, not this. I can't do this anymore.

I drew in a deep breath and rubbed my forehead. "It doesn't matter. You and I aren't possible."

"Please be honest with me."

The time bomb inside me threatened to explode once more, and I gripped the knotted wood railing. Sergei wasn't going to relent, but if I told him the truth, it would just get emotionally torturous between us again.

"I don't know why you want to dwell on this—"

"Because I need to know," he said with urgency. "I need to know how you really feel."

His desperation pained me, tearing away at my resistance. I bit my lip but couldn't hold back any longer. "No, I don't believe it!"

Sergei exhaled and closed his eyes. When he opened them, they glistened with tears. I immediately wanted to take back what I'd said. It would've been better if he thought I still had doubts.

"I do believe you should be with Liza, so I know this is the right thing," I scrambled to say. "And now that you're moving to New York—"

"What? Why would you think that?"

It's not true? A tiny drop of optimism seeped through the dark fog. "Someone on the internet said you were touring the rink there."

"I wanted to see where Liza will be training, and I asked

about teaching a few camps, but I'm not moving there."

"I thought you wanted Liza to come to the Cape so you'd be close to her?"

"I did, but..." Sergei said in a rush and then slowed himself down. "Elena and I had a long talk, and we agreed this shouldn't be about what I want or what she wants. It has to be about what's best for Liza, and she belongs in New York. She loves her school there and her coach, and it's the place she truly feels at home."

"That's great. She must be over the moon," I said, trying to sound as upbeat as I could.

"Liza will only be a few hours away, so she can easily come up here to visit." Sergei kept his eyes on mine as he inched closer. "And we can go see her any time."

My heart jumped at the small yet very important word he'd uttered. "We?"

He further narrowed the space between us. His body heat and the scent of his woody cologne circled around me, creating an enticing cloud. I wanted to lean into him, to bury myself in his arms, but I had to be sure I'd heard him right.

"Elena realized she's been holding on too tight to Liza, just like her father did with her," Sergei said. "She doesn't want to cause the kind of pain he did. She doesn't want to keep us apart any longer."

"So we... we can be together... and see Liza, too?"

He cupped his hands under my chin and brushed my face with light caresses. "If you'll still have me."

I stared at him, holding my breath, afraid I was experiencing an impossible dream. I put my hands on top of his. They were so strong and warm. This had to be real.

"Yes!" I cried. "I want you. I want Liza. I want all of it forever."

Sergei grinned and touched his lips to mine, and his tender passion sent my frayed emotions over the edge. I wept into his mouth, my salty tears mixing with the sweetness of his kiss.

Sergei enveloped me in his arms and showered me with more kisses on my forehead, my cheeks, and my hair. I smiled and rested my head on his chest, listening to his heartbeat pound against my ear. Ten minutes earlier I'd been lost in despair, unable to see beyond the moment, and now I was overflowing with hope for the future.

"I have something of yours," Sergei said, reaching into his pocket.

He pinched my diamond ring between his fingers and took my left hand in his. "Promise me you'll never take this off again."

He slid the ring onto my finger, and the emptiness inside me filled with joy. I felt whole once again.

"I promise," I said, joining our hands together.

We melted into another kiss, and I hummed quietly as Sergei's stubble bristled my skin. No dream could feel this good. This was definitely real.

I tilted my head back to look into Sergei's eyes. Their glow had returned, so bright and alive. I smiled and shook my head. "I still can't believe this. When I talked to Elena, I didn't think she'd ever change her mind. And then I thought you were leaving."

"I was never going to give up on us. I would've gotten on my knees and begged Elena if I had to. I couldn't lose you." Sergei's voice rattled.

"I didn't know what else to do," I said. "Everything was so screwed up, and I thought I had to walk away from you to make it better."

Sergei pressed his mouth to my forehead. "Us being apart… it never makes anything better."

"I tried to picture my life without you, and I couldn't because everything I wanted in my future was with you."

"Our future's going to be a little different from what we planned, but I promise I will always be there for you and I will give you all the love that you deserve." Sergei lifted my chin and locked his gaze on mine. "I don't want you to ever doubt how much I love you, how much I want you, how much I need you."

I blinked back more happy tears. "I love you so much."

All the anger and sadness weighing me down had disappeared, leaving me so light and free I thought I might fly away. I wound my arms around Sergei's neck and held onto him. Wrapped in his embrace, I still felt like I was floating among the stars.

CHAPTER TWENTY-SEVEN

"ARE YOU READY, SWEETIE?" DAD TOOK my hand.

I had never been more ready for this day. My wedding day. As I stood in the rear of St. Leonard's Church, I trembled with excitement and a bit of nervousness. I was about to begin a whole new life.

An unbelievably wonderful life.

I squeezed Dad's hand. "*So* ready."

Aubrey carefully swept my hair over my shoulders and lowered my blusher veil, readying me for the big entrance. Meanwhile, Liza scooted around the bridesmaids with her small basket of white rose petals, and she looked up at me with wide eyes.

"There are a lot of people here!"

She was beyond adorable in the dress Louann had hastily made to match the bridesmaids' seafoam green dresses. I grinned and touched one of her raven curls.

"And they're all going to agree that you're the prettiest flower girl in the history of weddings."

Her cheeks turned pink, and per Aubrey's command, she returned to the rest of the bridal party. My maid of honor was taking her role very seriously as she organized Marley, Courtney, and my cousins Bri and Bella into a line. The musicians in the choir loft began to play "The Rain" from the movie *Kikujiro,* and Aubrey signaled to Liza to start down the aisle.

One by one the girls departed, soon leaving just Dad and myself. Through the sheer tulle of my veil, I saw Dad's eyes misting. I took deep breaths and hurried to think of something funny to distract me from getting emotional. One of Chris's jokes from his best man toast at the rehearsal dinner popped into my head—*I'm gonna be skating with an old married lady now.*

The blare of the trumpet cut short my internal laughter, and Dad led me to the edge of the long aisle. I gazed toward the altar where Sergei stood with a smile bigger than any I'd ever seen.

I could barely hold back my emotions. I gripped my bouquet and Dad's hand tighter as we began our slow march down the white runner. The faces staring at me on either side of the aisle were a blur. All I saw was Sergei in his black suit and silver vest and tie, looking like a vision of the perfect groom.

When we reached Sergei, Dad lifted my veil and kissed my cheek. "I love you, sweetie."

"I love you, too, Dad," I squeaked.

He hugged Sergei and joined our hands together. "I know you'll always take care of her."

"I will," Sergei said, not taking his eyes off me.

Dad sat in the front pew with Mom, and Sergei leaned his head down to mine. "I have no words for how beautiful you look."

I resisted the urge to reach up and kiss him. That had to wait until after the "I do's."

"You look pretty hot yourself," I whispered.

We stepped up to Father Donovan on the altar, and Aubrey fanned out the train of my dress behind me. Father

Donovan had baptized me and had been a family friend all my life, so I couldn't imagine anyone else performing the ceremony. He smiled at Sergei and me, and I awaited one of his usual witty comments.

Clapping his hands, he said, "Let's get you two kids married!"

"I PRESENT TO YOU—Mr. and Mrs. Sergei Petrov!"

Upon the DJ's introduction, the wedding guests broke into applause and a few whistles. Sergei and I walked across the mahogany floor of the State Room and prepared for our first dance as husband and wife. Through the floor-to-ceiling windows, the pink sky of dusk over Boston Harbor provided our backdrop.

Sergei took me into his arms as "When We Dance" filled the large room. We swayed in time to the music, sharing what felt like an intimate moment even with hundreds of pairs of eyes on us.

"I thought the day I met you was the best day of my life," Sergei said. "But today will be hard to top."

"And there's still more amazingness to come later." I tickled the nape of his neck.

"It's going to be incredible," he said, his lips grazing my ear.

My stomach fluttered, and I pulled Sergei closer. It was going to be a long limo ride from Boston to Hyannis after the reception, but I wanted to spend our wedding night in our home. A hotel wasn't special enough for the long-awaited occasion.

Our song ended, and Sergei and I split up so I could dance with Dad and Sergei could do the same with Anna. On the edge of the dance floor, Mom dabbed at her eyes while watching us. She'd been weepy since I put on my gown at her house. I'd lost count of the number of times she cried, "My little girl!" when I was getting dressed and primped for the ceremony.

When the DJ invited the guests to start dancing, Sergei and I moved into the crowd and were bombarded with well-wishes from family and friends. We circled around the room, collecting congratulatory hugs and kisses, and eventually ended up at the reserved tables by the windows for the bridal party and immediate family.

Finally with a moment to take a breath, I looked around and admired the décor I'd designed with the wedding planner. Every table in the room featured a centerpiece containing blue and white hydrangeas, and small candles surrounding the flowers provided a soft glow. Night had fallen, so the Boston skyline had become a sparkling sea of lights all around us. I couldn't picture a more romantic setting.

Anna and Max rose from their seats at the main table, and Anna hugged Sergei and me at the same time. "My beautiful new daughter! I know you and Sergei be happy always."

"I wish you could stay longer to visit," I said.

"We return at Christmas, and I stay to watch you at national championship." She stepped back and smoothed my veil. "I want to spend much time with Liza, also."

Anna and Max had been in the States for a week, and Liza had quickly charmed them. Sergei said he hadn't ever seen his father so jovial.

Sergei asked Max in Russian, "Will you be able to take off work that long?"

"No, I can come for only a few days, but I'm looking forward to it," he said with a softness to his gruff voice. "I'd like to have more time with my granddaughter, too."

"She's pretty special, isn't she?" I said.

Max looked at me. "Sergei is very lucky. He has two special people in his life now."

Max's rare expression of affection touched my heart and

prompted me to throw my arms around him. He felt stiff with surprise at first but then returned my hug. When we parted and Max reached out to Sergei, my emotions soared again. Anna and I exchanged teary smiles as we watched an embrace that had been a long time coming.

Aubrey beckoned me to the dance floor to join my friends, so I took a quick sip of wine, tasted a few hors d'oeuvres, and then sashayed my way toward the group. I spotted Liza nearby, so I grabbed her hands and twirled her into the throng with me. We laughed and bounced around together to the classic party music, and as we left the dance floor I gave her a tight hug. It was hard to believe I'd only known Liza a few months. She felt like family I'd known for years.

"I'm so glad you were part of the wedding," I said. "It made today even more perfect."

Liza grinned. "Thank you for asking me to be your flower girl."

Sergei walked up and slipped his arm around my waist. "There's my gorgeous wife."

"I love the sound of that," I said and gave him a kiss.

"I bet you'll be kissing a lot on your honeymoon." Liza giggled.

Sergei and I laughed, and he said, "That's right. That's what honeymoons are for."

We gave each other knowing glances, unable to wipe the huge grins from our faces. We were still looking at each other when Elena broke through the crowd and joined us. Her blue silk dress matched the hydrangeas.

"I do not tell you congratulations yet," she said with a little smile. "It is beautiful wedding."

"Thank you," Sergei and I replied at the same time.

With all the heartache behind us, everyone had been able to have a fresh start. Elena was teaching ballet at Liza's rink, and she appeared happier every time I saw her. It seemed she was finally making peace with the events of the past.

"Liza, I save food for you at our table if you want to eat," Elena said.

"Yeah, I'm starving." Liza turned to me. "We can dance more later?"

"For sure!"

Liza went to follow Elena, but Sergei said, "Wait, I have something for you. I was going to wait until the end of the night, but…"

Reaching inside his jacket, he pulled out a little red satchel. He handed it to Liza, and she opened it to find a silver rose charm.

"I love it!" she said, already unhooking her bracelet. "Thank you!"

"I looked for a tiny basket of flowers but couldn't find one," Sergei said. "So, I figured rose petals… a rose…"

"It's awesome," Liza said as Elena helped her add the new charm.

When the bracelet was clasped around her wrist again, Liza hugged Sergei's waist, and he crouched down so he could swallow her in his arms.

"I love you," he said and kissed her head.

She clung to him for a long minute. "I love you, too."

Elena and I both sniffed back tears, and I rubbed Sergei's back as he released Liza and stood tall. Elena and Liza left us, and Sergei took my hand.

"Definitely the best day ever," he said.

"And this is just the start of a lifetime of amazing days," I said.

Sergei lifted my hand and touched his lips to my wedding band. "Forever."

I smiled. "Forever."

MORE BOOKS BY JENNIFER COMEAUX

Edge Series
Life on the Edge (Edge #1)
Edge of the Past (Edge #2)
Fighting for the Edge (Edge #3)

Ice Series
Crossing the Ice (Ice #1)
Losing the Ice (Ice #2)
Taking the Ice (Ice #3)

To stay up to date on Jennifer's new releases, join her mailing list:
http://eepurl.com/UZjMP

Jennifer loves to hear from readers! Visit her online at:
jennifercomeaux.blogspot.com
www.twitter.com/LadyWave4
www.facebook.com/jennifercomeauxauthor
www.instagram.com/jcomeaux4
jcomeaux4@gmail.com

Please consider taking a moment to leave a review at the applicable retailer. It is much appreciated!

ABOUT THE AUTHOR

Jennifer Comeaux is a tax accountant by day, writer by night. There aren't any ice rinks near her home in south Louisiana, but she's a diehard figure skating fan and loves to write stories of romance set in the world of competitive skating. One of her favorite pastimes is travelling to competitions, where she can experience all the glitz and drama that inspire her writing.

www.ingramcontent.com/pod-product-compliance
Lightning Source LLC
Chambersburg PA
CBHW031232120726
47905CB00002B/572